# UNMADE

Amy Rose Capetta

HOUGHTON MIFFLIN HARCOURT
BOSTON  NEW YORK

"Blessings from the Stars" from *What the Heart Knows: Chants, Charms, and Blessings* by Joyce Sidman. Copyright © 2013 by Joyce Sidman. Used by permission of Houghton Mifflin Harcourt Publishing Company.

www.hmhco.com

Text set in ITC Slimbach
Book design by Scott Magoon

*Library of Congress Cataloging-in-Publication Data*
Capetta, Amy Rose.
Unmade / by Amy Rose Capetta.
p. cm.
Sequel to: Entangled.
Summary: "Cadence is in a race against time and space to save her family and friends from the Unmakers, who are tracking the last vestiges of humanity across the cosmos." —Provided by publisher
ISBN 978-0-544-08737-8
[1. Survival—Fiction. 2. Science fiction.] I. Title.
PZ7.C173653Un 2015
[Fic]—dc23
2013050208

Manufactured in the United States of America
DOC 10 9 8 7 6 5 4 3 2 1
4500512274

This one is for my mom.

# Blessing from the Stars

*(after the Passamaquoddy song)*

We are the stars, who sing
from a distant place.

Yes, you are alone in your orbit,
as we are.
Yes, your light burns fiercely,
as fiercely as ours.

The thin wind of loneliness
may howl around you,
suck the breath from your fire.

But look before you
and behind you.
Look above you
and below you.
See how many other hearts are burning,
burning as brightly as yours.

We are the stars.
We sing with our light
in our vast, brilliant constellations:
alone,
       together.

DO I DARE DISTURB THE UNIVERSE?

—T. S. ELIOT

# PART ONE

# CHAPTER 1

The white planet looked perfect from far away.

Everyone should have been there when it slid and locked into view, but Cade was alone, so no one saw her in front of the starglass, hands capped to her chest. No one was there to hear the words that flooded out, the rich and steady river of curses.

"Snug. Snug, snug, *snug it all.*"

Cade stood at the center of the control room, not moving, but it reached out of her like rays — the need to get to the surface. To land on this cloud-breathing planet. Down there, somewhere, she had a mother.

Cade started to dance.

Hands first, shoulders, feet.

A few months ago, she never would have let this happen. It was a hard line she'd drawn in the imaginary sand a long

…me ago: No dancing. The music she'd pounded on her guitar had been for listening purposes. If other people dressed themselves in her rhythms, brushed and slid her notes against their skin, that was their choice.

But Cade's hips were breaking the old rules. Going rogue. Nudging air.

She danced to the song in her head, a song no one else could hear. It was ready whenever Cade reached for it, stitched out of the thoughts of the people around her. It wove brightly into her brain. Overwhelmed her, as much as the first time she'd felt it. But Cade had come back from the brink of death for that song, and she wouldn't stop listening until all of the humans scattered through space came back together, the way they were meant to be heard.

Starting with her mother. One slim thread of the song was formed out of notes Cade knew, captured in old footage of her mother and watched by Cade, every day for months. It hadn't been easy to pick her mother's notes out of the song and follow them across wide, dark bolts of universe.

But now they blared back at Cade from a white-clouded planet.

She bent and molded a hand to the floor. "This is the place, Renna," Cade said. "Res Minor."

The name of the planet splashed against the song in her head. She liked the way they sounded together.

"What do you think?"

The ship had nothing to offer, not after so many days and weeks of flying at top speed — toward Cade's mother, away from the Unmakers. Renna had done her best. Now the floor under Cade's feet rolled slow.

"Sorry." Cade patted Renna back into a resting state.

Cade picked herself up and pulled out charts, trying to set a course. But she kept checking the view of Res Minor in the starglass, and then the door, until she was turning in circles, waiting for someone else to get caught in her centrifuge of happy swears and dancing and almost-almost-there.

Cade had been in good company ever since she was peeled back from the edge of the black hole. There had been Renna to answer her moods with a fitting rumble, Ayumi to listen to her guitar with amber-wide eyes, Lee to poke into the bedroom three times a day with a questionable meal on a tray.

Cade had gotten used to having someone. But now there was no one, and now it was time.

She ran out of the control room, down the chute. The feeling in her wouldn't go quiet, and she needed a crew member to share it with. Lee and Ayumi were running Human Express deliveries, and Rennik had been avoiding her, and that left —

Cade almost clipped the point of Gori's elbow as she rounded a turn in the chute. In Gori's normal state, he could tuck into one of the small bunks set in the wall of the ship, with room to spare. But in a slight rapture state, with his gray skin swelled and stretching, he overflowed the bounds of the bed and got squarely in Cade's way. She knew he was tuned in to the movement of dark energy through the universe, but the puffed mass of his cheeks made him look like one big allergic reaction.

Cade reached for his shoulder, but the feeling inside her amplified things. She tried for a gentle tap and landed a super-charged punch.

"Wake up!" Cade said.

She had already punched him. She might as well commit.

Gori stared up and shrank back into himself, the blank of his eyes swapped out for a harsh, measuring stare.

"I have no use for sleep," he said.

Cade guessed he had even less use for dancing.

"I saw Res Minor," she said. "And heard it. It's the place we've been searching for."

Gori gathered his gray robes around his shriveled gray toes.

"We have to go," Cade said. When Gori made no move bigger than a robe-swirl, she added, "Now!"

"Now is an invention," Gori said. "All time is one time."

This was one of the Darkrider's favorite mottoes. But Cade was in no mood for mottoes and robe-swirls. When she came back from the black hole and found that her old, pinched ways wouldn't do, she had changed. Pried herself open. Gori could snugging well do the same.

She sat with him on the bunk. Closer than he liked — she could tell by the increased rate of his blinking.

"Did you have a mother?" Cade asked. "On your planet? When you were a . . ." "Baby" couldn't be the right word. Not for him. "A little pile of robes?"

Gori narrowed his eyes, and his face compacted into new wrinkle-patterns. "No."

"Well, then maybe you wouldn't understand."

Cade chose not to add that her own understanding of the mother concept was limited. For most of her life she'd thought her mother was dead, or run off, or that she'd never existed. Then came the revelation that her mother was a spacesick who, *again*, might be dead, and now her mother was a song.

How could Cade explain all of that? This was one of the worst parts of openness. It came with the burden of words, so many words, all of which had to be found and flattened into the right shape.

Cade closed her eyes.

"There's a pull in having a mother," she said. "A complicated pull. It knots you. In a good way."

Cade shook her head. She could name the loud feeling now — happiness — but only because it was leaving her. It scrubbed against frustration as it went.

"You wouldn't understand," Cade said again.

"I had no mother," Gori said. "But I did not spend all of this life in absence."

Cade chanced a look at his loose, non-raptured skin, the inward curl of his shoulders. Gori was a Darkrider — more connected to the infinite, snarled workings of the universe than she could imagine. He was also the most alone creature Cade had ever met. Gori had lost a planet. Cade had lost one boy, but sometimes he'd felt like enough to build a world on.

*Xan.*

This was the wrong time to think about Xan, about the

black hole and its bright heart. The boy she hadn't been able to save. Every time was the wrong time to think about Xan, so Cade didn't mind when the memory was knocked out of place by a gentle tap-and-slide.

A ship docking.

"See?" Cade asked as Renna perked under her feet. "There *is* a now, and a good one too."

She raced down the rest of the chute and let the news about her mother swell to the surface again. The dock sprang open. Lee — who, most days, could be counted on to haul even Cade's most complicated thoughts out of her head — made her entrance in no shape to listen. She swung into the main cabin with a bloody smile and a blackened eye.

"So," Cade said, news held back, even though it scrabbled at her stomach. "You had fun?"

Lee bounced on her toes, which added to her height, and tossed her hair out of the knots that she always wore. She flourished her fists, kicked invisible shins. "Best fight I've gotten into in years! Best kidney punch, courtesy of me. Finest drubbing in a public fountain, also my handiwork. Richest, blackest black eye." She pointed at the rim of dark shine. "Sweet universe, yes. It takes all the honors."

"Did you win or lose?" Cade asked.

Lee stopped pummeling the air long enough to pin Cade with a confused look. "I *fought.*"

Behind her, Ayumi whisper-stepped into view. She took up the smallest possible fraction of the dock frame even though she was taller than Cade, more fleshed out than skinny-sharp Lee. Ayumi's dark curls were slicked with reddish dust, her arms scored with bruises. She stayed quiet. A breakable quiet.

The lively flare of Lee's mood and the dangerous tremble of Ayumi's stretched Cade in one direction, then another. Keeping up with people's emotions was like being forced to make constant key changes.

"Someone came after us," Ayumi said.

"That's the Express." Lee fended off a new set of memory-foes. "Someone's always after us."

Ayumi shook her curls. Particles dropped to the floor, rust-flake red. "Maybe someone, maybe always. But never like this."

"Right," Lee said. "Usually we're beset by amateurs! But this crowd? They really knew how to beset someone."

Lee's bravado levels fell within the normal range. But Ayumi's concern rang a warning bell deep in Cade's system. "What happened?"

Lee headed for the center of the room and cocked her leg against the bottom of the chute. "We set up in Eastwall. Close to the crowds, far from the headquarters of the local force. Lots of new customers this time, but I don't complain. People need us to take their messages and most-treasureds, so we do." Cade knew how it worked. She'd been part of it once. But now that she was Unmaker-hunted, mother-obsessed, she didn't have the time or the freedom to help with runs. Cade never would have thought she'd miss the long lines and the hope-crusted eyes of the Human Express. People sick to connect with their families. But she did. "Pick-ups ran their course, no problem," Lee said. "Drop-offs were—"

"Fine," Ayumi supplied. She was Lee's partner now, and Cade had to admit, with a minor twinge, that they made as brass a team as Lee and Cade ever had.

Lee uncocked her leg. Sank into a deep crouch.

"It wasn't until we packed up and headed back to the shuttle," Lee said. "A commotion broke out, I'd say a six on the ruckus scale, and then . . . scraps! All around us! Someone ripped the pack from my hands, and you know I wasn't going to stand for that. I fought my way to the edge of the crowd. The pack was in the dirt, just lying there—"

"It felt wrong," Ayumi said, shaking hard against the dock frame. "Wrong, wrong, wrong."

Ayumi's fear hit Cade with the rip-and-ebb of an electric sound wave. All she could offer was awkward comfort of the flutter-pat variety, but she started across the cabin. Lee was already halfway there.

"Hey." Lee ran her hands down Ayumi's arms, and Ayumi focused. Cade didn't think she noticed Lee dropping blood into the space between them.

"I wouldn't let those slummers hurt you," Lee said. "You know that, right?"

"I'm strong," Ayumi blurted.

"Of course you are," Lee said.

"I'm capable," Ayumi added, and Cade had to agree. Ayumi hovered in the region of scary-smart, and she knew how to fly.

Of course, there was the little matter of her spacesickness, which only Cade knew about. "Today was just—"

"Wrong," Lee said. Ayumi nodded. "If you say it was, then I believe it was. So it double was."

Ayumi needed the calming down. She had more than earned it. Cade had no right to shoulder into the moment. But—

"I think I found her."

Lee broke out of the dock frame and pulled Ayumi. She had one arm around the shaking girl, and she put the other around Cade.

"That's brilliant!"

The words were right and the smiles were warm, but there had been a vastness to Cade's good feeling when she first saw Res Minor. It had swelled her cells to the bursting point. She needed more than smiles.

"So we hit the surface," Lee said. "Right? I'll prep the ship if you're ready."

Cade needed a wisp of her mother's song to follow, to make sure they put down in the right spot, but she couldn't sit still and wait for it.

"Right," she said. "Ready."

Lee and Ayumi headed for the shuttle, and Lee called back. "Tell Rennik."

Heat and pressure, everywhere. Cade still hadn't told Lee about what had happened in Hades, with Rennik. But she felt the held-in story through the low curve of her back, climbing hot up her neck.

"Right," she said.

She crossed the main cabin to his door. Knocking should have been as simple as hitting a downbeat.

Rennik had been there with Cade in the first days after the black hole, always there, looming tall and letting his nerves show through the hardened ice of his patience. He had administered the injections that smashed through Cade's system, leaving her all muscle-scream and blistered with strange fevers. He'd sat with her for hours and told her worn-in stories of when he and Renna first sailed the universe.

Then he had all but disappeared.

But the texture of the time they'd spent together — minutes thickened with long stares — had sunk into Cade. She let it rise now, never thinking that the door would open and she would be caught with Rennik so obviously on her mind.

He turned on a heel and headed back into the room like that had been the plan the whole time.

Maybe he was hoping that Cade would scurry to some safer place on the ship and pretend it had never happened. But she waited him out. Rennik made a show of calm to cover the impulse-burst, shifting papers across his desk.

Cade had seen the rivered muscles of his back close enough to fit her fingertips to them. Now anything else felt far, far, far.

"Hey," she said, running in — until there was no more room to run and Rennik had to face her.

The features that had been striking-strange the first time Cade saw them formed a well-known map. The sharp rise of his cheekbones, eyebrows, chin. The smoothness of the rest. His gray-brown eyes and hair set against the cool nonhuman tint of his skin. At the center of it were double pupils so dark they should have been another black-hole tumble. But since Rennik was Rennik, she never felt like she was sliding away from herself.

In fact, Cade's personality doubled when faced with Rennik's calm brand of reason, and at the moment that meant twice as much frustration. He gave her one of his best smiles, like he hadn't been avoiding her for weeks.

Like he hadn't just spun a frantic circle at the sight of her.

"Cadence?" he asked.

"Hey," she said. Again.

Unlike with most people, she knew what she wanted to say to Rennik. She just didn't know if she *should*. Words raced, faster than the eager slide of her blood. Cade told him the smallest thing she could find, because letting out one word more would drag the rest with it.

"We're getting the shuttle ready," she said.

"It's Res Minor, isn't it." Rennik didn't sound excited, or disappointed. He didn't sound anything at all. But Cade knew the signs: the pull of skin at his temples, the overstretched fingers.

Rennik was nervous.

Cade had gotten better at reading him, so she should have been able to figure out if the kiss she'd pressed on him in Hades had been more than an impending-doom-fueled mistake.

"Yeah," she said. "Definitely Res Minor."

"I can't go down there." Rennik's long four-knuckled fingers swirled a pen through the air. "Not in a capacity that will do you any good. The Hatchum have been on poisonous terms with Res Minor for centuries."

"So I'll go alone."

Rennik stopped the pen, mid-swirl.

"Lee and Ayumi have an Express drop, and I'm not asking them to cancel again. And you can correct me if I have this wrong, but I don't think Gori leaves the ship. At least, not bodily."

Rennik took his time and considered. "Do me a favor?" He put the pen down and set his fingertips against the wall. "Don't put yourself into danger if you can help it."

"Unfair," Cade said. "That's one thing I can't promise. I put us all in danger, just by having these particles." This topic had played out during her recovery — different verses and variations, but it all ended up sounding the same. The Unmakers had been successful in deleting Xan from the universe, and now they wanted the other half of the entangled pair. Cade couldn't stop them from wanting her. They would find her, like they had found Moira. The girl Rennik used to love.

Cade needed to stop thinking about Moira. Wondering about Moira. Worrying about whether she was too much like Moira, or not enough. The Unmakers were easier to focus on. They wanted to kill her.

"We've been on the move for seven weeks," Cade said. "No sign of them."

She couldn't find the Unmakers in the song, either. Their being human meant they were woven in there, somewhere, but no matter how late Cade stayed up, picking at the song like an over-worried knot, she couldn't tell how many Unmakers there were, or where to find them. For one reason: she didn't know what they sounded like.

But Cade knew Rennik. She didn't have to connect to him on a sub-everything level to know what was bothering him.

"You think I should stay onboard."

The little room pulsed twice, like a tightly held hand. "I think the longer you go without being noticed, the more likely it is the Unmakers will forget this and move on." Renna pulsed again. She was giving him strength. "At the same time, you're the only one who can locate your mother on the surface." Cade would have to follow the song, which left Rennik to sit on the ship and wait up for her.

"So?" Cade asked.

She would go down to Res whether he wanted her to or not.

"Well," he said.

She should have been able to leave the room.

Rennik looked up, and something inside Cade broke apart into music. "I think you should have what you need," he said.

She knew that he was talking about her mother, but—

"What I need." Cade traced the words with her lips. Tested them.

She needed what had happened in Hades to happen again. Cade reached for Rennik's arm, and found more than she'd asked for. He pulled her in with less-than-patient hands, lining her up to him. It felt perfect for a full measure. And then it felt safe. Cade tilted back. Turned her face up to him like sky.

Their lips fit together, found their own particular way of matching. Cade's skin was a shade warmer than his, and her breath came faster. She drove the kiss into crests. The universe started to split into sound, pound its needing strains, pour into her. And then — the notes Cade had been searching for sailed into her head, calling and clear.

"I can hear it," Cade said, slipping out of Rennik's hands. "I hear her."

He touched her cheek and tried to smile. "The next time we encounter trouble — the smallest potential for trouble — I want us to face it together."

"Deal," Cade said on her way out the door. She called back, "Don't spend all day worrying about me. I won't get hurt."

# CHAPTER 2

The little ship broke through cloud after cloud. Cade held tight to her guitar case as Ayumi's shuttle went down.

"You sure you need that?" Lee asked.

"Yeah." But the pile of reasons in Cade's head sounded shaky, and she didn't want to share. She had grabbed Moon-White so she could talk to her mother. If the woman blank-stared at Cade, or didn't believe the wild story about Cade being her daughter, the guitar might help. It was a language they both spoke.

"My mother used to play," Cade said, hoping it was enough.

"Oh!" Ayumi said. "I wrote that down." She turned from the work of piloting the shuttle to talk about her real love — scribbling things in her notebooks. "I wrote down every-thing we know about your mother. The color of her eyes. The instruments she can play." Ayumi fiddled with a button that was probably best left un-fiddled with. "And. You know. That she's a—"

"Don't you need to focus on the landing?" Cade asked.

Ayumi clamped her mouth shut. Her cheeks went even rounder than usual.

Lee twisted in the nav chair. "Never been to this planet," she said. "But I've heard things. Happy-type things."

Lee tended to believe the worst about every place she put down. She catalogued the dangers, ticked off all the possible ways to die. It was part of her job. Lee was making a shining-brass effort for Cade, but she didn't want to know more about Res Minor until her feet hit the dirt.

Lee and Ayumi focused on navigating, in zero visibility, guided by coordinates that were based on a song in Cade's head.

Cade focused on white—a clean, fresh, unmarked planet.

She let the goodness of that lift her as the milky sky thickened and the ship fell into a dead plummet.

Ayumi's shuttle put down in a field. An honest-as-snug *field*. Grass, even if it wavered thin. Flowers, even if their petals spindled out from dry white centers. Ayumi jumped out of the ship and pressed one between the pages of a notebook before Cade and Lee caught up. They crossed the field on a wind that whipped up grating soil but also stuffed them full of oxygen. Cade breathed deep, air-starved.

"Don't ever tell Renna I said this," Lee warned. "But there's nothing like a true lungful."

The field gave onto neat alleys, and the alleys fed thin streets. Res Minor didn't boast a large human settlement, but it was well populated. Cade had never tried to shoulder through such a mass. People hurried and kept their heads down.

Lee and Ayumi sheered off when they hit the market. "Back at the ship before sunset," Lee said.

Cade followed her mother's song alone. But she had plenty of company in her loneliness — a constant swap-and-swirl of humans, their songs so close they crowded out thought. Tempos rushed and spiking. Cade struggled to hold them all, to hear them without losing her mother's thread.

She ran in fits and bursts. The effort of listening almost cracked her mind into clean pieces. She cradled her skull as it split along lines that no one else could see. The song flicked down a wide street, around a corner, and then stopped.

She looked up and found herself within ten steps of a low building in gray stone. *Res Minor Home for the Old and Infirm.*

Music bled out of the rectangle.

Cade rushed the stairs, her steps ringing staccato. She stopped at a desk in a tiled waiting room. The home — if you could call a box that smelled like a century's worth of urine and cleaning products a home — was staffed by men and women in green suits.

"And you are?" asked a man with a mild voice and thin fingers of hair that reached up into his cap.

"Here to see my mother," Cade said.

"Name?"

Cade didn't know it. She should have plundered the records

on Firstbloom, the lab station where her mother had dropped her as a baby. Too late.

"My name?" she asked, vamping for time. "Cadence."

The man took in the torn hems of Cade's jeans. The trickled-out ends of her hair. Moon-White's case.

"I can smell the atmosphere on you," he said. "You must have come a long way." The man stepped close, inserting himself into Cade's space. No one else seemed to notice. Cade had no real love of fighting, not like Lee did, but if it came down to it, she would sweep the knees of the attendant and run.

"All right," he said. "I'll let you in. But you should know, here on Res Minor, we stick around. Take care of our own."

Cade didn't wait for permission. She took off the down the hall, and the man's thought-song followed. She didn't like the way it shivered as he watched her walk.

Now she wanted to sweep his knees just because.

But that would cause a ruckus, at least a four on Lee's scale, and her mother's song was close. Cade stopped outside a door three-quarters of the way down the hall. Here the music burned—a light left on to draw Cade through the dark, and call her home.

The door pressed open into a small room. Empty shelves, bare floors, a chip of window that showed the last of the afternoon sun-melt.

A woman in the bed.

"Mom?"

Cade slammed into the edge of the mattress. The woman rested on an ancient slab of white, more wrinkle than sheet. Her body screamed out the truth. This was Cade's mother; she held too many echoes of Cade to be anyone else. The most obvious parts of Cade, the green eyes and the light brown skin, came from her father. But here were Cade's hands, here was the grain of her hair. Cade's mother stared, her brown eyes open. Her fingers were dead on the sheets, music drained.

Maybe Cade was the echo—the left-behind scrap of a beautiful sound that had been made a long time ago.

Her mother was spacesick.

Cade knew that. She'd known it for as long as she'd known that her mother might be alive. But when she had forced herself out of the black hole, she had needed it not to be true. Besides. Her mother's song had been perfect. Thought-songs were still new to Cade, and she had hoped that a clear song meant a clear mind. But spacesick had done its work on Cade's mother. Cade hadn't let herself believe it.

Staring at this voided woman, she *still* didn't believe it. The truth hadn't caught up with what she'd let herself dream.

A hand shot out and grabbed Cade's wrist.

"Mom?"

Hope rose sharp and fast in Cade's throat.

She had to remind herself that her mother's wild reaching out was part of spacesick, too. She would touch anyone like that, to feel herself doing it. To fight her way back through the fog of her wandered-off mind.

But Cade's mother didn't look far from herself.

She looked gone.

Cade worked her arms under her mother's shoulders and pulled her loose weight up to sitting. With Xan gone, Cade had lost her bonus strength. Her mother was helpless, soft as a baby, and wilted against Cade's efforts. Cade wouldn't be able to hold her for two minutes, forget carrying her to the ship.

"You have to move."

But the words were stones hitting a smooth surface. Cade let her mother slump against the sheets and went to work, trashing the room, looking for something that might help save her. Because Cade *had* to save her—first from this terrible place, then from spacesick. All the room gave her to work with was one pounded-thin mattress, two old sets of clothes, an abandoned bottle of bleach.

The window showed the first creep of violet. Ayumi's shuttle was supposed to leave at sunset. This planet had spun away from the sun too fast.

And then the dark-molded curves of the guitar case reminded Cade that she'd brought what she needed.

She grabbed Moon-White, flashing on all the moments when she'd held off Ayumi's spacesick with a bit of music. Of course, Ayumi was ankle-deep in the disease, and her mother's head was under, but maybe if Cade played well enough, she could earn her mother a few clear-headed minutes. Enough to get her off Res Minor.

Cade sat at the bottom corner of the bed, near the twin lumps of her mother's ankles. She propped Moon-White on her thighs and paused her fingers in the still air above the strings. "Listen, Mom," she said. "Listen."

She picked one of the old Earth-songs she'd heard in her mother's head, hoping for a pinprick of recognition.

Her mother stared through the ceiling. Pulled in long, even strings of breath.

"This is a good one," Cade said.

She dug into new-old chords, ones she'd never played on Moon-White but knew because her mother had handed them down, in an accidental sort of way.

"You love this song," Cade said.

Her mother's eyelids sank. Which didn't have to be a bad sign — lots of people close their eyes. A solid half of Cade's old club crowds had looked like sleep-dancers, the slight sway in their knees and nodding of heads the only way to know they were with her. Cade watched for signs that her mother was taking in the music. A deepness of breath, the gathering of a whole person around a bright-beating heart of notes.

"Listen," Cade said. And then, "Please."

Her mother said nothing. The world was Cade's fingers, shifting on tired strings, until the bombs started to fall.

# CHAPTER 3

Cade thought she was coming apart.

The explosions heated and spread her, sprawled her across the floor of her mother's cell, and her mother was still on the bed, outlined in the red of dropped bombs and the fires starting outside.

Within seconds, it became a question of making it to the ship alive. Cade knew one thing: It would be easier to leave her mother. Easier, and impossible at the same time. Cade would have to twist off the faucet of caring.

But then her mother would die, and that wasn't allowed. There would be no more almost-but-not-quite-saving for Cade.

Not after Xan.

Cade grabbed her mother's hand and pulled her to the unsure ground. Loose tiles chattered under them. The old porcelain heated too fast. The building hadn't been hit—yet—but fists of red uncurled hot and close and hard.

Cade slung the guitar case across her back and used both arms to clap her mother to her side, but she couldn't move an unwilling body, not fast enough to make it to the shuttle and take off safely.

The hall passed in a fit of slowness. Cade tried not to think about the gone-mothers and fathers, the children and friends behind closed doors. Thought-songs slammed into her. Doubled the pain of each step.

When she hit the waiting room, she found no one out there to herd patients or shout lifesaving orders.

So much for taking care of their own.

Cade stopped on the steps of the building and pulled off her sweat-thickened T-shirt. The undershirt left her shoulders bare to the heat, its touch rising and wrong as the sun went down. Cade ripped fabric, fitted it to her mother's mouth, and tied a knot at the back of her flagging neck to shut out the worst of the smoke. A deep breath of cindered air would have to be enough to swim Cade safe past the fires. Bombs fell, a few streets away.

Cade secured her mother and headed into the street, braced against the rush of bodies.

Hot, close, hard.

She had to take the blocks as fast as she could to push the tempo. Cade didn't want to put Lee and Ayumi in even more danger. She had promised Rennik that she would make it back safe.

But a few minutes had blackened and changed Res Minor so much that Cade couldn't find her landmarks. The harder she tried to piece the city back together, the harder it fell. The market stalls made a fine bonfire. Windows flung themselves to pieces, giving up without a fight. Cade squinted up to trace the bombs to their source, but the sky had turned into a sheet of smoke.

Only the pain kept Cade alert and moving. The side where her mother hung, almost-dead, flared with life.

It meant a special kind of torture, but Cade reached and opened herself to the songs. It was the only way to pick Lee and Ayumi out of this mess. She stretched her mind outward in circles and found people moving fast, their songs spiked and threaded with fear. That's what Cade had been hearing since she landed on Res Minor. Fear. People had felt that something was wrong, but on such a primal level, so shoved-down deep, that they would never be able to name it.

Cade still didn't know what *it* was.

She forced herself to wonder, even though the thought mingled with the ash in her stomach and made her sick: What if this proved the Unmakers had been following her since the black hole? What if all those weeks had been waiting for the right moment to show she could be had, whenever they wanted her?

Lee and Ayumi burst into Cade's mind, their songs tangled but impossible to mistake. More songs clustered around them, pushing at their edges.

Another fight?

Cade pounded toward them, dragging her mother by the

shoulders, the waist. She told herself that the weight was nothing. That she didn't need Xan's strength twined with hers. People rushed by and screamed at her to move, to move, or they would all be dead.

Res Minor ended in a sputtered-out street. The shuttle waited across the field, past the kicked-up dust.

"I'm here," Cade cried. "Don't leave."

Fire and dust laced their fingers and reached down her throat. Cade gagged so hard that she fell, and even then she had to hold her mother up so she wouldn't choke to death on swallowed dust.

The little ship roared, ready to leave.

Res Minor burned.

Hot, close, hard.

Across the field, a wall of people climbed one another like stones, tearing each other down to reach the ship. This wasn't a fight. It was a mob. Cade was supposed to help these people, save them from their scattered fates, and now they would all die together and there was nothing she could do.

Cade's universe pinched down to two hopes. One chased the first, like a heartbeat: Live. Keep her mother alive.

She curled on the ground, threw up in the dust.

The door of the shuttle stood open, inhaling as many people as it could. But they were running out of room.

"Lee," Cade cried. "Lee, I'm here."

She needed her friends to hear her over the bombs and the screams of the people and the screams of the ship, taking off.

"Don't leave!"

Cade's voice was a handful of smoke-shreds. It would never reach.

So she tried music. No guitar needed — she could use herself to broadcast. Lee and Ayumi had heard her do it before. Maybe they were waiting for a sign to help them find her. Cade tried, but the field was littered with broken songs. It was too hard to sweep them out of her smoke-filled head and focus.

She crawled, dragging and pushing her mother in equal parts. Grass matted her hot skin.

"They're coming," Cade said, lullaby-soft. "My friends are coming for us." If she was going to die, she might as well do it believing this.

Cade limped a few notes.

The ship lifted in a churn of dust. People fell from the open door like drops of water. Cade waited for it to close.

It didn't close.

Lee showed her heat-shining face.

"Cade!" Lee screamed.

The ship swept toward them, heat from near bursts blasting it in one direction, then another. But Ayumi was a first-class pilot and held steady. Lee dropped to the open door and stretched an arm.

It felt wrong to leave when so many people would die, but that didn't stop her from pushing off the ground with one arm, the other lashed to her mother's waist. Cade rose with the heat.

She found Lee's fingers with the last of her strength. And with something more than the last of it, she pulled.

The inside of the ship was dark and moving. People stirring. Low sounds. Charred smells.

Her mother's pulse, under the fumble of Cade's fingers.

Once Cade was sure of the basics, she started to deal with the pain. She stretched against the curve of the hold, her muscles pulling apart with ache.

A shape moved next to her—Cade's mother, stirring out of sleep. Wrinkle-tugged by time and gravity. Hair starting the long slide to gray. Something gentle in the default settings of her face, even if she had left it long ago.

Guilt crawled through Cade. She was supposed to be the hope of the human race, and when it came down to it, all she could do was save her own DNA.

The other survivors didn't scald her with blaming stares. They were busy making space in the hold, trampling Ayumi's Earth-artifacts, ripping her posters and maps with their restless backs.

The ship cracked atmosphere.

Cade stood, knees searching out a new balance, and ran the short distance from the hold to the flight cabin. Ayumi and Lee were sunk in their chairs, so fried from exhaustion and staled with sweat that it looked like they'd been strapped in for weeks. Ayumi flew with the automatic ease of someone whose brain has no part in the process.

Lee shook—fingers on the com, voice filling the small room.

"Eighteen."

She paused.

"Nineteen."

Ayumi's and Lee's eyes passed over each other, caught.

"What are those numbers?" Cade asked, hoping the answer would never reach her. Because in a deep, shoved-down place, she already knew.

"Attacks on at least nineteen planets," Ayumi said. "Ships that match the Unmaker specs reported in the skies over ten." Her voice skimmed the surface of the facts. "All of the targets were human cities and towns."

Nineteen planets.

That pain, repeated nineteen times. Cade forced her mind around the math, but her body was too small to hold it. Still, it pushed its way deeper, lodged shards in each muscle, poisoned her blood, stretched the walls of her heart.

It left so little room for Cade that she fell down and didn't even feel it. Her face against the dull, boot-dirtied metal was a hollow fact.

Cade had wondered if she'd been followed. Found. But she had never let herself imagine—

"The Unmakers didn't come for you," Lee said. "They came for all of us."

# CHAPTER 4

*because it had almost killed her once*
*she kept the gold of that place inside of her*
*deep*

*it was the tide, sometimes low down in her*
*sometimes rising, but always leaving her*
*gold-flushed*

*deeper and closer were the same*
*beautiful and bursting-wide in pain*
*the same*

When Cade came to, someone had carried her back to the hold. Or maybe she'd carried herself. All she had was the fading of a dream-flash. Her head was a sour mess, and she half expected to see Xan.

But he was gone, like so many other people. Gone, and all she had left was this feeling that rose in her at the strangest —the worst—moments.

At least it had waited for her to get off Res Minor.

The shuttle docked and breathed its passengers into the main cabin. Renna took them in with a confused ache, clenched so hard that Cade lost her footing.

"You have some new people to look after," Lee said, kneeling to trickle calm fingers on the floor. "Don't be scared."

Cade and Ayumi stood in the dock frame, checking everyone's pockets to make sure nothing electric made it onboard and crashed Renna's systems. Cade patted her mother's loose clothes, and wondered why she hadn't thought to do it before. Maybe they hid something, a bit of information, a flash of insight. But they were empty.

"You made it," Rennik said.

He stared down from the top of the chute, his face like a blown amp—blasted to silence. Cade hummed with envy. She could have used a thorough numbing of her own. A small dark room where she could wait this out. But there was no room like that left on any planet, and there was no room like that inside of Cade.

"Twenty-three," Lee called up.

"Twenty-three," Rennik echoed down.

Almost two dozen planets, hit by the Unmakers. Every major human outpost.

"Meet in the control room," Cade said. "Ten minutes."

She didn't know what she would do with the crew when she

got there, but there would have to be a regroup. There would have to be a plan. Otherwise, they would float like space-trash, waiting for the Unmakers to come and clean them up.

Rennik looked over the new passengers. Women clutched children to their legs. A few people stood alone, sending out the first flicker-stares to the other alone ones. A little girl broke from the older girl who held her — a sister or half-known friend — and climbed the chute, running a hand over Renna's floor.

"Let me give you a tour," Rennik said, injecting warmth and welcome into his flat voice.

He showed them the cabins, the bathroom, the mess — a mirror of the tour he'd offered Cade when she first boarded. She hadn't been sure what to make of the living ship then, of the Hatchum in charge.

Now the need to touch Rennik hooked deep in her muscles, almost pulled her across the cabin and into his arms. But Rennik wasn't the make-a-scene type. Cade had gotten back safe and the best he could do was spare her a glance, one moment torn out of the fake-cheerful tour.

She felt as far away from him as she had on the surface of Res Minor.

Rennik trailed the thin line of men, women, and children, pointing out the features of their new home.

Renna was brave, and didn't complain.

That came later.

She unsettled the floor as the control room filled with crew members. Cade did her best to keep her mother from toppling. She'd brought her to the meeting, propped her against the wall in the hopes that something could reach her. She had been stuck in that slumming home for who knows how long. Maybe what she needed was stimulation. Good company. Sharp conversation. A kick-in-the-teeth reminder that they were all about to die.

Cade rode the waves of Renna's emotions. Ayumi sat on the floor, notebook to her chest, tears dropping fast. She had kept herself in one girl-shaped piece on the shuttle, and now it was her turn to fall apart. Gori lurked so completely against the far wall that Cade could barely pick him out.

Lee installed herself in the captain's chair. "First, we blaze out of here."

"That might not be possible," Rennik said. "Renna's carrying a lot more than she should be." The threat of the Unmakers ratcheted up, from a soft throb to an everywhere-pulse, lacing Cade's skull. But Rennik held steady. "The best we can do right now is regroup and form a plan."

Lee stood on the seat of the captain's chair for emphasis. "If that's the best we can do, then we're ten shades of dead."

Cade touched the pucker of skin at her mother's elbow. Renna had stopped pitching the room, but Cade still needed balance. "I underestimated the Unmakers," she said. "We all did. We can cling to the mistake or we can get clear."

When Cade added her voice, Rennik listened. He bent over the controls, muttered to Renna, adjusted dials. She picked up speed. Lumpy speed, but still, it put some distance between them and the white planet.

"So . . ." Ayumi said, her lap full of open notebooks, all turned to blank pages. "What now?"

Cade didn't think anyone was ready for that question. But Lee stepped from the seat of the chair to the arm and proved her wrong.

"We delete them from the universe."

Ayumi crawled out of shock just far enough to sound disappointed. "*That's* your plan?"

"It's out of the question," Rennik said.

"Why?" Lee asked, jumping down so she could prowl the room. "That was a massive bombing on twenty-three fronts. If there was ever a time to attack them, it's now, before they get their evil back in order."

"We don't need a cause to die for," Ayumi said, staring out at the darkness like it might peel itself back and offer her a bright new solution. "We need to live, and that means cutting out of space as soon as we can."

Ayumi wanted a new planet. It was what any spacesick with half a brain would want, and she had brains to spare. Not to forget that Ayumi's old job as Earth-Keeper made her more than a little planet-oriented.

"I don't think it's about putting down fast," Cade said. "We have to find the right place."

"And what do we do in the hellish meantime?" Lee asked.

The need to have answers got its claws around Cade.

Wasn't she supposed to be the great hope for the human race? Had she let all the promises of entanglement get sucked into a black hole with Xan?

Gori, of all creatures, bought Cade some time. He cleared his throat, and it sounded like the shifting of continents. "On a cosmic scale—"

"You tell me it doesn't matter," Lee said, "and I'm going to punch your withered face."

Ayumi stood up and dusted off her legs, and Cade figured she was about to pull Lee back from yet another ledge. Lee was all ledges. But Ayumi bobbed her chin and said, "I can get behind that."

"On a cosmic scale," Gori repeated, "this is as important and unimportant as any other thing."

The Gori-ism rubbed Cade wrong. "Is that how you felt about your own planet?"

He stutter-blinked, and Cade knew she'd gotten to him. "This is best left to those with a stake in it," he said.

Rennik stepped forward. "I agree."

Cade and Lee turned on him together, a united front of *What-the-snug.*

"I wouldn't go quite so far," he said. "But I do think this decision belongs to the humans on the crew." He pointed a look at Cade. "I'll do whatever you think is best." Renna thunderclapped to show her support.

Cade had the ship on her side, and it looked like she had the captain, too. Ayumi would want to believe in Cade's new plan and Gori wouldn't care either way. They would all do what she thought best.

Now she just needed to know what that was.

Cade left her mother standing on the wall and entered the starglass. The living hologram rippled and closed around her like dark water. Points of brilliance—planets and suns—swam in loose patterns. One of them could be Earth. Dead, cold, so far from where she stood.

"Cadence?" Rennik asked.

She almost had it. Another moment. Cade held her breath and surfaced with a new sort of truth. Those stars had been packed together once, before the force of dark energy flung them apart. Someday they would draw together again. Scattered once doesn't mean scattered forever.

The stars spread in front of Cade and the words welled up. "We find the rest of the humans," she said. "We bring them back together."

That was her task—always had been. It didn't change because the Unmakers had attacked. The need only got louder.

"I have to connect all of those people," Cade said. "I think I *can*."

Ayumi's pencil came alive against the notebook page. "That sounds . . . incredible."

"We're decided, then?" Rennik asked. He found new footing as Renna resettled the floor.

Gori shrugged.

"That looks like four in favor," Ayumi said. "Lee?"

Lee glared at everyone from the depths of the captain's chair, the only holdout. Cade didn't need her vote to keep things fair, but she wanted it anyway. She tried to tug Lee over to her side. "We'll be stronger when we're all in one place."

"We'll be stronger when you admit this is a fight." Lee hoisted herself up. "Anything else, you're fooling yourself."

She slammed past Cade and out of the control room.

Cade ran, and almost heel-nipped Lee down the chute. She needed Lee to go with her plan. She needed Lee *alive.*

"It's all right," Ayumi said with knowing eyes. "She just needs to storm around a bit."

Cade pushed out a dark sigh.

"Don't let it bother you," Ayumi said.

Cade tried to hold on to the good of her idea, but it was slippery. Her hands were too full of the attacks, the Unmakers, the spacesicks. And now Lee's words. She didn't have space for good.

But she could fake it if she had to. No matter how grim things got, Cade could always put on a show.

She closed her eyes.

Stretched her mind, cracking through the layers of exhaustion and brain-rust. She hit the songs of the people onboard —the known songs of the crew, the tired songs of survivors —and slid over them.

That was the easy part.

Now it was a matter of finding more thought-songs, and the people attached to them. On Res Minor the crash-and-crowd of human thoughts, the volume of their need, had made her claustrophobic and nosebleedish. Now, the space around her birthed silence.

Silence. Silence.

Cade walked through it like new-fallen dark.

And hated herself for the relief she felt. Washed it down with so much guilt that it sank. That silence meant death —people missing, torn out of their lives by the Unmakers. The weight of this new quiet fell on Cade. She doubled over, fighting to keep her mind clear. To keep looking.

"Are you all right?" Ayumi asked.

Rennik rushed to her side, repeating the question in low tones. "Are you, Cadence?"

She fought all the way to standing, but she had to start over. Crew-songs. Survivor-songs. The silence.

And then—

In clusters of ones and twos, tens and hundreds, islands of melody pricked the surface of a silent-dark sea. Cade stretched her limits to hold more. The highs and the lows of the songs. The unbearable lows, shuddering underneath. Notes wandered on their own paths but found strange ways to weave together.

The human race was a small, broken orchestra.

Cade heard it all.

She reeled her mind back, listening for the humans closest to Renna. If she wanted to gather everyone, she would have to start with the survivors she could reach fast, and work outward from there.

"I feel something," Cade said. "A few somethings." The words were harder than the reaching.

"There's a . . . ship. I think."

The songs were clustered. Planet-bound survivors would spread, cover more territory. Cade couldn't explain it, but this *felt* like a ship.

"There's another one," she said.

It came a good stretch beyond the first and was headed in the same direction. Just a few songs this time, all of them shimmer-faint. And then, a swarm. Four songs danced around one another, moving too fast to be doing it at a human speed.

"And four little ships."

"Are you certain?" Rennik asked.

Cade didn't know what to do with that word, *certain*. It made even less sense than being able to hear songs inside her head.

"I know they're out there," she said.

"Incredible." Ayumi's voice was tightly packed with wonder. Like she had touched ground for the first time. Tasted water. Felt sunlight.

"It's not much," Cade said. "But it's enough to get started."

# CHAPTER 5

The first ship came and went in a cheap-metal blur.

It was stolen, no doubt. With a crew a lot like Renna's, on the surface—black-market traders who'd gotten caught between planets during the bombings.

"You want us to do what now, little miss?" the captain asked the first time Cade tried to explain it.

She had to repeat the message five times, each one slower, ground to a more frustrated edge. The captain almost buried her under a pile of idiotic questions. Cade had to get this across, and hope other captains would bring a few more brain cells to the process. When he had finally absorbed the minimum amount of information, Cade gave the ship a means to keep in touch with Renna and instructed the crew to spread the word. She performed a careful reading of the coordinates where all of the human survivors would meet, as soon as she'd found them. She asked if there was room to pack a few more passengers onboard.

That answer came back fast enough.

"No room."

After Cade described the position of the second ship in mind-breaking detail, and Rennik translated the description into a course, and Renna argued with half of the decisions, and Ayumi brokered a peace, the crew dispersed into tired clumps and headed out of the control room. Cade shouldered her mother's weight.

Heading down the chute to sleep felt like going home.

But as soon as Rennik pushed past Cade, she knew the night would be an endless toss-and-turn.

Cade slid the wall panel that led into the bedroom and hung around, waiting for Ayumi. "Can you set her up on the free bunk?"

Ayumi acted as though Cade's mother was made of some heavy, awkward precious metal. "I'll make sure she rests." Ayumi climbed into the tunnel and did her gentle best to pull Cade's mother in behind her.

The lack of her mother's body was as obvious as her pressing weight. It felt like Cade had been cold enough to beg for a blanket, and then ripped it off. But she didn't have time to change her mind, because Rennik walked with purpose. He made his way down the chute toward the main cabin, where the survivors looped in aimless circles. But instead of walking all the way, he pushed aside a wall panel and tucked into the tunnels that laced Renna's insides.

Cade followed.

The tunnels pulsed, slow and regular. Renna's walls gave a soft-ice glow — Cade's favorite color, because it reminded her of Moon-White. Here it was bright enough to see by. The *shush* of Rennik's steps told Cade where to go.

She wasn't going to wait for him to come to her. He'd proven that he could put it off for weeks. With the new state of things, it wouldn't be hard for lifesaving activities to keep them apart until they were both dead.

Cade chased the fade of footsteps deeper into the ship. If Renna didn't want her there, she would tighten the tunnels, flush the walls with heat. *Subtle* was not in Renna's vocabulary, and that suited Cade fine. It made it easy for her to know where she stood. She wished she could say the same about Renna's other half.

The tunnel opened up into a stooped but sweeping room. It housed one object that took up almost all the space — a pounding, churning, spreading-and-shrinking collection of tubes that fell somewhere between an engine and a heart.

Rennik looked up, a cut-short glance. Cade figured she would have his attention here, away from the survivors and the crew and the constant worries of what came next, but Rennik was focused on the heart, his hands fitted to its pulsing curve.

"What are you doing?" Cade asked.

"The same thing I've been doing every night for weeks," Rennik said, not looking up from his fingers. "It's a sort of calibration, but more intimate." The word left traces in the air. Cade's breath sped to meet them. "Renna is pushing herself past all reasonable limits. I have to do my best to keep her from bursting apart."

Cade wasn't sure if Rennik meant that literally, but he had never been known to tamper with the scale of the truth.

"Let me help," Cade said.

Rennik's face softened, and all of Cade rushed to do the same.

"It's not that simple," he said. "Renna isn't just a ship." He reconfigured his face to neutral. Cade couldn't tell which was worse — ignoring her because it came easy or because he thought he should.

"Stop telling me things I already know and let me help," she said.

Rennik inched one step to the side and made room.

"So how do we calibrate?"

He pressed his palms against the engine-heart, kneading until it went soft as clay. Cade tried to mimic him, fingertip for fingertip, but Renna resisted. "Like this," he said, hand spread over hers, pressure light.

Renna trilled her happiness in quick beats. "She thinks very highly of you," Rennik said.

Cade quick-shuffled through all the good things she could say about Renna.

"I love her."

⌐|⌐

It was the first time Cade had said those words, out loud, about anyone.

She and Rennik worked in silence, circling the heart in opposite directions. Cade wondered at how it worked — the layers of muscle and strategic rushes of blood that somehow kept them all alive. When she met up with Rennik on the far side, he put his hand over Cade's again, even though she got the feeling she was a natural at Renna-calibrating.

"Cadence . . ."

Her fingers paused on the rough-stubbled surface. "Yeah?"

"I meant it when I said I want to help you. But I don't know what will happen if Renna has to carry this many people without rest."

The walls drew tight, thinning the rim of space around the heart. Cade pressed close enough to feel the *in-out, in-out.*

"What happens if we can't find them a new ride?" Cade asked.

Renna's answer was hot-tense-squishy-cold.

"She's never done this before," Rennik said, "so I can't be sure of the outcome. But I know it isn't safe."

That was how Rennik needed things — safe. Cade's hate for the Unmakers doubled in that moment. Every one of the bombs that had fallen on Res Minor proved the universe would never be safe.

Cade's mother had already made a dent in the bed, and settled her breath into infuriating patterns. Cade was starting to wonder if she would look the same in any room in the universe.

But end-of-the-worlds or no end-of-the-worlds, Renna was an improvement on Res Minor. Her mother would know that as soon as she woke up.

Cade picked up Moon-White. The heat on Res Minor would have warped the wood of any other acoustic, but Renna had made this guitar for her, special. For all of its delicate looks it was the sturdiest one Cade had ever settled her hands on. She couldn't think of a better instrument for calling a person back to the love of all things human.

She brushed her thumb against the strings and poured herself out for her mother, one chord at a time.

She used soft finger-picking, the kind that spells comfort. It came out smooth, like a hand waterfalling down someone's back. This was different from the music she'd built her name on at the clubs, but she couldn't rest on old melodies. Cade had to pull out everything she had ever learned or thought of trying. If there was a right song to bring her mother back, Cade would find it.

Her tiredness was so complete that she didn't remember setting the guitar down. She fell asleep in a swelling of dark.

When she woke up, there were spacesicks all around.

Ayumi had come in at some point and glassed out. Cade's mother turned to the wall and back in a slow, even rotation. Ayumi's wrist hung over the edge of the top bunk, her hand curled like a half-dead leaf.

No Lee in sight.

Cade reached for Moon-White and played one of Ayumi's

old favorites until she snapped to sitting in her bunk. "Cade." Her voice sluggish, all underactive tongue. "Is anyone else — ?"

"All clear," Cade said.

Ayumi hugged the nearest blanket.

It was double luck, really, that Cade knew Ayumi's secret, and could play her back to a connected state.

Lee crashed through the tunnel that led to the bedroom, a few seconds too late to catch Ayumi's spacesick act.

"Night shift?" Ayumi asked.

"Better," Lee said through a yawn. "I was seeing if anyone from the Res Minor batch has fight training. A few decent pilots, trained on planet-skimmers. Close to no combat skills —"

"You didn't," Ayumi said.

Lee kicked off her boots. "What?"

"You didn't keep those people up all night. Not after what they've been through."

"They're not *done* going through it," Lee said, cutting Ayumi a sharp look. "Not even close."

Ayumi's eyes blurred and Cade's fingers jumped to Moon-White's strings. But it wasn't glass this time. Just tears. Ayumi buried herself in a notebook, and talked to the pages because she couldn't look at Lee.

"You can stop treating me like some idiot slummer," Ayumi said. "I've lost as much as you have."

Lee climbed into the top bunk and put her arm around Ayumi. "I'm sorry." Lee mumbled into her shoulder. "Sorry."

It was a good thing Cade had Moon-White in her lap.

She needed something to focus on, since she couldn't look squarely at Lee and Ayumi. Cade hadn't lost anyone in the attacks. So many families gone — and Cade, who'd never had one, had found her mother. Friends were dead or impossible to track down, and Cade's were all safe on one ship.

But she *had* friends, for the first time, which meant that she could be split open in the same way as Lee and Ayumi were now. Terrible things could happen to the people Cade cared about, and leave her pounding notes to an empty room.

The threat of spacesick blared, loud as death. Being entangled was supposed to keep Cade safe from it, but she didn't know if that held now that Xan was gone. Besides, it wasn't a single shred of comfort to know that she'd get to wait while the people around her glassed out one by one. Once the Unmakers forced the human race off planets and into the dark fringes, it was only a matter of time before spacesick came. Climbed into their minds and cut them loose.

Cade's fingers twitched across the fretboard. "Did you notice any spacesicks down there?"

"None that I could see," Lee said, running a hand down Ayumi's back. "But you can't always tell."

"No." Cade's eyes worked hard to keep from sticking to Ayumi. "Not always."

The second ship came on fast.

It had been slammed together from scrap metal and covered in the strange salvage of ten planets. A junk barge out of the Tirith Belt. It looked, for all the universe, like it was limping.

"Permission to board?" Lee asked.

A single word strained through the com. "Granted."

Renna's crew pushed down the chute, parted the survivors, and formed a breathless line at the dock, but no one from the junk barge came to meet them. Cade crossed the dock-line first, and found the air so thin that she had to suck ten breaths to dent the need in her lungs. She ran through the hold of the junk barge. Tubes and gears and clusters of wire barnacled the walls.

The crew had strapped into their chairs and were nodding in and out. That's why their songs had felt so faint.

Renna pumped fresh air into the ship, but all it did was remind Cade how much more she needed. Cade fished out a knife and sawed through straps; Lee followed her lead. Rennik and Ayumi hauled survivors back through the hold.

"We have a girl minus breath over here," Lee said as she cut a small figure out of a chair. Her pale brown hair tangled in the straps, and Lee had to remove a chunk of it. The girl couldn't have been more than ten, eleven if she was small for her age — not hard to imagine for the underfed, space-raised daughter of junk traders.

Cade grabbed the girl from Lee and lowered her to the floor, pressed the center of her chest, bone-deep, forced air into her stubborn lungs.

Cade needed this girl to live.

If she did, Cade might start to forgive herself for all the

people she'd left on the dust field. The ones she hadn't gathered before the Unmakers got to them. It wasn't right, mathwise, but it made sense in that place where scale and meaning slid away from each other. Where one girl mattered.

Cade's arms gave out. Her lungs were still smoke-sore from the attacks. Her body and her breath weren't enough. She hauled the girl, in the grasp of a strange idea. Cade nodded at Lee to help, and together they lumped the girl into Renna's cabin and set her down.

"Renna," Cade said. "She needs air."

The walls of the ship bent inward with the effort. Ayumi ran to Cade's side and dropped to her knees. Rennik set down another survivor without taking his eyes off the fast-unfolding scene. Even Gori peered down from his bunk. Survivors formed a crowd. The silence and the tense lines of sight and the leaning bodies, everything focused on one small girl.

Air stormed from all parts of the ship into the girl's rib-laddered, lifting chest.

She coughed once. Twice. Her eyes, even greener than Cade's, flickered open.

# CHAPTER 6

"Who does she belong to?" Cade asked.

The wreckage of the junk barge was a day behind them, and the girl still wouldn't talk. Cade didn't think she'd slept, either, unless she'd done it on the table in the mess where she sat now, prodding a bowl of grain-mash and swinging her legs. They scraped air, a few inches from the floor.

Cade rounded up the other survivors from the barge. No one claimed the girl.

"Were her parents left behind in the attacks?" Cade asked.

The man who stepped forward had the worst breath and the largest share of confidence. "If she had parents, I never met them. She bartered for passage. Tanaka to wherever the hell wasn't Tanaka. Didn't seem to care where the ship was headed, she just wanted to be on it."

"She bartered," Cade said. "With what?" If she got even the smallest pricking sense that the people on that ship had taken advantage of a ten-year-old girl, Cade would bury them alive, under mountains of space.

The mold-breathing man stirred in his pocket and came up with a small purse. He shook out coins.

Cade studied the fare, studied the girl. She hadn't spent time around children since her own days in the Parentless Center on Andana.

"Where does a girl as small as that on a planet as terrible as Tanaka come up with coin?" she asked.

Cade hoped the girl had a talent, like Cade did with music, something that people were willing to put up a front for so she could trade on the black market. Maybe she knew a craft —candles, dyework. Maybe she'd been saving the wages from a dreg-bottom job.

"Took the coin, carried the girl, didn't ask questions."

"You probably skinned her on the fare, too," Cade said.

The man shrugged. "Rates go up and down." Smiles cropped up on his crewmates.

Cade stepped closer to the man, even though it meant getting friendly with his smell. "And none of you feels like you should—now that the human race is exploding into tiny bits all around us—maybe take care of her?"

The junk traders looked at each other and pretended to consider it. Cade thought about tossing them into the cold black for the crime of being worthless people who had survived when so many others were dead.

"Here." Cade flung the purse back and headed for the mess. "Have fun finding somewhere to spend it."

The man lowered his voice to that special pitch that begs to be overheard. "Wouldn't pay for the privilege of a ride on this beast. Or that piece of girl-filth, either."

Cade turned on a heel and drove her knuckles into the man's throat.

The girl stood on her chair, pinned to the aftermath — the man clutching for breath, his crewmates scrambling after Cade to start a fight, Renna shaking them to such a pulp that they changed their minds.

The girl sat down cross-legged. "You know how to throw a punch."

"And you can talk," Cade said. "We're both full of surprises."

"It was even a half-decent punch."

Cade rubbed her knuckles and tried to look like she hadn't enjoyed hitting the mold-breather too much.

"I know how to defend someone, if it comes down to it," Cade said. "What's your name?"

The girl dropped a beat. "Mira." Being alone in the universe, she must have have known that acting too free with her name could end in trouble.

"You're from Tanaka?" Cade asked.

The girl plopped grain-mash from spoon to bowl. "Not born there, no."

"What happened to your family?"

Mira worked her pale brown hair into a quick braid so the ends wouldn't dip into the bowl. "Never had one." The lack of a torn, missing edge in the girl's voice made Cade believe her.

"I didn't have one, either," Cade said. Memories of An-dana caught in Cade's throat and swelled there, stuck so they wouldn't come out. She didn't tell Mira how she'd slept under a single blanket, feet raw with blood and sand, every night for months before she found her bunker. Didn't mention how she'd invented a new set of parents every day, only to talk herself out of them at night.

"Isn't that your mother?" Mira asked, nodding toward the door in the direction of the main cabin. Ayumi had taken charge of the spacesicks and was trying to engage the sick-est one in some kind of talk. She held a cup of tea—her own special grass-flavored recipe—to the woman's lips. It dribbled in little streams down her soft face.

Was that woman Cade's mother?

"Technically speaking."

The girl tapped her cheek, thoughtful. Like a tic.

"If you need anything—" Cade said.

"I don't."

Mira got the words out too fast. Cade knew that quickness. It was like tossing a particle-thin sheet over a deep hole. Cade waited. The inner drum that drove her around, all day, all night, slowed to a steady four-four. She wondered if this was what patience felt like.

"Here."

Cade got up, snagged a tin of raw sugar from a cupboard, and pushed it across the table at Mira. It was the only thing that made the endless bowls of grain-mash edible. Mira sprin-kled on a few crystals and poked her tongue at a spoonful.

Two bowls later, she looked up.

"Could use some quiet," she said. "These people won't stop crying."

The words should have sounded harsh, especially in Mira's clear-piped kid register, but Cade understood. The survivors had all gone through the same thing at the same time, and it had glued them together. Mira had lost everything a long time ago, with no one there to listen when she cried.

Cade led her out of the mess, through the main cabin, halfway up the chute. She pointed out a bunk to the right of Gori's.

"This one's yours."

No matter how many survivors packed onboard, no one ever claimed the bunks next to Gori. Cade wondered if he issued specific threats, or just stared at people until they felt the sudden need to drain.

Cade pulled Mira to the edge of his bunk.

"This is Gori. He doesn't say much. Well, he says the same things over and over, and you don't have to pretend they make sense." Cade inspected his dark-orb eyes. "If he knows how to cry, I've never seen it."

"Darkriders do not —"

"— cry, on pain of death, I'm sure," Cade said.

"Darkriders do not form bonds with children," he said, looking Mira over with disinterest. "Childhood is the shortest phase in a Darkrider's life."

"How long does it last?" Cade asked.

"Seven days."

"Never seen one of these," Mira said, prodding at Gori's midsection.

Gori flashed murder-eyes at Mira, but she didn't notice. She was too busy stubbing a finger at his raisinlike feet. Cade leaned in and whispered, "He's boring for the most part, but if you keep touching him, he might kill you."

Mira's eyes went wide and a little bit gleeful. She experimented with how close she could hover at the foot of Gori's bunk, while Cade headed down the chute.

She ran into Lee at the bottom.

"Making new friends?" Lee asked.

"No," Cade said. "The ones I have are enough trouble." Lee perched her fists on her waist, clearly taking it as a compliment.

Cade wanted to get back to her mother and try a few more songs out before they ran into the last set of ships, but Lee didn't budge. She was staring at Mira, her eyes cranked narrow. "There's something odd about that one."

A prickle spidered up Cade's back. "She's a little girl."

"Right," Lee said. "A severely odd little girl."

"She doesn't have to scream normal to *you*," Cade said. "You grew up with things she didn't. Family. Friends. Regular meals."

"Right, the glamorous life of a Human Express kid. Feet in your face every morning, the desperate hopes of humanity resting on you by mid-afternoon. And don't even talk to me about the slop we ate at night. It made grain-mash look like steak cooked in butter and dry-rubbed with gold."

Cade watched as Mira climbed into her new bunk, folded small. "So you're saying she's lucky?"

Lee shook her head. "I'm saying none of us are."

"Mira will be fine," Cade said. "We'll all be fine." But she heard her own doubtful undertones. The raw pitch of what she wanted to believe.

Cade had barely gathered her mother and Moon-White and found a place to sit when Renna clenched. Cade thought she was sending a warning and then remembered — this was the signal. She set the guitar down with care.

Cade corkscrewed up the chute. By the time she made it to the top, her guts were twisted, palms slicked.

Rennik, Lee, and Ayumi stood in the starglass. The entire view was filled with old, gray, crusted metal.

A ship. So big that it took Cade a full minute to understand what she was looking at.

"Is that . . . ?"

"It's human-made," Ayumi said. "Normal human. Not Unmaker human."

Cade let out her panic in shallow gulps. "Next time? Mention that part first."

"I got so caught up in looking at it," Ayumi said, putting up a hand to the image of the ship. It was spotted with lookout towers, cannons pointed like fingers in every possible direction. "It's so—"

"Brilliant," Lee finished.

"Impossible," Cade added. "That's not what I heard. I heard four tiny ships."

Or at least she'd *thought* she heard four tiny ships. Maybe what she'd actually heard were four people, spread out and moving all over one huge vessel. Still, even if that was true, "Humans don't make ships that big," she said.

"Not for centuries," Ayumi said. "But they did. During the nonhuman wars, when they still had big hopes for curing spacesick. My father . . ." She chased the coarse note out of her voice. "My father took me to see one of them when I was little. There were only two . . . or maybe three left in the whole universe. The *Persephone* was the one I saw. And there was the *Greystone,* and the *Everlast.*"

A word slid into view along the bottom of the ship. The paint had thinned in a few places, but the letters were unmistakable.

"You're telling me we're looking at a warship?" Cade asked. "An honest-to-universe warship?"

"One that hasn't been used in over three centuries," Ayumi said, "but—"

"Yeah," Lee said. "We are."

Cade ran for the com, but she didn't take her eyes off the starglass. Her dream of gathering the rest of the human race had a shape, and a name stamped in white letters on time-eaten metal.

*Everlast.*

• • •

Cade and the rest of the crew ran for the dock and pulled themselves together, although Cade had to admit that after weeks of running at top speed, and a bare minimum of showers, they looked dreg-poor.

The dock swirled open. The woman who greeted them on the other side wore an official-looking flight suit and braided twists of light red hair. "We're so glad you found us," she said, pressing hearty handshakes on all of them. She even hugged Cade. "I'm June."

She led them across the dock, into the body of the massive ship, where so much metal curved around them that Cade felt like she'd been swallowed.

"You must be knee-deep in the battle," Lee said.

"Oh, not me," June said. "I'm in charge of tasks and organization. I keep things in *ship* shape." She pressed hard on the pun. When it was met with silence, she added, "Mostly I maintain a chore roster."

"But this is a warship!" Lee cried. "A beautiful, cannon-bristly warship!"

June scrunched her forehead and kept walking, leading them down long metal halls crossed with structural beams. Lee touched everything she could reach. Ayumi drank in the details, then poured them out into a notebook.

June's voice bounced around the near-empty ship and came back without losing a bit of chipper shine. "*Everlast* has four levels — engine, operations, crew, and flight. With a protective sounding-hollow above to absorb blasts, and a triple-thick hull. All of the glass on the ship was made from sands of the Wex system, which are known for their . . ."

June went on about the building materials and their near-magical properties. Cade grabbed Rennik's arm and pointed out empty bedroom after empty bedroom. There were even fresh sheets on the bunks.

Perfect for unloading passengers.

June pounded the stairs from the crew level to the flight level. A man met them at the entrance to the control room with more handshakes. He had dark skin, easy-to-meet eyes, and the first rumblings of a stomach. Gray hair clung in stubborn tufts to his scalp. He looked a little old to be captain of the *Everlast*, but maybe that meant he had lots of years of captaining behind him. Maybe that was a good thing.

"I can't tell you how glad I am to see some life out here," he said. "You're the first people we've run into since those hellish attacks. Sorry, introductions first. Difficulties later. Matteo Campbell. Head of the *Everlast* Preservation Society."

Lee almost choked on her own spit. "You're *historians?*"

"I'm afraid so," Matteo said.

Lee hadn't been the only one hoping for a fully armed, defense-ready *Everlast*. But a floating museum of a warship was better than no warship at all.

Cade sat June and Matteo down, and laid out her plan to gather the rest of the human race. She didn't go into the details of the ex-quantum-entangled side effects that made it possible. But she sketched them. Lightly.

"We can't get to all of the survivors ourselves," she said. "Not with one ship. We need to spread the word, establish com patterns." She saved the most dangerous part for last. "There are some planet-side rescues to run." Matteo raised his peppery eyebrows. "Short version? We need your help."

Matteo nodded. "*Everlast* will give you everything she can."

Cade sighed, and even returned June's hug. It might have worked out in Cade's favor that these were historians instead of crust-hardened, military types. Lee, on the other hand, was still looking them up and down like she might have to throw a neat little coup and install herself as captain.

"This is your entire crew?" Lee asked.

"There are two more," Cade said. She'd heard four thought-songs.

"Right," Matteo said. "Four in each team. We rotate with other teams . . . or we used to . . . to keep the chances of spacesick low. And the ship sits in planet-dock for half the year so people can climb around on it, see what life was like on one of these old monsters during the wars." Matteo patted Cade's shoulder and leaned in. "I'll admit, I was never too eager to find that part out myself."

# CHAPTER 7

The survivors had ten minutes to gather their things and say their goodbyes—not that many had gotten attached to living on a ship that was also alive. The children loved Renna, especially Mira, who Cade caught running up the chute like a cut-loose animal. But the rest seemed itchy to leave for the known comforts of metal walls that don't talk back.

Besides, there was plenty of room, near-endless supplies, and a good welcome on *Everlast*. Cade decided not to mention that it was crewed by soft-in-the-stomach historians.

Matteo stood with Cade and her crew at the dock and watched the survivors pour in. June kept a list of names scribbled on her chore rotations.

"It's not too many, right?" Cade asked.

"Are you kidding?" June said. "The ship is outfitted to carry seven hundred into deep space and keep them alive for years." She consulted a list on an old-fashioned wooden clipboard.

Everything Cade had seen served as proof of the ship's age. "This is going to help so much with the mess shifts. And oh! Window cleaning." June scribbled harder.

Another rush of survivors pulsed across the dock. Cade sorted them to make sure her mother hadn't gotten mixed into the crowd.

But what if she did? What if Cade's mother disappeared into the clean, waiting rooms of *Everlast*? Cade had impossible amounts of work to do, and she could collect her mother when the fleet came together. Rennik would see the reason in her choice. Gori couldn't get his shriveled brain around the idea of "mother" in the first place. Renna needed a bare minimum of passengers to keep flying. But Cade worried that a new wince would crowd Ayumi's light brown eyes. She was the only one who knew that Cade's music might be able to cure spacesick. And Lee—would she wonder what all that searching was for if Cade gave up on her mother so easily?

Two new people in flight suits rattled the nearest stairs and came to meet them—a thirty-something man with beige skin and a blaring bald spot, and a girl with short white-blond hair and metal in every pierceable sector of skin.

Matteo waved them over.

"This is Green, our specialist on tech both ancient and modern. And Zuzu. She's in charge of weapons."

Lee's eyes went bright at the mention of weapons. She rushed Zuzu so fast that she almost toppled backwards.

"So what's the missile-per-minute capacity here? How

much gunfire can the hull take? What would you do to arm a small civilian ship if you wanted to add it to *Everlast*'s defense matrix?"

Zuzu twirled a silver ring in her lip and fired answers. "Twenty-three. Up to a thousand direct hits per sheet per week, double that for indirect. Rig the blast-wipers to fire small projectiles. Just as an idea."

Lee clapped her hands to her heart.

Ayumi cleared her throat and said, "We really should be helping with—"

"What? Survivors? They know how to walk across a dock." Lee turned back to Zuzu. "We're going to have a fleet soon, and we need them armed."

"Oh, right," Zuzu said, tugging at an ear stud. "I'm used to *thinking* about weapons. Not so much actually using them."

"Well, things are about to get really hands-on," Lee said.

Ayumi looked four different kinds of upset.

The last of the survivors from Res crossed the dock, and on the other side, Renna let out a full-ship sigh.

She wasn't the only one who liked things quiet. Cade had spent years kicking people out of her dressing room, slapping threats on anyone who stared at her for too long. Her new urge to bring the human race together wasn't the same thing as wanting them all within touching radius.

Cade took a walk, admiring the acoustics of the emptied ship. She was so tuned in that she heard the dull knocking right away. It was coming from the common room, behind one of the cushions that survivors had been using as make-shift beds.

Cade pushed aside a wall panel and found Mira, knees shoved to her face. She stared out, all green eyes and defiance.

"What's this about?" Cade asked.

Mira pulled her crossed arms tight and Cade noticed the places where they were still dotted with baby fat. "I don't care about that other ship. I like it here."

Rennik and Lee had been doing a maintenance round, and hooked around the door frame at the sound of voices.

"Who are you talking to, Cadence?" Rennik asked.

She stepped aside to reveal Mira.

Lee didn't look surprised.

"We're still close enough to *Everlast*," Rennik said. "We can hail them and have them here in—"

"No!" Mira sprang out of the panel. "Please."

"She has no reason to go with them." Cade's own past rose again. Andana, in all of its anti-glory.

"The girl needs to speak for herself." Lee retied an errant hair knot and did her best to look wise. "State your case."

Cade got the feeling anyone with a semi-functional heart wouldn't be able to turn Mira away once they heard her story. Wanting to know what had happened to her was like wanting to hear a sad song—Cade got the feeling it could drag her under, but it would also scrape her against something she needed to feel.

Mira didn't pour out a story, though. She kept her eyes hard and put a hand to the wall. "Renna let me stay."

Renna *was* the ship—she had the first and last word on the subject.

That was enough to take the air out of Lee's objections. Under normal circumstances, Rennik would have let it go at that, but he was still sizing up Mira as if every pound she added to the ship had to be worth it.

"If you want to stay," he said, "you'll be counted on to help."

Mira nodded like he'd handed her a hot meal, a birthday present, and a kitten all at once. She skittered out of the common room and turned back when it became clear that no one was following.

"All right, then!" she said. "What do we do?"

"*We*," Lee muttered. "Universe help us."

Cade didn't bother hiding her smile.

Mira's first job was to grab tables from the storage closet and set them up in the control room to help turn it into a center for the finding and gathering of the human race. She rushed, a blur of pale brown hair and bright eyes, so eager that she brought five more tables than Cade needed. Lee unrolled charts of all the known systems. Ayumi tore blank pages out of a notebook, which Cade patched with tape so that the huge sheet laid flat, taking up a good portion of the floor.

She kneeled in front of it, pencil in hand. Rennik claimed the starglass. Lee and Ayumi manned the charts. Mira sat across from Cade, ankles tucked under, and watched.

Cade didn't know a better feeling than having her strange little band assembled.

She snapped from the soft brightness of Renna's control room into the song-strewn dark. It was easier to do this time —leave the ship, press through the silence, find the humans. But Cade had new challenges. With the nearest ships located, it became a matter of getting to everyone else, pinning them to specific spots in the universe. Figuring out how to reach them fast, before the Unmakers did.

"What is she doing?" Mira asked.

"I'm listening," Cade said in a low, even voice.

She balanced the song-map in her head with the realness of the room around her. The smooth floor under her. Lee and Ayumi's footsteps. The pencil twirling.

Her wrist flicked, and the pencil landed over and over. Cade marked down the locations of songs, paying special attention to how far the clusters were from each other, how fast they moved. The first piece of information would make it possible to match her sketches to the charts of the known systems. The second would tell them whether the survivors were space-bound or planet-side. Some darted, or moved in strong, fast lines. Others sat, almost still, but when Cade focused she could feel a curved inching, the slow nudge of orbit and rotation.

"How many planets?" Ayumi asked.

Cade found one, then kept it in a loose mind-grip as she moved on and counted the others.

"Three," she said. "I think."

"Can that be right?" Ayumi asked. "Not that I know any-thing about how this works, besides it being incredible, but —"

"It doesn't sound right," Cade said. Of all the human out-posts, only three had survivors still clinging? Cade washed her mind over the songs again, but that was all she felt.

Lee's voice wormed into the dark. "Where are the Unmak-ers in all of this?"

"What are Unmakers?" Mira asked.

Ayumi shifted closer to the girl. "That's our name for them. The people who attacked."

"People?" Mira asked. "You don't mean humans."

"Bet your brass we do," Lee said.

Mira's voice twisted and tightened. "Oh." Then she went quiet. How was Cade supposed to explain to a little girl that her own kind wanted her dead?

"So?" Lee asked. "Where are they?"

The pressure of the songs rose, and Cade felt like her jaw might snap. "I don't know," Cade said. "I can't care about that right now."

"They're coming for us, whether you care or not." Lee's words were too loud. They pushed hard, toppling the balance in Cade's head. When she opened her eyes, the light in the control room attacked them.

"If you don't want to help, you can drain," Cade said.

Ayumi leaned over the tables. "Cade, she's just asking —"

"—a question I don't have time for."

Lee didn't storm out. She left the control room at a slow,

sure pace, her eyes dusted with disappointment. Ayumi hovered on her toes, ready to follow.

"Don't," Cade said. "I need your help."

"You needed her, too," Ayumi said. She didn't sound mad with Cade. She sounded reasonable, which was even worse. Ayumi settled back on her heels and stuck with the charts, but Cade had the feeling she didn't deserve it.

"Thanks," Cade muttered.

She got back to work fast. Reached out, translating songs into smudges on a blank white page.

The plan to deal with the ships came first. Renna would sail in one direction, *Everlast* in another, hailing as they went. They would spread the message that it was time for the survivors to gather, and give the coordinates where they would meet. A simple, open patch of deep space.

Cade got on the com and explained the plan to Zuzu.

"We'll have to have someone on hailing at all times," Zuzu said. Cade heard the nervous clatter of a tongue stud.

"Tell June to put it on the chore rotation," Cade said. "She'll love it."

Cade didn't mention that they wouldn't have the same issue on their ship. Renna was more than capable of sending out a hailing code all day and night to act as a beacon.

Ayumi's pencil flew over the projected paths. "It should take less than a week, if we do it right."

"All right," Cade said. "Now planets."

She described them—location and size, tilt and rotation speed—and Ayumi and Rennik matched them to the charts.

Cade started with the biggest planet, the one with the greatest number of songs swarming on it.

"That has to be Cass 12," Ayumi said.

"We'll ask *Everlast* to run the rescue there," Rennik said. "There are too many survivors for us to pick up."

The second planet was smaller, much smaller, but with a stubborn clutch of songs, huddled close, flaring bright.

Ayumi did a quick check against the charts. "Rembra." She choked on the name of her planet. "It's Rembra. I'm sure of it." Tears slid down her cheeks, skirting the corners of a smile.

"Do we set a course?" Cade asked.

"There are still too many people," Rennik said. "We couldn't pack them in."

"Of course. Right right right." Ayumi sniffled against the back of her hand. "We'll spread the message, and tell them where to meet us. We have our own ships on Rembra. There'll be a resistance there. A fierce one."

Cade reached out and pulsed strength into Ayumi's hand, the way she used to send it to Xan.

"You'll see your people soon."

Cade returned to the black to find the last planet. Medium-sized, with a strong tilt, a slow orbit. Songs like a scattered handful of sand. Cade's memories filled in the rest — a raking wind, the dry stick of a throat that hadn't felt the touch of water for days. She didn't need anyone to check this against a chart.

It was Andana.

# CHAPTER 8

"Not so fast," Lee slurred.

She had waited until the rest of the crew drained and came back to the control room, her feet moving in unbalanced patterns.

The scent around her was so strong that Cade didn't have to lean in to take stock. Mint, and something stiff and woodlike, and another hint, strong and reaching up like a hand through the other layers. Every night in the bar on Andana piled into Cade's head at once.

"Peace offering?" Lee pulled a bottle from behind her back. It was filled with burnished green, only a few sips missing. Either Lee had zero-gravity for tolerance, or it was strong. Very strong.

"Where did you get a thing like that?" Cade asked.

Lee waved a vague hand toward the rest of the ship. "Was

Moira's. She kept it in the highest cupboard in the mess, for *emergencies*. Never used it, not once. Not when I almost got thrown in a torture cell on Tirith. Not when wassisname told me it was time to settle down and *stole* my *pack* because I made it clear how many times and in what fashion he could snug himself. Not once!" she roared, like it was a point of pride, and Moira might be taking notes somewhere.

"So why do it now?" Cade asked.

"Dregs." Lee set the bottle down with a solid glass thump. "Every second of now is an emergency."

Cade swiped the bottle, and thoughts of Andana drove her lips to the rim. She took a swig so deep it seared her from the throat down.

Lee whooped and put an arm around her.

Maybe if Cade got Lee fuzzed, she could convince her to let up on all of the attack-mongering, and see the good in Cade's plan. With Lee on her side, she could face anything.

Cade swigged again, and Lee sloshed a smile. "I knew you hadn't gone over to the wet slummer side."

It hit Cade a few seconds later. Fire first, and then a warm gut-spread. Much nicer the second time around.

Lee's hand fluttered on her wrist. "What say we skip stones?"

Cade touched her burning-tender lips to the back of her hand. "Do *what?*"

"Skip stones!"

Lee clumsily wove her fingers through Cade's, and led her

to the starglass. They took their shoes off and stretched their toes in front of them. Lee pelted the image in front of them with a little paper ball, and it rippled like dark water.

"So," Lee said. "You and Rennik . . ."

Cade waded through the warmth of her brain and found herself deep in concern. Had Lee rigged this whole situation just to ask her about Rennik? If she asked, would Cade be able to lie? She held her green-heavy breath.

"You and Rennik," Lee repeated. "Did you chart it?"

Maybe that was some kind of new slang. "What?"

"A course."

Cade sighed. Lee slung a paper ball, and a far-off galaxy trembled. She started in on another white scrap, molding it small, but her fingers were disconnected from their function. Still, she kept at it, battering the paper into an ever-smaller shape.

"Yeah," Cade said. "We're going to Andana." She *hated* Andana. If she couldn't get herself to like her own plan, how much of a chance did she have with Lee?

"What about the Unmakers?" Lee asked.

Cade thought back to her time in Hades, opening up to it even though she didn't want to. She was back in a small white room with a woman who didn't think much of the human species.

Her own species.

"They made their big move," Cade said. "Now they think we're crushed and done."

Lee's voice was quiet, but impossible to ignore. "You don't know that."

Cade wondered if Lee was back in her own small room, her own past moment — the one where she'd watched Moira die.

"They might come back," Lee said.

"Then we'll be ready!"

Lee stood up and paced sloppily. "If they come for us, they'll do it on their own terms. If we attack them now —"

"Wait," Cade said, and the room went sideways.

"What?" Lee asked.

"Did you get me to drink with you so I would change my mind? So you could get all 'Hey, die' on the Unmakers?"

"Admit it!" Lee cried. "You wanted me to change my mind too."

Cade laughed and walked away, slopping each step like she was liquid coming out of a pail. She stood in the starglass. The stars were moving. Or maybe she was moving and the stars were telling her so.

Cade didn't know how to make it clear that she couldn't let Lee die. With Xan gone, Lee was the strongest connection Cade had. She should have been able to open her mouth and say that. But all she did was stare, farther than far.

She stared, farther than far. At brightness and dark, the beauty of the two even better when they sat so close like that. Every good thing was out there, waiting. The universe was wide and wonder-stuffed and Cade wasn't done with it. Not even close. "But the most important part," Cade added, like she'd said the rest out loud and was just picking up where she left off, "is that you and I are here together. You know that, right?"

Lee squinted. "We're missing something," she said. "Very important. Must right this terrible wrong." She scrambled for the door. "Don't. Move."

"We're on a spaceship!" Cade cried. "Where am I gonna go?"

Lee ran back with Ayumi, and a smile Cade hadn't seen in ages.

"She told me there's something not to be missed," Ayumi said, tipping back and forth on her toes.

"It's like she came pre-fuzzed!" Lee said.

Cade raised her eyebrows — and the bottle.

Ayumi happy-sighed and hugged it like a lost cousin. She lofted it high. "To the fleet."

Cade went still, waiting for Lee to insist on a different toast. Instead, a smile tugged at Lee's cheeks and snuck into her eyes, without ever forming on her lips.

Ayumi pulled the drink down in remarkable gulps. "This-isfantasticwheredidyougetit?" she asked. Less than a minute later the green was gone, and it had turned Ayumi into a warm blanket of a girl. "Fantastic," she said, and hugged Lee so hard, for so long, that it looked like dancing. "We need music!"

"Yes yes yes." Lee turned to Cade. "Music."

Cade rushed to get Moon-White. She could almost feel the curve of the guitar against her body.

"No!" Ayumi's eyes stopped Cade, then stretched serious-wide. "I have something to show you."

Ayumi led them into her shuttle and sacked the hold for ten minutes. At least, Cade thought it was ten minutes. She couldn't feel time anymore. Dregs — she couldn't feel her own face anymore.

"Here it is!" Ayumi shouted. Cade and Lee leaned over her cupped hands.

"What in the name of all things shiny is that?" Lee asked.

Ayumi offered up a fat metal rectangle, stubbed at the corners, with a small glass inset window. Another rectangle, this one of clear plastic, was fitted inside, and housed a thin spool of film strung between two toothy circles.

"One of my artifacts," Ayumi said. "Electrical, so I can't bring it onboard. But I've been waiting for a reason to share it." Her finger sought one of the buttons along the top.

"Listen."

She held up a foam-coated pair of headphones and stretched the old metal so Cade and Lee could each use one. The arc of the headphones drew them in, and they huddled close.

A song crackled into Cade's left ear. Well, it fit the basic definition of the word *song*, although it stretched that definition as far as it could without cracking the concept. All she heard was a simple bouncing bass line, the scratch-and-shine of primitive percussion, and a man's voice, moving over simple lyrics. On the chorus, men's voices doubled and tripled.

Singing about dancing.

About dancing and moonlight and warm and bright.

*Terrible*—but also fantastic.

"Thank you!" Cade shouted, and it felt good to shout. She could feel her throat when she pushed the words. And the more she felt, the better everything felt.

Oh, dregs. She really *was* fuzzed.

"Thank you for what?" Ayumi asked.

Cade knew, but she couldn't say. The green had locked away her words and set her feelings loose.

Ayumi took the headphones and set them down, pushing the volume all the way up. The music came out small, like a few streams of light on a dark, dark night. Just enough to dance by.

Cade and Lee and Ayumi claimed a small patch at the center of the hold, which only a few days ago had been stuffed with the survivors from Res. Ayumi balled her hands and shook them in the general vicinity of her shoulders. Lee shuffle-jumped through the chorus. Cade dropped back and kept it simple. But the more she moved her hips, the more she felt the lack of certain other hips.

She ran back toward Renna.

"Hey!" she cried. "Wait here." But Lee and Ayumi didn't look like there was one place in the universe where they would rather be.

• • •

The green was against Cade now. It had wiped the clearness from her head, and crashed her mission to change Lee's mind. Now it worked in partnership with gravity, making it hard to stand up. But that couldn't keep her from her course. She threw open the door to Rennik's room.

"You!"

He looked up from his desk, his fingers light on the barrel of a pen.

"Cadence?"

Looking at Rennik steadied her. She didn't need the door frame to help her stand, but she held it anyway — just in case. Rennik put the pen down, forgetting to find a proper place for it.

"What are you . . ."

One beat for his mind to catch up. One more for his face to do it. He knew exactly what was going on.

"Well?" Cade asked.

Ink pooled on the desk as she waited for an answer. The look Rennik gave her wasn't a yes. It wasn't a no. It was a want, strong and unformed.

So Cade tried to give it a shape. "Do you want to dance?" she asked.

"Do I want to — ?"

"Dance," she said. "With me."

". . . Perhaps this isn't the best moment," Rennik said.

"But you do!" And then she could tell she was yelling, so she dropped her voice to a whisper. "Want to."

Cade ran off, feeling triumphant. She loved the drink for letting her say what she meant. Loved Lee for giving it to her. Loved the night for not ending, because she got the burning-green feeling that all that love wasn't going to last.

When she crashed back onto the shuttle, Ayumi and Lee were still dancing. Cade sat and drummed her hands against the floor, throwing too many glances at Renna, hoping for a last-minute entrance from Rennik. Instead, she found round, dark eyes peering around the corner of the dock.

"Gori?"

He moved into the lighted rectangle.

"All right, all right," Lee said, treating Gori like a shriveled uncle. "We'll keep it down."

He picked at his robes, pinched his gray lips. "May I join you?"

Ayumi kept dancing, but Cade and Lee stopped short.

"Are you sure you want to?" Cade asked.

"*What?*" Lee said.

"Cade needs a partner!" Ayumi cried.

"Not dancing with him." Cade snatched her feet underneath her. "He'll rapture all over my toes."

"No, no." Gori waved a hand through the air. "I was referring to the—"

"Libations?" Ayumi asked. Three gulps, and her fancy words came out in force.

"Really, Gori?" Cade was impressed, not so much that he wanted to get fuzzed as that he wanted to do anything close to human.

"Sorry," Lee said, tipping the bottle. "All out."

Gori shuffled over the line and crossed into the shuttle. "That won't be necessary." He stood near the girls and breathed deep, puffed out.

"Hey!" Lee cried. "You said you would have fun."

"This is my form of fun," Gori said. "It is also my form of communion. It is also, as it happens, a fine way to become intoxicated." He wobbled on his feet.

Lee and Ayumi cheered. Gori sat in a circle with them, rapture-breathing and sinking into his new state in small increments. Lee and Ayumi laughed until their voices thinned and then failed altogether. The silence deepened.

Ayumi leaned her head on Lee's shoulder, curls spilling everywhere.

And then Cade blinked and Lee and Ayumi were gone.

And Gori was deep in a rapture.

And Cade was alone.

She didn't remember falling asleep.

She was in a bunk, but it felt distinctly not-hers. The inside of her head fluttered and twisted like a broken compass needle as she tried to get a lock on her new location. Her body sounded out the lumps.

Not Rennik's bed. That didn't have lumps. Not any of the bunks in the hidden bedroom. This was set into the wall, not stacked.

"Really?" Cade whispered. She had fallen asleep in Gori's bed. "Snug."

A voice came out of the dark, somewhere near her elbow. "I hope not," Lee said. "For your sake."

Cade jumped, and her stomach lurched an echo a full ten

seconds later. She looked over and found Lee kneeling at the side of the bed.

"All right," Lee said with a dimly lit grin.

"All right what?" Cade asked.

"I'll go along with your plans."

"You'll . . ." Cade strained for eloquence. *"What?"*

Lee pointed a *take-this-seriously* finger. "I still think it's a bad move. I want that on the record."

The mission to change Lee's mind had died a wretched death around the fourth swig, or so Cade had thought. "What changed?"

Lee clutched Cade's arm. "I want to tell you. I absolutely can't tell you. Yet. Okay, here's what I can tell you. *It's great.* The reason. If you piled all the reasons in the universe on top of each other, it would be the best and finest and prettiest one there is."

"Sounds good," Cade groaned.

Lee jumped up and left, happiness spilling everywhere.

# CHAPTER 9

When Cade woke up, happiness was a planet, and she had drifted millions of light-years away from it.

Of course, *now* Rennik came down the chute.

"How are you feeling?" he asked.

When Cade opened her mouth to say something scathing, she threw up. She crawled out of Gori's bed, waving Rennik back, but he followed her to the tucked-in spot inside the control room where she rushed to deal with another foul-rising wave. He stood behind her, lifted her hair off of her neck, and ran his patient fingers through it. This was so far from the closeness Cade wanted with him. She hated her body for soaking it up anyway.

Pride knocked Cade back to standing. And then something else tugged her away from Rennik—a sense that the control room had changed. Not the light, or the layout, or the slight, organic Renna-smell.

Cade almost walked straight into the captain's chair before she figured out that her mother was sitting in it.

Her arms had molded to the strict lines, and her head lolled back so her neck couldn't hold it up.

"What is she doing?" Rennik asked. With a nervous smile, he added, "Not trying to fly the ship, one would assume?"

Cade clipped a half-smile. "That would be brass." A bold way to come back to life and announce what she needed. But her mother was too far gone for that. She faced the wide black of the starglass, barely breathing.

"She's in love with *that*," Cade said, waving at a smear of space.

"Bewildering," Rennik said. "Space is good for getting from one place to another. It's nothing, in itself."

Cade squinted until her eyebrows hurt. She'd kept the idea of spacesick at a safe distance for as long as she could. But it made sense, under the skin of things. "My mother's brain cracked itself on nothingness. Whatever was in there before ran out, and nothingness worked its way in."

Cade stepped toward the starglass, and the white rushed her, more stars than all the notes she could play in a lifetime. "Can you imagine letting in something that huge, and then trying to shut it out again?"

"Yes." The word brushed low and quick, and by the time Cade turned to Rennik, he'd cleared his throat and tripled his politeness. "Shall we find a better place for her to rest?"

Rennik and Cade lugged her mother to the common room, their hands shifting and swapping her weight. When they almost touched, Cade's nerve endings sang like they had.

Cade installed her mother in the middle of a small universe of cushions.

"Better," she said.

She didn't tell Rennik the one good possibility that sat like a pit at the center of her feelings. Cade had to be sure before she would let it grow into something like hope.

She asked every member of the crew, down to Mira, but no one had moved her mother. She must have walked, on her own steam, from the bedroom to the control room.

Something in Cade's mother was waking up. Cade had to grab it while she could, and drag it into the light.

She found Ayumi in the hold, surrounded by notebook pages spread thin and everywhere. Ayumi hopped from one blank floor space to another, crouching over pools of her handwriting, taking notes on her own notes.

"We need this," she muttered. "We need this now."

Cade stared down at the scribbles, but she couldn't figure out what *this* was. She made a small nonverbal sound and caught Ayumi's attention.

"I thought you might be able to help me," Cade said.

"With what?" Ayumi's attention fluttered from Cade to the notebook pages and back again.

"A song."

"I'm not, strictly, musical," Ayumi said with a frown. Then she brightened. "I do have a minor amount of training on the *slyth*. It's a double-reed instrument we use on Rembra, with a flat tone that sort of splits your nerves down the middle—"

"Not like that," Cade said. "I mean, I don't need you to *play* the song."

"Oh." Ayumi's fingers stopped in the middle of their demonstration of the air-*slyth*. "That's probably for the best."

Cade sat down at the edge of the papers. "I was hoping you had a song I could play on Moon-White."

"What kind?" Ayumi asked.

"An old one," Cade said. "My mother loves Earth-songs. Or she used to. So I thought—"

"I have a few," Ayumi said. "Here. Somewhere. Songs and poems and story-bits . . ." But she was so distracted with her own work that she didn't offer to help. She turned pages, fluttered notebooks.

Cade kneeled, unable to avoid the rustle. "What are you looking for?"

"A planet." Ayumi's fingers fast-skimmed a margin.

"What kind?" Cade asked.

"One we can live on when the fleet's gathered. We have a plan for how to pull everyone together. We need a sub-plan for what to do with all those people and ships, and I don't sleep so I figured . . ."

She laid one page on top of a slim pile, and threw the others back into the general mess. "We need a location outside of the known systems. Lee and I talked about it, and we can't see nonhumans letting us start new colonies on top of the old ones. Especially not if it means a threat from the Unmakers."

"So we need something new," Cade said.

Ayumi nodded. She held up a page from her little pile. "How does this sound?" She put on her most convincing voice and tried to sell it to Cade. "Forty-five degrees cool side, five thousand hot side. Methane issues. Snappish and hungry nonhumans."

Cade couldn't keep the sourness off her face. Ayumi crumpled the paper and threw it.

"There's got to be something in here," Cade said. "A song for me. A planet for all of us. Right?"

Ayumi perked up on her knees, brightened her eyes. She was so used to being the source of constant uplift for everyone else, and she looked relieved that someone else had supplied a little bit for her.

Cade sifted through pages looking for an Earth-song, while Ayumi hunted for the vague scent of something habitable.

"Caves?" Ayumi said. "Inhabited, drippy, prone to flooding."

"Maybe," Cade said. "Inhabited by what?"

Ayumi squinted. "Doesn't say."

"Never a good sign."

"How about this one? Land and water reported, but the planet was never settled due to . . ." Ayumi turned the page and deciphered the back. "Brain infestations by the local empathic bacteria species."

"Pass."

Cade went through page after page, and found that most were filled with splinters of information about Earth. The names of ancient countries: Nigeria, Ireland, Venezuela, Japan. Recipes for food that probably hadn't been cooked in a thousand years.

Paella. Something called a cheeseburger. A short and mostly crossed-out description of the smell of Earth-grass. Sweet and mild and mixed up with dirt. Bitter-bright when you cut it. The names of wars, the names of battles, the numbers of the dead. Half a poem about the question of being or not being. What the sun looked like when it touched the sea.

Cade was so attuned to the details of a planet she'd never seen that she almost missed a page of what looked like songs. "London Bridge," and "Ring Around" something called a "Rosy," and "Twinkle, Twinkle, Little Star."

These told Cade nothing about Earth, plucked no deep chords in her. But they were Earth-songs, so maybe her mother knew them. Maybe they would trickle their way in through her cracks.

Cade read "Twinkle, Twinkle, Little Star" with more interest than the others. It didn't sound like it had anything to do with real stars, not the way Cade knew them. But she got caught on one line: "Up above the world so high." It made her think of lying on the ground, on that bittersweet Earth-grass, staring up into a white-freckled night, seeing stars the way humans were meant to see them.

Cade looked up, and found Ayumi watching her with a specific sort of dreaminess on her face.

"It gets in your head fast, doesn't it?"

"What?" Cade asked. "The lyrics?" She scanned them again. "They're catchy. In a boring sort of way."

"No," Ayumi said. "Earth."

Half an hour went by. Cade counted the time in paper cuts.

She was supposed to be looking for songs, something that could reach through her mother's disconnect. But Earth kept drawing her in.

Cade found a page that she knew was important before she even started reading it. Something about the careful handwriting, the way the block of words was centered and set on its own page.

*"They left before the asteroid hit. They told their children how blue it was, how green."*

Cade slammed the notebook shut.

This was an account of Earth's last days, and there was nothing dusty and distant about it. Cade had almost been able to see it — the colors of the planet, ringed in pure space-black. She'd almost been able to feel it — there, and bright. Then gone.

Back to the search. Cade shifted a few pages aside, and underneath them, found another notebook.

"Don't open that one," Ayumi said, even though it looked like every other one.

"What's in it?" Cade asked.

Ayumi's face welled pink. "Details of spacesick, what it's like to be spacesick, very personal stuff."

When Cade had first met Ayumi, she'd been so calm about the whole thing, treated it like part of the human condition — a sour fate, but unavoidable. Now she looked like she wanted to find a way to hold spacesick down and punch it in the face.

"You can talk to me about it," Cade said. "If you want."

Ayumi shook her head, so sudden-hard that Cade worried she might bash it against the nearest surface.

"I don't want to talk anymore," Ayumi said. "I want it out, out, out."

Cade told the entire crew to meet in the common room — no exceptions.

She sat down, stuck the little paper with the Earth-songs on top of her knees, and settled Moon-White across her lap. If a guitar could sigh, that's what Moon-White did. The smooth body found its home against Cade's, and the warm-ups hummed through her with a sort of rightness that she hadn't felt since before Res Minor.

"I don't get it," Mira stage-whispered from where she sat, half-sunk in cushions.

Rennik stood propped against the wall. When he spoke, Cade heard a grace note of pride. "She's a musician."

"She's the most finger-destroying guitarist in the known systems," Lee said, not to be outdone. "And, since it's hard to imagine people coming up with guitars in the unknown systems — maybe something *like* guitars, but not the same — I think it's safe to say that she's the best there is."

Mira stared at Lee, the green of her eyes struck through with stubborn flint.

"Don't worry," Lee said. "Cade will convince you."

This was bigger than Cade's reputation. She had to tell the

crew the good her music might be able to do. There was no point in bringing the human race together if they celebrated by glassing out.

"Do you remember the footage from Firstbloom?" Cade asked. "When the scientists said music was tested for its effect on spacesickness?"

Lee downshifted from praise to scoffing. "It clearly didn't do the trick, or we would all know about it."

"What they heard back then wasn't enough," Cade said. "But they never heard me."

And she went to work.

Simple chords first, and then more complicated finger-weaving. It was all fine and building until she transitioned to the Earth-songs. Cade started with "London Bridge," but she couldn't force the words out. They were too ridiculous. She tried "Twinkle, Twinkle, Little Star." She "Ringed around the Rosy."

Cade looked up, and found her mother as gone as ever. Mira frowned with special, intense boredom. Ayumi and Lee traded glances. Rennik's neck corded as he turned his head toward the door, like he could hear more important things happening somewhere else on the ship. He had told Cade once that he didn't feel music the same way she did. Now she was nerve-sick, and she needed to go back a few minutes and un-demand that he come. She didn't want Rennik to see this happening.

Cade never lost her audience.

Even if she did, they had never mattered as much as the music. Cade had been willing to drop the crowds in the club, and if they found their way back to her, brass. If not, she would hit the next song without thinking.

This was what it meant to care—to know that if she lost these people, it mattered. Cade shifted the chords, disrupted her patterns, tried harder, but not with the Earth-songs. There was no space in their simple melodies. Cade let the page drift down from her knees. The song chose what it wanted to be. It led, and Cade followed.

The crew went with her.

And Cade's mother did, too. She wasn't moving, but energy swirled below the surface. Cade couldn't explain it. She felt her mother, a presence in the room where before there had been nothing and no one.

Her mother—

Thrashed out of stillness, and her breath tore the air. Drowning. She looked like she was drowning. She grabbed the nearest solid thing—Mira—and battered her down. Tugged the girl's clothes, anchored fingers in her hair.

Mira loosed a scream, cold as space on bare skin. Cade dropped Moon-White with a hollow bang. She grabbed Mira out of her mother's soft-desperate arms. Mira slammed into Cade's shoulders, and ran. She turned in the door frame and stared at Cade's mother, her features bunched and set, her voice chilled metal.

"Don't touch me."

The fight had passed out of Cade's mother, but Rennik held her hands behind her back. Cade followed Mira across the main cabin, where she spun, cornered by the harsh realities of space. There was never anywhere far enough to run to.

"No one is allowed to touch me," Mira said, the small points of her teeth showing.

"That's okay," Cade said. "That's fine." She held both hands in the air to prove that she wouldn't try.

Rennik carried Cade's mother in the bracket of his strong arms and set her down on his own bed. They stared at her like she was a picture of a woman, taken a long time ago.

Rennik asked his question to a vague patch of air. "Do you ever worry that it might happen to you?"

"No," Cade said. "I'm entangled."

She and Rennik kept a tight hold on her mother's arms, pressing her into place.

"You don't ever worry that it will . . . expire?"

Rennik's politeness could act as a balm on the wounds of a torn-open universe. It could also suffocate.

"Do I think that I'm going to glass out now that Xan is dead?" Cade asked.

Rennik winced.

Cade shook open a roll of tightly wound bandages. "No." She had felt it on the shuttle coming back from Res Minor. Entanglement wasn't done with her. Her muscles might have drained of the extra strength, her mind reshaped all the spaces where Xan's thoughts used to fit. But he was still with her, always with her.

Cade started to wind the bandages around her mother, tying her to the bed, but she couldn't keep her brain on the task.

At first she thought it was the leftover feeling from the common room, clouding her.

But this was different.

*it came*
*gold and perfect*
*and pulling her inward, to something even more*
*perfect, the point*
*the center of it*
*all she would have to do was wait*
*with him stripped*
*down to particles*
*there at her side*
*or closer*
*and still she couldn't think about him*
*because even more than the gold*
*he was the reminder*
*of what she had left*
*for this red*
*for this burning*
*this life*

# CHAPTER 10

"What's happening?" Rennik asked.

Cade blinked at him.

She had felt this before, but never in a moment that she shared with someone else. The black hole had clung to the edges of her life, slipped into quiet moments. It hadn't cut in. Until now.

"It only lasted a few seconds," Rennik said. "But you looked like you were entirely somewhere else."

Cade set a hand to the wall, like she'd seen Rennik do so many times, for strength. Renna's confusion leached in.

"I was."


The day started with sickness and throat-sting and never let up. Lee found Cade piling comfort food in the mess and lured her out into the main cabin with a chorus of *You owe me*'s.

The rest of the crew was assembled there in a loose knot. The belt at Lee's waist dripped with knives.

"What the snug is this?" Cade asked.

"Fight training!" Lee said, launching herself at Cade. She latched on with her knees at Cade's waist, her arms in a death-hug around her neck. Cade dropped Lee like a sack of grain-mash.

"Not bad," Lee said, dusting off her shoulders.

Lee had marked the floor, as if she was turning the cabin into some kind of arena.

Lee paced up and down the ragged line of crew members. "I said yes to all this fleet-gathering," she said. "But there's no way I'm letting anyone take one more step without proper lessons in defense. We have no idea where the next attack will come from: Unmaker, nonhuman, space-bound, planet-side."

Ayumi shivered. "That's a happy little speech."

"You know what I mean," Lee said. "We have to be ready for anything." She slapped her palms together. "But Andana first." Cade's desert home came to her in all of its awfulness. She could feel the memory of the sun on her cheeks, sweat pushing down her arms.

"It's a slummer-filled planet." Lee flicked a glance at Cade. "Sorry if that sounds harsh."

"I think you're giving it too much credit."

If Cade was really going down to Andana, she needed the warm-up. She still knew how to fight, technically, but she hadn't done it since before the black hole. Cade had all these people to save, and she wouldn't do them any good if she got sliced clean through.

"Today, we'll train for a planet-side fight," Lee said. "Starting with hand-to-hand, and knife work."

For the first matchup, Lee paired herself with Rennik.

Cade tried to shake the feeling that it was more than an easy way to get started. She couldn't count all the times she'd seen the two of them together, Lee boiling with fake anger and a very real blush.

Rennik and Lee met in the center of the cabin, shook hands, and circled. Slowly at first, then with a swell of momentum. Lee came at him, all spitfire, hard-slamming kicks and sharp angles. Rennik stepped around her in patterns, graceful. He made fighting look like some kind of elaborate dance. They had known each other so long that there was a simple harmony to the two of them together. In skill, they were well matched — until Lee stepped out of it, panting.

"All right," she said. "Show me what you can really do."

Rennik frowned. "Is that necessary?"

"This is the fight of our lives," Lee said.

"*For* our lives," Ayumi corrected.

Lee circled him again. "Do you really think it's the best time to hold back?"

Rennik went to his room and returned with two long, leaf-shaped double blades that hung from his hands, the weight making itself obvious. Cade had fought a lot of people, human and non, and she'd never seen anything like them.

Lee homed in on Cade's interest. "Hatchum ceremonial blades."

Rennik stood at the center of the cabin, flipping the handles a few times until he found their balance. Then, without any intro, he swung so hard and fast that the blades blurred, more like traveling light than long knives. The work was effortless. A crowd of people standing in his way would have been cut down.

"All right," Lee said. "That's enough."

Rennik let the blades swing to a stop. "I'm glad it meets your approval."

Lee sailed a playful punch to his shoulder.

She moved down the line and found Gori raptured as big as a pillar. "Really?" she said. "That's your defense mechanism?" She poked him in the vague area of what were probably his ribs. "Dead. You'd be dead. Moving on."

Lee slid down the line to Ayumi. "Hit me," she said.

Ayumi winced, and no one had even thrown a punch. "I can't . . ."

"All right," Lee said. "Hit Cade."

"How is that—" Cade was about to say *different,* but a fist connected to her face. "Ayumi!"

The Earth-Keeper hid behind one hand and pointed the other at Lee. "She told me to."

"All right, then." Cade pushed up her sleeves and drew Ayumi out of the line like a magnet.

As soon as Ayumi lost the element of surprise, she lost the

fight. Cade came at her with a series of moves that she'd more or less invented in the Parentless Center and perfected at the clubs. Andana had been a terrible place to live, and a first-class place to fight.

Still, Cade could feel that she wasn't half as good as she used to be. Her strength needed building up, but it was more than that. There was a relentless pull at her center, and it ruined her balance.

Having a black hole there wasn't the same as having a boy.

"All right." Lee waved them apart and set a hand on Ayumi's arm. "We'll work on it." Ayumi nodded like she'd known that all along. She ran back to the line, shaking off nerves and energy.

"You need help too," Lee said. So she could tell that there was something different about the way Cade fought now. Something *less*. But Cade couldn't add one-on-one training to the endless list of things she had to do to save the human race.

"I've got this," Cade said.

Lee gathered all of her doubt in a dimple. "Try it against Mira." Cade's eyebrows did a quick *you-can't-be-serious,* but Lee stuck to her decision. "You need to practice, and I need to see what she can do."

"I'm not fighting a little girl." Cade had all kinds of noble reasons, and they leaked into her stomach, churning together with memories of fighting when she was Mira's age. For everything. Food, soap, guitar strings. All she'd had to her name was a seven-blade knife and a stubborn unwillingness to die.

It didn't have to be like that for Mira.

The little girl bounded into the ring. "I'm not scared," she said with a rubber-band smile—stretched wide, then gone. "Are you?"

Cade would go easy on Mira. Easier than easy.

She shook the girl's small hand and circled her once, twice. Mira slashed with her arms, drove with her knees. She fought cold and constant. When it became clear that Cade was gaining, and would win no matter what, Mira pushed harder. It was just a practice fight. Maybe she knew she wasn't going to get hurt. Maybe she could feel Cade's hesitation, the pull-back when she worried a punch would land too hard.

Cade's muscles kept up the work but her mind went further, trying to see into Mira and figure her out. People had never been Cade's strong suit, but now she had a shortcut. Mira's thought-song would teach her more than a lifetime of small talk. Cade chose her moment, closed her eyes, and cast herself into the space right in front of her shifting feet.

She listened.

But Mira didn't have a song.

Just silence, a not-song so obvious that when Cade sailed across it she noticed, like hitting a patch of bad atmosphere. It had a shape to it, weight, different shades of silence like all the hues of dark.

The absence smacked into Cade, and now Mira's arm flew and hit Cade's nose. Hard.

It ran thick with blood as she blacked out.

• • •

Cade's face throbbed an evil rhythm.

Lee had cleared the rest of the crew out of the main cabin. She stood over Cade, one foot planted on either side and a clutch of cold towels in her hand.

"I told you to fight her, Cade. I didn't think she would *win*. What is she, some kind of violent prodigy?"

Cade tamped fingers to her face, and her nose groaned against the pressure. "Worse." She got up and dragged Lee into the mess, sweeping the area to make sure it was Mira-free. "You were right."

Lee crossed her arms. "It's the natural state of things."

Cade swiped a cloth and set it on the place where the pain bled over into her cheek. "Consider the universe back in order, then." Mira's non-song stuck to Cade like sweaty droplets of fog. When Cade told Lee about it, she shivered, and it was only half overacting.

"What does that mean?" Lee asked.

"I don't have that part worked out," Cade said. "I was too busy getting punched in the face." Lee did an impatient shuffle-dance while Cade thought. "The way the thought-songs work . . . every species is like a frequency band. I tune in to the human part of the universe."

"So she's *non?*"

"I don't know." The pain in Cade's nose light-speeded around the rest of her head. "There are exceptions, like if I'm standing close to someone I know. I can hear Rennik's song."

"What does he sound like?" Lee asked.

Cade managed a micro-shrug. "Like you think he would."

"Neat? Precise? All little boxes and well-kept rows?"

"Right." Cade kept the rest to herself—the chaos she felt under the table of Rennik's neatness.

Lee squared Cade's shoulders, as though the next part was very important. "What do *I* sound like?"

Cade closed her eyes and tapped in to Lee's song. The wild highs, and the plummets that should have bottomed out into sadness but caught updrafts and flung themselves high all over again.

"You sound like flying."

Lee's posture sparked, a sure sign that she loved the answer. For the first time, Cade's mind ran into the question of what her own song sounded like. Would it be the same now as the day she was born? Had it morphed since she cleared her own personal sand-hell and found Renna and the rest of the crew? What about the black hole? What had *that* done to her song?

"What does Ayumi sound like?" Lee asked.

"We don't have time to do this for everyone on the ship," Cade said. "We have to deal with Mira."

Lee plunked herself into a chair. "Right as radiation."

Cade didn't want to believe that Mira's non-song had a dark meaning, but she couldn't ignore the possibility, either. "We need to know if Mira's a danger."

"What category of danger?" Lee asked, switching to instant Express mode. "She's not here to start a fight. Your nose aside, she's pretty amateur."

"She could have a tracker," Cade said.

"The only way to tell, without a specially rigged light, is to do a manual check. An *everywhere* manual check."

Protection took a strong hold. Cade knew what it was like not to want strangers puncturing your space with unwanted hands. "You mean strip-search a girl who told us she hates being touched?"

"I mean get creative."

"This is not normal," Mira said, her voice muffled through the wall.

Cade and Lee had stuffed her in one of the tunnels and were crouched on the other side, in the main cabin.

"Don't worry," Lee said. "Renna knows what she's about."

Like most of the plans Cade and Lee formed together, this was half bold, half unstable. They had built it with the knowledge that Mira liked the ship more than she liked any of the crew.

"Renna will do a full-body scan," Cade said, "and then you're official. It's like having a uniform, but more . . ." She dove for the right word and came up with "unique."

Cade and Lee had asked for Renna's help, and after a twitch of hesitation, she'd agreed. Lee had stamped an old dead tracker against the wall so Renna had a basis for comparison.

"How does she scan me?" Mira asked.

"Just sort of roll around," Cade said.

"Right," Lee muttered. "Because that sounds official."

"Do you have a better plan?" Cade whispered. "Because any second before now would have been a nice time to bring it up."

Lee shrugged. "Desperate times call for weird measures."

They divvied up Mira's old clothes, checking for any information about the girl who was drumming her skin against the wall. Cade hoped that Rennik wouldn't pass by and question them with that amused look of his.

"Both of you have done this?" Mira asked, mid-thump.

"Oh, sure," Lee said. "Once a year since I sprouted teeth."

Cade tended to stumble all over herself if she veered too far from the truth, so she kept as close as she could. "I'm newer to the ship than Lee is. Grew up on Andana with no one. It was me and sand and more sand."

"No parents?" Mira asked.

"No." Mira's shirt was neater than Cade would have thought—no niggling-loose threads or chewed hems. It held no clues that could lead Cade to a new understanding of the girl. "No parents, and slummers used to call me nonhuman every chance they got. Not that it would be a sour thing, if it turned out to be true. But people got some kind of sick gossip-thrill out of it."

Mira's voice came through the wall like a cold shove. "So?"

Cade closed her eyes and prodded at the non-song. It was still there—or painfully, noticeably not there. Cade needed to know what could do that.

"If someone was nonhuman I wouldn't care," she said.

"Me neither," Lee piped.

"Obviously," Mira said. "You both look at that Hatchum pilot like he spins the suns."

That shut Cade up. Lee didn't seem to care; maybe her feelings were so obvious she had no fear in broadcasting them. Cade wondered what that felt like, and if she would ever get there. With Rennik. With anyone.

Lee finished rummaging through Mira's clothes and looked at Cade with a shrug. *"Clean,"* she mouthed.

Cade didn't know where to go from there. She still had doubts — and Mira stuck behind the wall.

"Hey, did you ever get knocked on the head?" Lee cried. "A solid sort of thump that could really clear it out?"

Cade grimaced at the quality of Lee's idea. Lee mouthed, *"Worth a shot."*

A pierce of sound cut through the wall.

"Renna, stop! Stop!"

Cade ripped the panel aside and found Mira's arms crossed tight across her chest, fingers stuffed into her armpits.

"She was tickling me," Mira said.

Cade shook her head and Lee patted the wall. Mira came out a minute later and Lee tossed her a set of clothes. It became clear that they used to belong to Lee when Mira tugged them on. The waist pinched one size too skinny, and the legs trailed three sizes too tall.

"Now you're officially official," Lee said.

Renna rippled the wall, cheering.

Cade's nerves eased down from high alert. She didn't know how much she'd wanted to be wrong.

"Don't see why it mattered," Mira said, rolling the pant legs into cuffs. "Renna has been treating me grand since I got here."

"She's the best ship in all the systems," Lee said. "But don't worry if she grumbles at you. Her language is grumble-based."

"I'm *not* worried," Mira said with a sharp gloss of pride. "We talk all the time. Renna tells me plenty."

"Like what?" Cade asked. She couldn't imagine what Renna would keep from her own crew but confide to the girl.

Mira ticked items off on her fingers. "She hates it when everyone's asleep and she sees a comet and she wants to wake all of you up but she knows that no one will thank her for it. And she loves foggy atmosphere and rain. And she gets scared, a lot."

Lee's face crumpled and her hands hurried to the wall.

"Anything else?" Cade asked.

Mira nodded. "She's hungry."

# CHAPTER 11

Renna's fuel needle wobble-pressed dangerously close to the empty line.

Cade and Lee and Mira watched it in a solemn lineup. Rennik and Ayumi, who'd been hailing nearby ships, hemmed them in.

"Did you know about this?" Cade asked Rennik.

He went a special shade of death-pale.

"How did it happen?" Cade asked. "I thought you had enough fuel for a whole run. What is that? A year's worth?"

"We did." Lee patted Renna with an absent hand.

Rennik's face clenched tight. "Renna isn't a machine," he said. "Her fuel is food. She's usually efficient in the extreme, but all of this fast-and-hard flying puts stress on her systems. Sometimes the only way to compensate is increased intake."

"So she's stress eating?" Lee asked.

"Essentially," Rennik said.

"Fan-snugging-tastic." Lee broke out of the little group and walked off, possibly to hide the dots of water at the edges of her eyes.

"So we put down," Cade said. "Refuel."

"We can't." This was no auto-argument. Lee hunched forward, feeling every word in her gut. "The nearest planet with the right supplies is too far. We'd spin out before that."

"What are the right supplies?" Cade asked.

"Organic matter, vegetable in nature," Rennik said. The crew—minus Lee, who must have already known—united to stare at him. "Cabbage, if we can find it. Renna loves cabbage."

"We're only a day out from Andana," Cade said. The only thing worse than putting down on her least favorite planet would be putting down to find everyone dead. "There's no way she can make it?"

Rennik answered her question with a hard stare.

Renna would fly anywhere, at any speed, if that's what Cade needed. But she couldn't bring herself to ask. She knew what it meant to be stretched too far, too thin, all the time.

Lee turned to Rennik, fear swapped out for grim sureness. "You know what we have to do."

"No." Whatever Lee was about to propose, Rennik had seen it coming, and he stood firm.

Lee turned to Ayumi, to drum up support. "There's a trading post—"

Rennik cut in. "A *nonhuman* trading post—"

"Between here and Andana. It's almost completely on the way."

Renna slid the floor a few times, up, then back. Like a shrug. Not a vote of confidence, but at least it wasn't a doom-laden rumble.

"It's too risky," Rennik said.

But Cade couldn't ignore the change under her feet.

"There's risky and there's dead."

"Stop. Wriggling."

Lee stood on a chair above Rennik, trying to drop gold tent-like material over his head. Ayumi and Mira waited on the ground to help pull it into place.

"Hatchum don't *wriggle*," Rennik said.

"Well, you're not much of a Hatchum," Lee said. "Hence the robes."

The cloth, instead of a graceful flutter-and-fit, slumped. Stuck in odd places. Ayumi fiddled with the sleeves, which gaped three times too large at the wrist. Apparently, Rennik kept his old ceremonial robes hanging around, in case he needed to add a legitimate air to his diciest missions.

If Cade had ever needed help finding Rennik less want-able, these robes were made to order.

"You look very nonhuman!" Ayumi said, working against the sleeve-droop. Rennik adjusted the robes and ignored the compliment.

Lee jumped off the chair. "Now there's the question of who goes with him."

"I do," Cade said.

"No one," Rennik said at the same time.

Lee pursed her lips. "See, that's where I think you're both wrong. I have a grip on how these trading stations work."

"I won't let anyone risk their life," Rennik said, tugging at his wide collar.

"No one will," Lee said. "But you're an outlaw too, and if there's trouble, it's not the kind you want to take on with two hands. No matter how good those hands are at swirling blades around."

Cade rolled her eyes.

"Renna has been risking her life for us every day," Cade said. "We can give her a few hours."

"A fine point," Lee added.

When Cade and Lee pooled their stubbornness, Rennik didn't stand a chance. He slid a glance between the two of them. "It should be Gori who comes with me. He's nonhuman. Darkriders are rare, so he might draw some attention, but less than I'd get with a human on my arm."

"Great plan," Lee said, "except it involves two impossible things." She ticked them off on her fingers. "Waking Gori up when he doesn't want to, and getting him to leave the ship, which he never does."

Rennik's fancy sleeves crumpled as he put his hands up in surrender.

With that part figured out, Cade and Lee locked eyes, mouths set in harsh lines, wills matched.

"I can disguise myself as nonhuman," Lee said. "Plus I have the flight skills. *And* the spaceport experience."

There was no way Cade was letting them go without her. It looked like she was beat, but she still had a card to play. "Rennik told me the next time there was danger, he and I would go in together."

Rennik looked stricken, but Lee broke into a smile. "It's settled, then," she said. "We're both going."

"Me, too!" Mira said.

"No," Cade and Lee said chorused.

Rennik kneeled in front of Mira. "It's more than possible that you saved Renna's life." Cade looked down on the scene and her chest swelled tight. "I'd like to ask you to stay here and take charge of keeping her safe."

Mira's face twitched in an odd pattern, computing. She put a hand to the wall and struck a nod.

"All right," Cade said. "Let's move."

Ayumi, who had been quiet since the control panels, chose this moment to speak up. "You're sure you have to?" she asked. "Those attacks changed things for the human race. I have notes, I have stories, all of which back up the basic premise that, historically speaking, when things get bad for our kind, they get really bad."

Lee pried Ayumi's fingers out of her curls, pulled her hands close, and centered them between her long fingers.

"If things want to sour on us, we just won't let them."

Cade wondered if Lee would live by those words. If they would really stand between her and a good fight.

The meeting broke up, but Lee turned back and made one more dive at the bag that held Rennik's Hatchum finery. "Oh, wait, this is the best part!" She produced a slew of silver bells.

Rennik's sigh came from the depths of his gut. "I had hoped you would forget those."

"Never," Lee said.

She tied some around Rennik's neck, and others in circles around his upper arms, accenting the puff of his sleeves. Cade laughed once, and it sent Mira into fits. Ayumi pressed her lips together. Even Renna quivered.

"I hope you appreciate this," Rennik mumbled to Cade as he passed her on the way out.

"Me?" she asked. "I'm not the one who pulled those things from storage."

"No, but . . ." Rennik's scowl faded. "You're the only human I would act like a Hatchum for." He headed for the control room, ringing all the way. Cade's heart kicked out of time, a little too hard. She told it to calm down. They had people to save. Vegetable matter to locate.

The trading station was bigger than Cade had imagined. In terms of size, it could have been a small moon, but it was wheel-spoked instead of round, with long arms spreading from a central point. The arms alternated, some lined with docks, some with shops where nonhumans could trade for what they needed on long space runs. Sharp lights — red, blue, green — outlined the metal in the dark.

It was beautiful.

Cade didn't waste a lot of time being jealous of nonhumans, but the trading station gave her good reason. Without spacesick, nonhumans could live in the black as long as they wanted. Since they weren't being hunted out of the universe, they could fly without the constant fear that crept over Cade's minutes and days.

Lee eased Ayumi's shuttle into the long rows of docks. Cade had never seen so many small craft in one place, not even at the spaceport on Andana.

Lee gave the shuttle's control panel a *good-ship* pat.

"This is one of the reasons we avoid space refuels," Lee said, low enough that Rennik wouldn't hear. "Renna is one-of-a-kind when it comes to ships. On most of the planets where we put down, she's a curiosity, nothing more. But here we can run into Hatchum, and that starts the questions up right."

It was true, Ayumi's ship blended with the others, but Cade knew that she'd be able to pick it out of any lineup. It didn't have distinctive markings from the outside. The difference was in the scale, the proportions. Something about its humanness.

Cade picked a corner of the hold and helped Lee into the form-fitting Saea outfit that would keep her safe in the nonhuman crowd. Lee had insisted on Cade wearing it, and Cade had counter-insisted, which led to a coin toss: loser wears the suit. Cade rolled the light blue skin-film over Lee's freckled shoulders, and pasted the bonus eye to the back of her neck.

With Lee transformed, they met Rennik at the back of the hold. He'd slid into a different personality easier than he'd shrugged on the robes. He was hard-faced, calm, twice as unreadable as the real Rennik.

The dock swirled open.

Rennik and Lee went in first, and Cade ducked around their shoulders to get her first true look at the trading station. Low ceilings, bright lights, glass walls, the stir-and-bustle of shops. It made the black market on Andana look like an old smudge.

Years working in space meant Rennik and Lee were used to this. Cade would have to make up for her limited experience with a quick stare and a touch of brass. But as soon as she stepped in sight of the nonhumans, she knew that no amount of posturing would do. They stared at her and the air went flat, like someone had strangled everything that was good to breathe out of it.

Lee checked a map at the center of the hall, so casually that Cade thought she might start whistling. Lee had lots of practice in pretending that her plans were solid and intact when they had already unraveled.

"Organics are in row 4, section 19," Lee said, in Saea. Cade understood the words, which gave her a little scrap of meaning to hold on to. Saea was one of the languages she could mostly understand, and sort of speak. It was something Cade had always done on Andana, at the club, picking up bits of dialect like dropped coins.

Lee led the way, and Rennik stayed close to Cade as they turned into row 4. He tried to hide her but it was useless. A fresh group of nonhumans stared. Saea detached themselves from the crowd, and two walked right up to Lee and hailed her as one of their kin.

Rennik stepped forward and put his most intimidating calm into effect. "It's a great pleasure to meet you," he said in their language. The vocabulary was basic and Rennik's accent was clean. Cade had no trouble following along. "I'm Nesko, of Hatch." He nodded at Lee. "This is my second in command."

"And the human?"

The sleeping air bristled.

"She's Hatchum," Rennik said. It was a bold lie, and Cade couldn't imagine him getting away with it. But if Rennik had the same worry, it didn't show in the smallest crease of his skin. It looked like he wasn't done lying. "This is my new wife." He clutched Cade to his side, where she fit perfectly.

Cade blushed so hard that it added weight to Rennik's absurd story. "She's shy," he said. "Doesn't speak much."

"Only when I need to," Cade added, speaking Saea — which Rennik didn't know she could do.

His calm took a direct hit as Cade watched him figure out that she must have understood the part about being his wife. Lee forced a laugh down her throat.

The impatient foot-shuffles of the Saea pulled Cade away from her friends' reactions. "Where are your orbitals?"

"Sending messages at the post." Rennik's answer came fast, but not too fast. He was good at this game, and the Saea could sense it.

So they doubled their efforts on Cade.

One of them stepped forward, nudged into her space. "She's short for a Hatchum. And her eyes are—"

Rennik caught the Saea's hand, half-raised. "Not yours to inspect."

His killing grip turned the Saea's fingers white, and all of row 4 trembled, on the edge of a fight. Cade had a knife in each pocket, and her hands hung loose at her sides. But she didn't let them travel the last few inches. Not yet.

The Saea backed off, summoning fake smiles. "All the happiness in the universe to you." They turned to leave, but Cade didn't feel one bit safer until they were around the corner, their bonus eyes unable to track her.

Lee leaned into Rennik, then Cade, with an impish twist of a grin. "That's a timely match."

Of course, that was the real brilliance of Rennik calling Cade his wife. If anyone tried to touch her, or even stand too close, a Hatchum would take it as an insult to his honor. And insulted Hatchum were famous for hacking into people.

Rennik, Lee, and Cade took the halls at a fast-tapping pace, but not a run. Cade's mind rushed ahead, pushing at the self-imposed limits of her feet. She started to hate the low, bright halls.

They made it to section 19, then the shop.

It was filled with Hatchum.

"Snug it," Rennik said as he snatched back from the door. Cade had never heard him swear, and maybe it should have rattled her, but she couldn't help liking it. It reshaped his blank, beautiful face into an over-the-top expression. She found it strangely adorable.

Rennik steered Cade and Lee backwards, into the nook outside the door. It was a good thing the shop had actual walls, not just glass.

"Wait here."

Lee primed herself to argue, but Rennik was right. Lee couldn't leave Cade alone to fend off the nonhuman crowds, and there would be no marching in the shop and telling the Hatchum that Cade was one of their kind.

Rennik flashed a look at Cade. "Don't get yourself into trouble." He flashed a much more serious one at Lee. "Don't get her into trouble." Then, with a robe whisk, he was in the shop.

"Don't worry," Lee said, settling deep into the nook with Cade. "We've done business with this trader before."

"Does he know about Rennik?" Cade asked.

"Of course. This fellow does a strong and shady business. He'll keep our secret to himself." Lee punched the words to make them sound extra-true.

Conversation drifted out of the shop in a language Cade had never heard. It sounded basic. Unctuous. Like bites of raw meat. Lee stood within whisper-distance and translated into Cade's ear. "There are four others," she said. "Ordering the same thing we are, for their orbitals. Well, they're ordering about as much for a year as Renna eats in ten minutes."

Cade picked out the four other voices. Then the trader's, lower than the others.

A fifth voice.

"That's Rennik," Lee said, as if Cade wouldn't know his voice anywhere, in any language. "He's ordering Renna's food. Now he's making some kind of excuse about going on a long trip to explain why we need a million pounds more than we should."

The trader filled the orders for the other Hatchum first. They came out of the shop, orbitals spinning. It was like seeing four of Renna in miniature, each one so tiny Cade could have covered it with her palm.

As soon as Rennik was alone, the trader switched to English. Cade's sore brain thanked him, but Lee's face bleached the dirty white of bone. "That's as much as calling him a human-lover."

The volume of the conversation dropped, and the trader's voice sounded like a scraped knee. "I heard there was a Hatchum running around this trading station in the company of a human girl. Now if I was that someone, I would be quick about changing my mind."

"This is not good," Lee muttered. "This is exactly as not-good as Ayumi said it would be."

"What . . . and who . . . I carry, is none of your business,"

Rennik said in a soft tone, just this side of a threat.

"I thought you'd like to know." Cade heard a false smile changing the way the trader shaped his words. "The other ones, the kind that wiped the humans clean, were in here a few days ago and I must tell you, I prefer their business. They're smarter, stronger, have much better sense than humans. No species in any system that wouldn't prefer them. It's why so many went back to finish the job."

In that moment, the rest of the trading station didn't exist. Just Lee's hand, slipped into Cade's.

"What do you mean?" Rennik asked.

"Cleared up two problems at once, didn't it? No new fight on their hands, no humans crawling under their feet."

So that was why Cade had only heard survivors on three planets. The original attacks were intense, but not enough to null and void whole cities. Not unless nonhumans went back for the survivors.

"That's sickening," Lee said. "That's pure, utter sickness. That's . . ."

No word existed for how bad it was. But it wasn't the only thing that stuck wrong-side out in Cade's brain.

"They can't tell that the Unmakers are human?" she asked. "Really?" She had seen one under the robes, a small woman with red hair, nothing special about her.

"I don't know," Lee said, with an empty shake of her head.

"It's a bunch of costumes," Cade said. "It's an act." But the disguises had fooled her for a long time. The Unmakers didn't act human, didn't talk like humans. Maybe there was something in it. Something that went deeper than metal voice boxes and costumes.

"It's a good thing I'm a bad sort," the trader said, "or I wouldn't sell to you at all. But I need the money. And I must say, there's a bit more pleasure in taking it off the likes of you."

Lee strained toward the door. Cade clamped her hand tight, held her in place, Lee's pulse leaping in her wrist. Her need to start a fight sat too close to the skin.

Rennik came out of the shop, moving fast. "It'll be loaded by the time we get back." They turned the corners, hurrying down the same halls in reverse. Nonhumans stared at them, and more stopped to watch every minute.

By the time they made it back to the ship, they were running. The four Hatchum from the shop stood at a window not far from their dock, then stepped into the middle of the hall, stretching across it, forcing Rennik, Cade, and Lee to a stop.

"That's a nice piece of metal," the tallest one said, in English. "Human-made?"

So Cade wasn't the only one who'd noticed.

Lee peeled back the blue skin-film at her neck, freeing her head from the Saea costume. "Why don't you ask me that again?"

"*Two* humans?" the tall one asked.

"You're making it even harder," said the one at his right, with the brightest eyes. "Which do we kill first?"

"The quiet one."

Cade's hands shot to her knives.

As Rennik stepped between her and the tall Hatchum, he loosened the collar of his shirt. Cade had never thought bells could sound threatening. "If it's Hatchum honor you're concerned with," he said, "you kill me first."

"He's right."

Three of the Hatchum cornered Rennik, leaving the weakest-looking one to stand guard over Lee and Cade.

Lee smiled like she couldn't believe her luck.

Cade threw herself into motion, knives flashing as Lee sprang onto the back of one of Rennik's attackers. She toppled him, and Cade moved on to the third, barreling headfirst so that the surprise snugged his balance. She knocked him down again, this time cold. Lee claimed the fourth, who stood there too idiot-faced to defend himself. Rennik rushed to pull out his double blades, but by the time he'd balanced them in his hands, the last Hatchum had hit the floor.

Cade sat in the hold, cabbage-smell surrounding her, rank but soothing. Lee and Rennik talked back and forth in low voices. It was a short return flight, and the shuttle wasn't being followed. Those Hatchum would be out for hours, and no one else hated them enough to risk being killed by two human girls.

Rennik came back to the hold and double-checked the crates to make sure the trader hadn't stiffed them — not that there was any going back if he had.

"Do you mind if I . . . ?" He lifted a pinch of robe-cloth.

"Oh," Cade said. "No."

Rennik gathered his normal clothes and stood in the far corner of the hold, facing away. Cade knew that he hated the robes, but did he really need to make her watch this? She kept her eyes on her knees.

"Thank you," Rennik said. No matter how hard she tried not to look, she caught a second of the muscle-shift in his back.

"For what?" Cade asked. "Saving your nonhuman skin?"

His shirt drank the sound of his voice as he pulled it on. "That," he said, clearing the neck-hole. "And for making sure Renna doesn't spin out, or run out of fuel and spend the rest of her life half-buried in a desert."

"I know what it's like to get stranded," Cade said.

Rennik turned, dressed in a black shirt and stone-green pants, plain and comfortable. Instead of going straight back to the controls, he sat down on top of one of the crates, facing in her general direction.

"You don't have to thank me," Cade said. "It wasn't all my choice."

"But it comes down to you, Cadence."

It was true. She felt the constant need to choose the right path for everyone. It kept Cade from Moon-White when she needed music. It broke her chances to be with Rennik. To be with anyone. The scientists had entangled her, the Unmakers had come after the people she loved, and she cared too much to turn her back.

So this was her life.

"I have to help. Renna, the people on these ships, even the ones on Andana. I can't let anyone else get hurt."

It was Xan all over again.

No — that sounded off-key, even to Cade. Xan had chosen to be left behind. He had seen the universe, a small and twisted chip of it, but enough to make a choice. This was worse. The human race was having the choice made for them.

Cade's eyes flicked to Rennik and found a scratch at the corner of his mouth, sticky with blood. He must have gotten clipped by a fingernail. Or maybe a flying bell.

"You're hurt," Cade said.

"Oh." He put his hand up. "It's so small . . ."

Cade crossed the hold in a few steps and set a hand to the side of his face. "It's my fault," she muttered, tracing the spot to one side of his lips. There was nothing she could do to help, and no reason to touch him except that she couldn't stop her fingers from doing it.

Cade hadn't meant to show that much. To let Rennik feel what she wanted — even if it was just one fraction of her overwhelming need. She couldn't do this. Cade had to give and give and give. When she asked for something back, the universe handed her bombed cities and spacesick mothers.

But Rennik didn't pull back from her hand. He closed his eyes, and his long eyelashes bent over his cheeks. "It's not your fault," he said with a sun-warmed smile, though there was no sun in sight. "You're not the one who attacked me."

"No," Cade said. "I would have done a cleaner job."

"There are Hatchum who can back up your claim," Rennik said, "although I'm glad I'm not one of them."

Whatever warmth Rennik was feeling reached Cade, and she laughed.

"Did I ever tell you about the time Renna and I got into a fight on Esk?"

Cade sat on top of the crate. There wasn't technically enough room for both pairs of hips, even though his were narrow.

"No," she said. "I don't think I know that one."

"This was before I met Lee, when Renna was hardly big enough for me to sit in the pilot's chair."

And it was as if they were back in the days before the worlds started to end, when Cade was stuck in her sick bed and Rennik sat with her. When the universe shrank down to the size of a bedroom, and stayed that way for long enough that Cade had started to think Rennik might never leave her side.

He talked the whole flight, unfolding stories for her — ones she asked for, ones she never would have thought to request.

"Do you ever miss it?" she asked.

Rennik tapped his long fingers on his knees. "Miss what?"

"Home," Cade said.

"Yes." The answer surprised her. Rennik never spoke about Hatch.

But then Cade remembered why he'd been kicked out in

the first place. Not for associating with humans, not just that. He had cared too much, drawing strong lines between him and the things he loved. Maybe that included Hatch itself.

"It's quite a place," Rennik said, his eyes half squinting like he was looking at it in the distance, his cheeks tilted as if to catch a wind. "Most of the Hatchum live on plains, which sweep across to the cliffs, and the sea."

"Hatch has a sea?"

"It has twelve of them. Each one a different shade of blue. Some are calm, some are furious, and some are both, at the same time."

Cade thrummed with the need to see it. But they were both unwelcome on Hatch. Visiting Rennik's old home was one more item on the fast-growing list of things they would never do together.

"Tell me more about the sea," Cade said.

Rennik told her about tides, about waves, about blue that bled into sky. At some point Cade closed her eyes, but Rennik knew she wasn't asleep. Cade trusted that he wouldn't stop talking.

# CHAPTER 12

As soon as the cabbage was unloaded and Renna had been fed, everyone's focus turned planet-side.

Cade hailed *Everlast*, which was about to run its rescue on Cass 12, and let them know to look out for nonhumans, in addition to the Unmaker threat. Matteo didn't seem like a natural fit for his new position, and Cade worried that he would back out of the mission as soon as she gave him the bad news.

But he listened quietly, and then said, "All the more reason to get to them now."

Behind him, Cade heard Green and June fighting, and Zuzu shouting cannon-related instructions.

With the trading station behind them and Renna's course set, Cade and Ayumi attacked the mess. They laid out grain-mash and the last of the bin-hardened fruit, toasted bread, powdered milk, freeze-dried eggs.

"It'll give us strength for tomorrow," Ayumi said. "To gather the survivors."

Or to face down a fight.

But Lee, for once, didn't remind them how inevitable that might be. The crew ate with a minimum of talk, but it was a good quiet. Mira sat at one of Cade's elbows, and Lee did some hearty slurping near the other. Rennik smiled at Cade from across the table. A true calm settled over him instead of the Hatchum fakery of the trading station.

All around them, Renna digested with shivery delight.

Cade's food turned on her as soon as she stood up from the table. As she climbed the chute, her stomach twisted, and it tightened when she slid through the tunnel in the bedroom. She needed sleep even more than she'd needed a decent meal. But she sat at the lip of her bunk, feet on the floor.

Lee and Ayumi had stayed up late for fight training. Ayumi needed it if she was going to be part of the rescue party, which could use all the hands it could get. Cade's mother had been moved to the common room and was strapped down on a semi-permanent basis, in case she went on another grabbing rampage.

So it was just Cade in the little room.

And then, when Cade couldn't stand it anymore, she left too.

Renna had dimmed the main cabin, and Cade crossed it on bare feet. She didn't knock on Rennik's door, because that would have announced what she was doing to the rest of the ship. She slid into Rennik's room, and the door found its home in the frame. A soft darkness soaked into Cade. After the eye-smarting black of space, this felt like a place where she could rest.

But her skin would not be quiet.

Her heart had no such plans.

Rennik slept on his back, arms set in clean parallels on top of the blanket. He bunked in a small bed, not designed to be shared, but he had found room once, for Moira. Cade wondered if Rennik remembered her in those pre-sleep moments. She wanted to know. Not just the surface of him, but every deep thing.

"Cade?" Rennik asked, his voice sleepy but certain. He must have known the sound of her footsteps.

"It's me," she said, like she hadn't taken a wild leap by coming here, with no invitation, in the middle of the night. She moved across the small room, until she stood so close to the bed that Rennik could touch her.

All of Cade's words were there, waiting for him.

*A kiss and a half is not enough. We almost died. Again. We're going to die. Soon.* Too many choices, and Cade hated them all.

Rennik shifted against the sheets, propped himself on an arm and studied her. No shirt, just darkness on the canvas of his skin. Cade thought of his little stunt that afternoon, how he'd shed his clothes in front of her, like it was something they were free to do. Before she could change her mind, Cade lifted her shirt. Edged her pants down, until their thin weight pulled them the rest of the way.

Rennik looked at her like she was impossible. That's how Cade knew that she hadn't made a mistake coming to his room. When she'd dreamed this, in none of the variations had Rennik ever looked at her like that. Even with all of her night-sneaking and clothes-shedding, there were things she wasn't brave enough to hope for.

"Cadence, we can't," Rennik said.

That was how fast he shut the whole thing down.

He sat up, his arms slack at his sides.

Cade stood there. Naked.

"I thought . . ."

He reached for her wrist. Not a weighted, wanting reach. Slow and careful. An apology.

Cade snatched her hand back. "I thought you . . ."

She wanted to stop talking. She wanted to stop *existing*.

Rennik stared in the direction of his knees. He couldn't look at her anymore, and she didn't know if that was a good thing, or a very bad one. "I know what I want," he said, and her knees almost gave. "But . . ."

The cold hit her skin all at once. She needed her clothes.

"But the end of the world. But you're still in love with Moira. It's a simple enough tune, Rennik. I catch on fast."

She folded in a shape that hid as much of herself as possible.

Rennik's words lumbered out, tired. "Let me explain."

Cade wasn't there for a lecture on all the reasons they couldn't. She grabbed at her clothes—all puddles of same-looking fabric. She fought each one and still ended up with the shirt inside out, scratching at her skin.

The walk back to her bedroom was short, and Cade's clothes hadn't caught up to her. She still felt naked. She clamped the shirt to her skin like it didn't count unless she could feel it covering every inch.

Cade slid through the tunnel into the little room, and she hadn't hit the floor before she could feel that she had company.

On the top bunk — the spreading-ink shape of two girls kissing, breaking apart, and coming together to kiss again. Ayumi's legs wrapped over Lee's hips, ankles knotted behind her back. Lee's head was a bare inch from the ceiling. She leaned in, her hands traveling well-known routes over Ayumi's body, sure even in the dark. Lee's smile was the brightest thing in the room. Ayumi's rose, sleepy-warm, to match it.

Cade didn't mean to watch them, but she couldn't *not* watch them. The beauty of what was happening collapsed her. It was one thing to run from bombs, to be sanded down by constant threats.

This was worse. This rattled a deep and empty part of Cade.

She tried to back out. One knee hit the tunnel at the same moment in which Lee sprang straight up and bashed her head.

"Dregs! Ugh. Hi, Cade." She fitted a hand to her skull and refocused. "Hi! Cade!"

Ayumi dove for all the sheets within grabbing distance. Lee dropped from the bunk to the floor, cutting the ladder out of the equation. She took Cade's shoulders in her hands, pinned her with serious eyes.

"Talk?"

Cade nodded, but she didn't really want to talk. She didn't know what they had to talk about, except kissing, and that would be like peeling her skin off one strip at a time.

As soon as they were out of the tunnel and in the main cabin, Serious Lee swapped out for the giddiest version Cade had ever seen. "I'm so glad you walked in," she said. "I mean, not glad in the sense that you probably didn't need to see that, but now we can *talk about it,* which is a neat workaround, since I wasn't supposed to bring it up."

Cade's head fumbled to keep up. "But I thought . . . Rennik . . ."

"Rennik?"

"I thought you had. You know. A thing."

"For him?" Lee asked, trapped between confusion and laughter. "When I was *twelve.* I had a big, dumb, twelve-year-old thing."

"But you're always fighting with him," Cade said.

"I'm always fighting with everyone. All you and I do is fight! I must really be wild about you." Lee cut off her own laugh, hung her head, and twisted her fingers. Cade had never seen her like this. Shy. "It's different with Ayumi."

Even with it barreling at her face, Cade hadn't seen this coming, and now she had one more aftermath to deal with. She rubbed circles at the corners of her eyes, but they clung to their stubborn ache. "Different how?"

"She lost her family too. Friends. A whole planet." With each word out, more softness seeped in. "But she's still so lovely, you know? Sweet. I grew up on the Express. I'm used to a lot of things. Sweetness is not one of them."

Cade understood in ways she didn't want to. Ways she wanted to cut out of her, precisely and surgically. The awfulness of the timing dug in all over again. "If you wanted to tell me, why didn't you —"

"This is *not* a secret," Lee said. "It's a good thing, but it's set in the middle of all of these bad things. Ayumi thought we should wait to tell people so it could be ours for a while before we let the rest of the universe in." Lee's voice shimmered, like the moon caught on water. "It sounded good, but most things do when you have skin contact and you can't breathe straight."

"Right," Cade said. Not because she knew, but because someone needed to stop Lee. She was killing Cade in small, happy increments.

There was no going back to the little bedroom that night.

Cade wandered the ship and ended up in the common room with her mother. Her cushion bed had sprawled, and she looked small at the center of it. The light that fell on her face was a dim, unshakable gray.

Cade held her mother's hand, squeezed her fingers. Squeezed them harder, hoping that it would hurt. She wanted some wincing sign that her mother was still in there.

Out of habit, Cade hummed a song, and she liked the sound

as it formed—it made her think of the soft upward swell of hills, dipping back to hard and reliable ground, or the rubbing back-and-forth of water. Cade added another verse, and another. But habit wouldn't bring her mother back from the place where she hung, not-dead, barely alive.

Cade and her mother sat, each wrapped in her own form of quiet.

An hour until they cracked atmosphere.

Andana loomed in the starglass, every shade of brown and beige and reddish-tan. Cade sat in the pilot's chair studying the planet's surface, pocked with sand-craters that might have held oceans once.

She was alone with her old planet until the hailing light came on, green and blinking. Cade hurried to the panels.

Green's voice came through. "Renna? Is this Renna?"

"You have us, *Everlast.*"

"Good." Green sounded like he'd been running up flights of stairs for hours. "Another twenty ships have been hailed."

"And told to meet at the coordinates?"

Cade felt the constant pull of those coordinates, the need to reach them and claim the safe harbor of space, away from the attacks, the constant hovering threat of more. What she really wanted was to skip this whole Andana business and gather the fleet.

"The other ships went ahead while we completed the mission on Cass 12," Green said.

Cade kept one hand on the com and braced the other

against the panel. Renna ran cool, pulling the itch out of Cade's sweating palm. "What happened there?"

"We got almost everyone off planet," Green said.

Cade felt the hollows, the hidden pain — all of the people who didn't fit inside of that *almost.*

"Not as many people in the town as we thought there would be," Green said. "You estimated eight hundred, but we only found four. Someone came back before we got there."

"Nonhumans or Unmakers?" Cade asked.

"Couldn't say. Attackers unloaded firepower and ran. But they left messages, scrawls saying they'd come back and deal with anyone who was left. We found people holding scissors, posts they'd torn off their beds. Little kids with kitchen knives. They were waiting."

Cade let herself breathe. Let herself believe that all of the work so far had amounted to one good thing.

"Did anyone leave the city?" she asked, thinking of the people *Everlast* might have missed.

"Unlikely," Green said. "There's water on three sides of it, and the roads on the fourth are always watched. It's how the Cassians controlled the human population."

"All right. Thanks, *Everlast.*"

The com switched to static, the light went dead, and Cade's finger let up on the button. She hadn't really wanted to thank Green for adding thickness and weight to her fears about Andana, but it wasn't his fault.

Cade turned and found Ayumi in the door at the back of the control room.

"Did you hear that?" Cade asked.

"Most of it." Ayumi pursed her lips at Andana, like she was sizing up an opponent. But when she talked, it was in a soft voice, to Cade.

"How are you?"

Those words were like the opening chords of an almost-forgotten song. Not the gut-pluck of "Who's Kissing Who Now." Not the harsh scramble of "We Need to Save Everyone." This was the sound of caring.

Slow, building, soft, sure.

Cade went looking for the right place to start, but when she opened her mouth, there was too much. The floor rushed away, ripped from her, and she wondered if this was what tides felt like as she fell.

*down*
*there in the place where she kept him*
*because he had to be kept*
*secret*
*because he couldn't be told to a moving-on universe*
*a needing universe*
*one that had fallen*
*down*

*and just when she started to pick it up*
*dust off its knees and tell it a new story*
*now he fell*

*and the dark center*
*that had been*
*down*
*there*
*waiting*
*wasn't waiting anymore*

*it was here*
*it was time*
*or it had always been time and she just hadn't known it yet*
*time to go*
*down and down and down*
*into that last dark*

When Cade came to, she was on her knees, with a sense that she'd struggled to keep her balance and won the last few inches.

Ayumi stared from a safe distance, worry trapped in the amber of her eyes. "What just happened?"

Double bruises formed on Cade's knees, large and somehow comforting. At least the bruises made sense.

"It's Xan," Cade said.

"Xan?" Ayumi edged forward, helping Cade to her feet. "I thought he left us back at the black hole."

Cade brushed Ayumi off, and tried to pretend it was a matter of smoothing the wrinkles from her sleeves. "He's not alive," she said. "But something lingered."

"Your entanglement?"

This kept happening. And it was getting stronger. Closer. Harder to ignore.

"Maybe," Cade said.

She turned back to the starglass, the red-brown hurtling close, and all she could feel was Andana.

# CHAPTER 13

Sand scattered in every direction as Renna put down on Cade's old bunker. The spaceport in Andana was too far, and run by nonhumans, and there were no landing fields near Voidvil. So Cade had offered the one place she could think of—but as soon as Renna rocked to a stop, Cade regretted it.

The starglass showed sand, just as endless as space, just as everywhere. Renna tried to cheer Cade up with ripples under her feet as she left the control room. Cade pretended it was working, but nothing could shift her into feeling good about all of that sand.

The rescue party had gathered in the main cabin, where the walkway would uncurl. Rennik stood at the head of the group. No Hatchum ceremonial robes, but the double swords hung at his belt. Lee made herself busy cleaning her gun. Ayumi clasped a knife in one hand and a notebook in the other. Mira stood off to one side, drawing circles with a foot. Her fingers were stretched out and twitching.

When Mira had asked to be part of the mission, Cade had almost knee-jerked another *no*. But if Cade couldn't see the girl, it would be impossible to keep her safe.

Gori's bunk was Cade's last stop. He sat cross-legged, half-raptured. There was no getting him off the ship, but as long as he was going to stay, he might as well make himself useful.

"I need you to look after my mother," Cade said, hoping that it was for an afternoon and not the rest of her life.

Gori breathed deep and didn't move.

Cade marched on, whispering to Renna. "You'll probably have to take care of both of them." A reassuring tap sounded on the soles of Cade's feet.

As soon as Cade joined the group in the main cabin, Renna opened herself to the elements. Rennik tried to set his pace in time with Cade's as she headed down the walkway, but she shouldered ahead.

Heat smacked her in the face. The walkway was the last bit of firmness, and then her feet sloshed into the hot, moving grains that made up ninety-eight percent of Andana's surface. Sand lashed at Cade's ankles like it was trying to make up for lost time. She had to remind herself every five seconds that this condition wasn't permanent.

This wasn't her home.

Mira struggled against the sand. Lee strode hard, one arm wrapped across Ayumi and raised to eye level to keep the coarse wind out of their faces. Rennik cast a glance back at

Renna, to make sure she was waiting there, unbothered. Then he turned to Cade. She could see that he wanted to talk, but the sand gave her an excuse. If she tried to speak, it would crust her mouth at the corners.

Voidvil came into view over a dune, shining and rolling in the heat. If Cade hadn't spent so much time there — scorching days and loud nights — she wouldn't know if the city was real or a heat-snugged dream.

By the time they reached the outskirts, Cade was sweating, with the faint edge of a chill that rose from the depths of certain desert afternoons. The streets were in worse shape than she remembered. Pavement spidered beneath her feet. Shops stood open, wares looted, most doors clean off their hinges.

"Where is everyone?" Ayumi asked.

Cade knocked on an intact door. Maybe people were hiding, unsure if the crew on the street was there to round them up for a rescue or a quick death.

Cade wandered into the next apartment and found an empty box — flimsy walls and stale sheets, spoiled food on the counter, as if someone had raided their own kitchen and decided none of the plunder was worth eating.

"No one's been here for days." Cade swung back into the street. "Keep moving."

The crew trailed behind her in a loose line, Rennik at her heels, Lee bringing up the rear. Cade chose alleys that cut through dead-asleep sections of the city. She looked for signs that their presence was pricking Voidvil awake. There was no noise, no movement, and the absence kept Cade alert. She felt as though she would have noticed one arm hair ruffled in the wrong direction.

"Where did everybody go?" Mira asked, a few steps behind Cade.

"Maybe they pulled back to the center of the city, to make it easier to defend." Maybe they had barriers. Walls. Knives, guns, explosives. "Be ready," Cade said.

"For what?" Ayumi asked.

Lee pulled her gun. "People in this town might shoot first and check species later."

Cade paused at the mouth of the alley. "No one." The crew spilled onto a wide street.

A hard shiver in Ayumi's voice made Cade think of cold, even with the sun pouring heat. "Let's drain. Can we drain?"

"No," Cade said. "I heard people here." It had been less than an hour since she checked the position of the songs. That wasn't enough time for an attacking force to hit the city, kill everyone, and leave. Even if they had, there would be signs of a recent strike. Freshly destroyed buildings. Bodies.

"They're here," Cade said. "They have to be here."

"Can't you do the thing where you listen?" Mira asked. "You know." She pulled her face solemn and closed her eyes. "Listen."

"Good call." Lee patted Mira on the shoulder. Mira's spark-green eyes blinked up at Lee, confused.

"What?" Lee asked. "Is me giving a compliment really the wildest thing that's happened today?"

It *was* a good call. Cade fought the useless *I-should-have-*

*done-that-sooner* itch. She spread herself out, tracing every inch of Voidvil. Her brain pinched, searching for the smallest bit of music.

Nothing.

Cade sank to the pavement, but it was too hot. Her shins couldn't stand it. Her palms boiled against the sticky black. She shot back to standing.

"What?" Lee asked.

Cade had been reaching in the wrong direction. She blinked sand and sun out of her eyes and started again. This time, instead of working out in circles, her mind plummeted to her feet and kept moving. There it was. Straight down. A rash of music under silent streets.

Voidvil had gone underground.

The city had been built deep as well as high. Most of Cade's time living there was spent in cavelike rooms — from the black markets to the clubs — tucked under the city's hot, seething skin. Now the humans of Andana had shed their aboveground presence and burrowed as far as they could into the dark.

Cade listened to the songs until she found a natural place to start. She led the crew two blocks west, to one of the tallest apartment buildings in Voidvil. This was Humanscape, the last place where Cade had seen the traveling black market.

"What's so special about this one?" Mira asked as Cade slid them in through a concrete door that opened onto a flight of urine-soaked stairs.

"Seems like a good spot for a resistance," Cade said.

"It doesn't hurt that we're intimate with the ins and outs of the building," Lee said. "Especially the outs."

Their voices dropped down the stairwell like stones. Cade found more signs of a human presence on the staircase landings than she had in the rest of the city. Meat-shreds on bone. Heaps of old clothes, toothbrushes. In one corner, blankets. Still warm.

Cade turned a tight corner, but she snatched back as soon as she saw a man across the diagonal. She held herself against the wall and waited for him to make a move.

"Show yourself," he said, in a voice that rattled like a key in a wrong-fitting lock.

Rennik's hand fell on Cade's upper arm, staying her for a second, but Cade stepped onto the landing and blinked her palms open. She had her crew and an impressive array of weapons behind her. It didn't make her feel any less exposed.

"Look," she said. "We're here to help. To take you —"

"Cade?" Her own name sounded through the stairwell. "Is that Cade?"

She pressed forward another step, and the man's face took shape in the dark. A squashed nose, one eye thickened to a blind white. The sort of memory-laced smile that Cade had seen on plenty of faces over the last few weeks. The smile of someone who was spending quality time in the past.

"Do I know you?" Cade asked.

"No," he said. "But I went to see you a few times."

At the club. This man wasn't a regular, so Cade didn't know

his face, but he knew hers. She stumbled over the strangeness of the idea. Even after the end of worlds, she still had fans.

"We're looking for the market," Cade said. "Or whatever's left of it."

"Right this way," he said, and his nostalgic smile morphed into another one, a little too eager.

Cade motioned the crew to follow, choosing to ignore the concern on all of their faces. She wasn't in love with this plan either. She had the feeling that back in her club days, this was one of the men who might have knocked too long and loud on her dressing room door, and now she was following him into a cold, twisting dark.

The market had been moved, and only the ribs of the stands were left. People huddled in corners, creating shells of stink. Cade tried not to cover her nose. She waved at the men and women who stared at her, recognition reshaping some of their faces.

This was Cade's planet. These were, in some unshakable way, her people.

The man, who called himself Till, led Cade and the crew to a small group who seemed a little cleaner than the rest, a little more awake. Cade knew at least one of them — a small man who used to run a secondhand clothing stall in the market. Now it looked like he was wearing all of his wares at once.

"Look what I found," Till said, his proud smile showing the dark kernel of a tooth gone bad.

"Cade," the small man said, pulling at the fingertips of his non-fitting gloves. "I heard you were gone, long before everyone else."

"Well, I'm back." Cade slapped on her old stage attitude like a quick layer of makeup. "Call it an encore."

"We're here to get you off this sand-heap," Lee said. She was back to her old ways too, strutting, hands all but glued to her hips, a take-charge gleam in her eyes. Cade hadn't known how much she'd missed that.

"You'll have to take serious care," the little man said, fiddling at one of his cuffs.

Cade didn't need anyone to tell her that. "We have a ship waiting outside the city. Start spreading the word and we'll meet—"

Till cut in, stubbing at the ground with a foot. "Some here have it in their minds that it's best to join up with *them*."

A strong smell wandered over from the nearest clutch of survivors.

"*Them?*" Cade asked.

"The ones that done it," Till whispered. "Some would rather be on the side of those who wipe us out than be wiped."

Cade stared at him like too much time underground had choked his higher brain functions. "And what makes them think the Unmakers will do anything but pitch them out of the nearest airlock?"

"They must have heard about us," Till said. "Our situation here, the number of us still living. They sent the ships back. Except this time, there was no killing. Just a woman, looked near to human. She used some pretty words to convince the tired and weak that they could get in on something new."

Cade sorted through all the bad things Till had said and found herself staring at two small words.

*A woman.*

"Was she small, with light skin, red hair?" Cade asked. "A little bit of white streaked in?"

"That's the one," the little man said, the stack of hats on his head bobbing as he stepped in. "You two aren't close personal friends, now, are you?"

"We shared the same patch of universe for an hour. That's it." Cade didn't add that it had been one of the worst hours of her life, with the woman trying to sell Cade on the idea of throwing herself into a black hole.

"She doesn't have a name," Cade said. "And she doesn't want to do us any favors."

The little man cast his eyes around the open room, the large circles of people, the smaller satellite clusters. "There are those here that might think bringing them a human trophy will win favor."

Cade shook her head, swallowing against a new sort of foulness. In a universe thick with enemies, Cade should have known Andana was the one place she'd end up fighting her own kind.

"We spread out in teams," Cade said. She included Till, the clothing-stall man, and the others in the group, even though she didn't know if she could trust them. She didn't have much choice.

"Take until nightfall, find everyone you can. Tell them to meet . . ." She needed a place underground, one that wouldn't draw attention. One that she knew, inch for inch. "Tell them to meet at Club V."

"How do we dodge aspiring metal-breathers?" Lee asked.

"They're not making a secret of it," Till said, pushing his tongue against his rotten tooth. "Trying to turn themselves into monsters as we speak."

When no one moved, Cade said, "Look for bad actors in big robes."

The group cracked into pieces, and Till headed off by himself. He didn't look like the kind who lived by the buddy system. Lee grabbed Ayumi's hand and ran, calling back over her shoulder, "Last one to the club's a fake Unmaker!"

That left Rennik, Cade, and Mira. Rennik tried to ask something with his eyes, but Cade avoided the question.

"I know the planet. I'll take the girl."

Mira followed her across the ruinscape of the black market and out of the building. As soon as they were in the open air, her voice tugged at Cade. "Why did you want to get away from the Hatchum?"

The street under Cade's feet had split a long time ago, and now it looked like a burst and blackened lip. Cade stumbled to one side of it as Mira walked the center. Her whole face puckered with focus. "I thought you liked him."

"I did. I do." Cade cut for the nearest apartment building. "He's the one who doesn't feel things."

"Not true," Mira said. "He steals looks at you all day and his eyes get big and his breath goes weird. Those are signs. I know."

Cade had to bite back a laugh. She couldn't believe she was talking about this with a little girl. She dropped into a new staircase and followed the thought-songs down.

"Stay behind me," Cade said.

Mira stuck like a shadow that was too good at its job. "You like the Hatchum too." Her words seemed bigger in the dark. "Every time he comes into the room, you make an angry face. Like this." Mira tapped Cade on the shoulder and treated her to a miniature version of her own scowl.

"And that's a sign?" The humor in Cade's voice was cut with gritty irritation.

"Yeah, it lets me know you're having a feeling, a big one, and it doesn't have anywhere to go, so it turns around and attacks you. So you get angry and you look like you have a stomachache all the time. But you don't. You're in love."

Cade crouched on the landing and listened for the rustle of people below. "Oh, really?" She almost asked where Mira had gotten her manual on human behavior. "What else do you know about me?"

Mira paused, out of ready-made answers. "You don't make sense. None of you do."

Cade merged the thought-songs with the sound of footsteps

and the soft rub of voices to create a living map. She held it firmly in her head as she led Mira into a slimed honeycomb of basements.

"Agreed."

The people they found there fell into different categories: eager to follow, suspicious of every word, itching to fight. So tired that they could barely lift their heads. So foul that Cade wanted to cut her nose off. Mira had promised to stay behind Cade, but she edged out with her voice, talking to people from behind Cade's back.

"Space is a lot nicer than this," she said. "You'll like it."

"We have lots of grain-mash on the ship, and even sugar to put on it sometimes."

"Don't make me fight you," she said, which was met with laughter — grimy as old coin, but true underneath.

Sometimes all Mira had to do was smile and activate her dimples. Cade let her go a short distance in one direction while she took the other, staying close enough to keep a watch on the girl but far enough away that Mira could double the ground they covered. She was so good at reading people that Cade wondered if soon, with the fleet gathered and her strange skill set put to bed, she'd be able to retire.

The thought was cut off by a long scrape and a cloth-dampened scream.

Cade ran and found a man dragging Mira into a sub-basement. The smell of turned meat leaked from the entrance. Cade lunged with her knife, but the man was more alert than she'd given him credit for, and when he spun, he caught her across the cheekbone.

"Give me the girl," she said. Her voice was a fierce, pulsing thing.

"What girl?" The man stared at Cade as he gathered up Mira, holding her still and much too close, a long needle at her throat. It was dull at the point, no shine. It could have been a knitting needle in another life. But with enough pressure—

"Let me have her," Cade said. "She's mine."

"No idea who you're referring to." The man's eyes were pasted over with madness. But there was a hint of a smile, too, like he dared Cade to argue that Mira was real, when in his mind she was a piece of meat.

"It's okay," Mira said. "You can go. Make it to the club. Gather the fleet. That's what you're supposed to do, Cade." She swallowed hard, and the needle bobbed against her throat. "So do it."

Cade shifted her weight, testing the man's readiness. He read the signs, predicting all of her possible attacks. Cade backed off, each step boiled down to glue, the sticking awfulness of letting Mira believe for even ten seconds that she would be left to die.

Cade stopped with her back turned. She closed her eyes, and the sounds of dragging scratched at her like fingernails. Cade settled into the wide, balanced stance that she used for playing *hardfastloud*. Music swept like a strong wind through her mind, gathering fury and force as it went, and she sent it out, out, out.

The man's mind wasn't open to her, but she wrenched it open, and turned to find him on his knees, silent-screaming. Mira wriggled away from his grip and ran clear. Cade moved in and sliced the man's calf just above the ankle.

Then she ran.

She kept Mira in front of her, little heels slapping. As soon as they were up the stairs, Mira turned and looked at Cade with awe.

"You came back for me."

Cade ruffled Mira's hair, and it was strange how natural the impulse felt. "You know, this isn't the first time I saved you."

"But before, I could have been anyone. This time you came back. *For me.*"


The staircase that dropped down into the club felt the same as it always had. The rest of the city around it had changed, but when Cade circled those stairs, she could have been on her way to play Club V on a Saturday night.

The chairs and tables at the back of the club had been overturned, stripped, broken down for parts. Some of the table legs and curtains from the stage had been thrown together to form what looked like small huts. Leading with her knife, Cade checked them one by one. If there had been buzz-fiends living here, they were gone, leaving rows of empty bottles behind the bar.

Cade slapped her palms on the stage, pulling herself up by her arms. By the time she rose to standing, she was drenched in memory. All of those Saturdays, all of those songs. Everything strong — the stage lights, the crowd-stares, the drinks.

Cade hadn't picked this place so she could swim around in old times, but they came back anyway. The brass, and under it, the loneliness. And then, the one good part: the pure rush of music.

Cade had been a guitar-slinger once, not a savior. But even in those old days, she'd been different from other people. Cade and Xan were already entangled, and he'd needed a kick start to the brain to wake him up from a coma. Cade had provided that with the loudest, hardest, best song she'd ever played.

It was while she stood here, on this stage, in this spot, that it had all started.

Cade shook off the memory and it broke and left her, like a shattering of droplets. But some of them clung, seeping into her as she set up the microphones, found the booth, and brought the stage lights back to life.

Rennik led in a group of survivors, and the club started to look like it always had on show night, thick with bodies and excitement.

"Have you done a sweep of the backstage areas?" Rennik asked.

Cade shook her head.

"I can do it!" Mira cried, running for the black-painted hall.

"Better let me," Rennik said. A few long strides and he passed Mira with a pat on the shoulder.

Cade tried not to think about him in the dressing room, every turn of him reflected in her mirror. Now she was the one who wanted to knock on the door, impatient, press him back against the wall.

Putting her wants away was easier work than usual. Cade couldn't change what had happened, but at least she could promise herself not to make the same naïve stumble twice.

Lee and Ayumi thundered down the stairs with a set of survivors. Till and the man from the clothing stall and the others followed with their own groups, until there were fifty people, maybe seventy-five.

A full house. Cade slitted her eyes against the stage lights, really looking at her audience for the first time. The survivors. The spacesicks. The exhaustion that sat on people as clear as grime-layers. Cade's crew lined the room, looking triumphant in the case of Lee and tense in the case of everyone else.

Cade rushed to set the rescue in motion.

"If you're here," she said, "it's because you want off this planet as much as I do."

Cade had it all planned, the brass speech, the quick flight to the outskirts of the city.

But the floor had other ideas. It wavered under her feet.

*back where*
*things begin*

*packed infinities*

*trembling, like a word on the tongue*
*to grow*
*into the shape of itself*
*careen out —*
*be the air and fill it*

*waiting*
*to wild-expand*
*to*
*become*


Cade held the stage as this streamed through her.

She managed not to fall to her knees, and that felt like a victory. She cleared her throat and got ready to move on to the rest of the speech.

But then a ruckus — a full ten on the scale — broke wide at the back of the club. People dressed in robes rushed in and spilled forward, swirling the crowd like dark paint. The figures came first, and then the sounds. Grunts, knives, skin.

And everything inside of Cade exploded.

# CHAPTER 14

She felt like she was being torn in thousands of directions, from the center outward. Every time she closed her eyes, she was in a strange world of violent expansion.

When she opened them again, she was in the middle of a bar fight. The fake Unmakers hadn't reached the stage yet, but Cade didn't have long. Robed figures crashed through the crowd, which was armed for the most part, thanks to the constant death threats.

Cade had just enough time to get clear. She had to. But she couldn't move. The wrenching apart of her particles was too much, too strong and painful. It flashed and strobed through her. Tore time into pieces.

*and inside things were moving*
*out fast white-hot*

*wild and spreading*
*everywhere*
*and she couldn't*

Stop it. She had to stop it.

The fight, the inner explosion, everything.

Cade opened her eyes. Knives flashed at her feet. All it would take was a few steps and she would be backstage, but she couldn't do it.

She fell to the floor, and crashed. Inside. Outside. Everywhere.

*the beginning,*
*all over again*
*the same as before*
*the same always*
*she could feel it*
*this time, she could feel*

Everything.

Beauty, pain, all of the things she hadn't been able to feel when she lived on Andana, when her life was loneliness and the scratch of sand.

Lee caught her eye across the room.

*"What's happening?"* Lee mouthed, clear as noon. She shoved a robed man off and put a knee to his stomach.

*What's happening?*

Cade didn't know. Something with Xan. Something with her particles. Something with the universe.

Exploding.

Cade tried to shrug, but her shoulders were made of parts that were moving away from each other too fast to act like a shoulder.

None of this made any snugging sense, and Cade had just enough of her brain functioning to know that. But it was real. It was happening. She tried not to blink, but that just dried her eyes out and didn't stop it.

*forcing her open,*
*and open,*
*and more open*

Focus.

Cade would have to smash herself back together. Fast.

She tried to follow the fight, find its rhythms, so she could throw herself back into it. She watched Till take down three fake Unmakers, only to get slashed in the gut. Ayumi and Mira stood behind the bar, smashing bottles and handing them to people who needed weapons.

Rennik had his double blades out and swinging, but he kept interrupting himself to toss concerned looks at Cade. They all did. Her inner disruption was throwing them off, holding them back from winning this fight.

Cade had to get it together.

She pulled out her knife, jumped off the stage, and was fighting before she hit the floor.

A fake Unmaker grabbed Cade by the shoulder. She hit him and sent him down. Easy. The hard part wasn't being strong. The hard part was keeping herself in her body. The hard part was staying in one piece when her connection to Xan was splitting her apart.

*farther and farther and father and*

Cade had to stop him.

*but this was part of her*
*how could she contain it,*
*how could she ask it to end when it was all starting*

"Stop, stop, stop," Cade muttered.

Rennik fought his way over to her.

"Are you all right?"

He planted himself in front of her, between the stage and the robes and the clash that wouldn't stop.

"Are you all right?" he asked, louder.

"I will be," Cade said.

*she let it stream and have her,*
*be part of her,*
*all of her*

And then she turned it off.

Dark, silent, done. It was as simple as telling Xan that he wasn't welcome anymore, which was something Cade hadn't been willing to do. Not after everything that had happened. But she couldn't hold this anymore.

And then—

Cade came up kicking, biting, swinging with all of her force. She fought with a cold intensity she had never felt before. She would get them out of this club, off this planet, away from here, forever.

Cade fought shoulder to shoulder with Lee. She nodded at Rennik to let him know that she was all right. Better than all right. She was back to herself—a Xan-less self, but she would deal with the loss later.

The fake Unmakers put up a fight. Still, under their robes, they were cowards, the kind who would turn on their own species to keep their skins intact. Faced with a serious brawl, they ran up the stairs.

Once the crowd was back to its original composition, Cade breathed out so hard she almost sank, but she braced her knees and kept it together. She decided to skip to the end of her speech.

"Let's get the snug out of here."

Lee fired her gun into the air and let out an open-throated sound, a pure rallying cry. Cade ran up the circle of steps into the warm night. Over the last stretches of sand, back to Renna, trailing all of the people who wanted to live as much as she needed to save them.

Survivors crammed every inch of the ship. They dimpled the wall with their elbows as Renna cracked atmosphere.

Lee and Rennik set the course to meet the rest of the fleet, but Rennik was distracted. His eyes stuttered over the crowded control room. Cade could almost see the worry expanding inside of him.

"It's just for a little while," Cade said. She patted the panels so Renna knew the comfort was meant for her, not her frustrating counterpart. "We'll get them onto *Everlast* as soon as we join the rest of the fleet."

It was one more stretch of black now, one good haul away. Cade needed to check and make sure the ships were all coming together the way that they'd planned. But first, she needed to find a minute for herself, curl her fingers around a little bit of time. She figured she had earned it.

Cade headed down the chute, toward the one person who might be able to help her understand what had happened in the club. Gori was still in his bunk, staring at his toes. The influx of survivors didn't seem to touch him.

Cade poked him in the ribs.

"I need your help," she said. No niceties, but no begging, either. Gori had a special way of making her feel like a gnat.

"I will do whatever I can to assist," he said.

"You mean, without leaving the ship or interfering with your busy rapture schedule," Cade said.

Gori sat up straight, radiating pride from his little bunk. "I will do what I *can*. This word implies parameters."

Cade sighed and launched into her story. Everything that had happened since Hades, everything about Xan. She told Gori about the lingering connection, the strong flashes that had nudged further and further into her life.

"Xan was in a black hole. And then he was—everywhere."

"Everywhere?"

Cade cupped her elbows with her hands. "Yeah. That's what it felt like." Xan—or whatever he had broken down to —had just ripped and spread through Cade with such force that she didn't know if she would ever feel whole again.

Gori sat up straighter, but this wasn't another injection of pride. He looked almost excited. "This human. This boy Xan. The particles that were once part of him made it to the center of the black hole." Cade had more or less put that much together herself, from all of the scraps of feeling, all the flashes. "It was an immediate process for the human boy Xan," Gori said, "but your experience of the same event unfolded on a much slower time scale."

"How is that possible?" Cade asked.

Gori looked disappointed in her, almost stung. "All time is one time," he said. The motto he loved so much had finally come in handy.

"So he made it to the center," Cade said. "Shouldn't that

have been it? Shouldn't I have stopped feeling him?"

Gori got up and paced in front of Cade, his robes sweeping, pebbly lips pursed. The crowd in the main cabin below angled their necks and took notice. It wasn't every day that you saw a Darkrider leaping around.

"The human boy Xan did not simply make it to the center," Gori said. "He passed *through* the center."

"Of a black hole?" Cade asked. "What the snug is on the other side?"

"There are many possibilities." Gori's dark eyes sparked and his fingers pulsed. "It sounds as if, in the case of this specific black hole, the human boy Xan returned to the beginning."

"The beginning," Cade repeated. Those words had been part of what happened to her in the club. "The beginning of what?"

"Time."

Cade sat down on Gori's bunk. It was as simple as that. Gori told her the truth, and she believed it, and her knees stopped existing.

"You're telling me that Xan's particles *time-traveled?*"

"Yes," Gori said.

"And the thing I felt was . . . ?"

"The universe starting again."

All of that bursting, spreading, growing—that was what Xan, or at least his particles, had felt. Cade had to feel it, too, because she was still connected to those particles. But there was a catch. She couldn't hold the entire expanding universe inside of her. She had barely been able to handle the black hole.

"So it's a good thing I shut it down," she said.

"Perhaps it is a necessary thing." Gori sat next to Cade, spent from his little burst of excitement. He would probably take ten naps in a row to recover. Cade didn't have that sort of time. She had to process the impossible-but-true. She had to keep her mind clear and her eyes on the fleet.

But she had one more question.

"What will happen to him?" Her voice pinched small. "The pieces that used to be him?"

"They will continue their journey," Gori said. "The same one that they have traveled, and always travel."

Cade nodded. That made sense. All of it made a very strange sort of sense. Xan would keep doing what he had always done. And Cade would get up from this wrinkled bunk and try to change the fate of the human race.

# CHAPTER 15

The ship was clogged with bodies.

With the common room retrofitted as a sleeping area, Rennik's cabin off-limits, and the secret bedroom full, the survivors from Andana were left to wander the main cabin and the common room all day. Maybe the control room, if Rennik didn't polite-stare them down and Lee didn't kick them out.

Cade needed peace and as much quiet as she could manage. It was time to check on the progress of the fleet. She tried the mess and found it full of survivors in various stages of stuffing their faces.

Mira bobbed in behind Cade. Since she'd saved the girl in the basements, it was like Mira had tied herself to Cade with an invisible string. As soon as Cade stopped moving, Mira felt the tug and came running.

"Do you need something to eat?" Mira asked. "Ayumi taught me how to make mash cakes. Oh, and tea!"

"Not hungry," Cade said, which she figured out was a lie as soon as her stomach twitched a correction. "Well, maybe. But right now I need to find the recipe for everyone leaving me alone."

Mira perked to her tiptoes and piped in a harsh-honest tone, "Cade doesn't want you in here! Clear out!" She sat at the freshly emptied table and folded her hands. Mira didn't seem to think *alone* had anything to do with her leaving, too.

"All right," Cade said. "Good enough."

She sat across the table from Mira and closed her eyes. Mira's chair screeched forward as she leaned in to watch. Cade settled her shoulders and sighed through her irritation. Her audiences usually gave her a little more breathing room.

Cade reached, knowing that the first thing she had to do was get past Mira's rough lack of music. The songs of the crew and survivors came back. She readied herself for pure silence, the reminder of every death, the dark outline of every failure.

Cade didn't have to go far to find the other humans, on their ships, all of them streaming toward a single point. She ran her mind over the songs. So many—but the experience didn't overwhelm her now. These songs were old friends. They had given Cade a small, care-worthy hope after the Unmaker attacks. And they were coming together.

It was real.

The fleet she had dreamed was real.

Once Cade found the right way to listen, to hold them all in her mind, space opened up. Time stopped pushing at her and streamed alongside, like a helping wind. Cade didn't need to rush. She could stay for a minute, linger.

"What does it feel like?" Mira asked.

Cade cast around for the right words. "It's like when you hear a song, and it comes with feelings tacked on, whatever you felt when you first heard it, and the place where you were, that gets twisted up in it too. It's like that, but happening a hundred times. A thousand times."

The eager scratch of Mira's chair went silent. "I'm not used to songs."

Cade clamped the rubbery inside of her cheek between her teeth. Of course Mira wasn't used to music. Cade didn't know what sort of life she'd had, but it probably hadn't come with lullabies built in. Maybe that's why Mira didn't have a thought-song.

"You can learn to listen," Cade said.

She hummed a few notes, and was surprised to find that the same bit of song she'd tried on her mother came back to her now. Even though she couldn't see Mira, Cade could feel her trying. The change in breath, the muscle-focus.

"That's not listening," Cade said. "That's clenching."

Mira sighed and gave up. When she spoke again, the words were fainter than far-off stars. "Do you ever wonder if you can be like everyone else?"

So Mira felt it too, their being different from the other humans in the fleet. She felt like she had to give Mira an answer, even if it was fractured and half wrong. Even if she failed.

"Take Lee," Cade said. "I don't want to be her. I don't even want to be *like* her. But for good or bad, I need her. I need to shove all the closed-up things inside me open enough to let her in."

Mira sighed again, harder. Cade had definitely failed. And now her mind had been stretched out for too long. It started its normal, automatic reeling-in process. But this time, it stopped short.

This time, Cade heard something new.

And near. And unsure. Like a fingertip trembling strings for the first time. The notes thin and faint, the sort of organic, fascinating mess that comes with being new and eager and needing music to fill certain spaces.

Mira-song.

Cade opened her eyes. Mira was focused on her, breathing hard through her nose. Whatever terrible thing had turned Mira into a song-less girl was being undone while Cade watched.

"You're looking at me with your face all weird," Mira said.

"I thought you could read people."

Mira drummed her fingers and ducked her head, taking Cade in from a new angle. "Not this time."

The feeling was complicated, even to Cade. "I'm happy," she said. "And scared." She knew that Mira's song had something to do with her, maybe a lot to do with her. What if she messed it up, or forced it into the wrong shape, or crushed it before it got started?

Mira leaned all the way over the table, drawing Cade in so

they met halfway. She whispered, like she had cracked open a secret and if she wasn't careful, it would spill everywhere. "I'm happy-scared, too."

Cade looked down into the mirror of her green eyes, and when she blinked, Mira's song leaped to meet her.

A semicircle of survivors crowded around the dock that led to Ayumi's shuttle. Cade almost passed them, but then she saw Lee coming through with an armful of supplies. Cade cut back, forced an opening in the crowd. "What's this?"

Ayumi stopped in the dock frame, her arms weighted with thick rolls of paper. "We're getting ready."

"For the fleet?" Cade asked.

"Even better." Lee popped into the dock frame and slung an arm around Ayumi's waist. Ayumi settled against Lee's side in a comfortable way. It looked like they were done keeping their late-night makeouts to themselves.

"We wanted to surprise you," Ayumi said.

Lee rubbed her hand from the curve of Ayumi's waist to her stomach, and Cade was envy-bitten because she made it look so easy. "As soon as the ships are gathered and safe, we're going to find a new home," Lee said.

"A place to live," Ayumi corrected.

Earth was the true home of the human race, according to Ayumi and all the Earth-Keepers who'd gone before her. Cade knew she wouldn't hand the title over to a planet that hadn't earned it.

"There's nowhere to take the people who came to this ship

looking for refuge," Ayumi said. The survivors around them shuffled out of their watching-state, and a few tried to cut in with questions. Ayumi plowed on, scattering uncomfortable truths as she went. "We'll have thousands more on our hands soon, a whole fleet on our hands and nowhere to take them. I've been through all of the notes. And not just mine. The Earth-Keeper archives date back generations. I went through every notebook I have. I've extrapolated up, down, and sideways." She handed Cade a scroll from her hoard. "This is the best we can do."

Cade unrolled the sheet and found a homemade chart, smudged with planets. A few of them had been circled. Lee and Ayumi tracked Cade's face as she took in their choices. Uninhabited planets with foul conditions, systems and systems away.

Cade's friends needed her to approve, but she couldn't.

"Don't leave yet," she said. "I'm not done with Moon-White." Cade pressed a hard look on Ayumi. She knew better than anyone that Cade's music could hold off spacesick. It was a brighter hope than another desert planet, where they could look forward to death by exposure or nasty native species.

Ayumi's whisper drew a small circle around the three of them, cutting out the crowd. "The music is a good thing, Cade," she said, "but it's not enough."

That was code — it meant Ayumi was still glassing out. But Cade's nerves took it the wrong way, twisting it into an insult to her music. Music had been Cade's safety once; it had kept her filled up when she went hungry, tethered her to the world when it didn't seem worth wasting another breath on.

Cade tried to twist things another half turn, from insult to challenge.

"Let me play," Cade said. "A few songs." She'd never had to beg before — her music had always been enough.

Lee's arm switched from Ayumi's waist to a defensive perch on her shoulder. "You don't like our plan?"

"That's not what I said."

Cade hadn't brought them all together just to watch Lee and Ayumi vanish into space for months, years. Or worse. She couldn't lose them to the empty promise of a not-quite-home. She needed them here.

Cade held out the map, but Lee wouldn't take it back. Ayumi's eyes were narrowed.

"One song," Cade said. "You'll feel it."

As soon as Ayumi accepted the map, Cade rushed to the bedroom and grabbed Moon-White. Back in the main cabin, the survivors and crew half-circled and curved so that part of the room became a stage. Renna had changed the lighting so that Cade would be easy for everyone to see.

A show. It looked, for all the universe, like a show. Some of Cade's old fans even swirled through the audience. But Cade was distracted by the new quiet inside herself. By Lee and Ayumi with their heads bent, closing the small space between them. By her mother sitting in the corner.

Still so unreachably far.

Cade had promised the song to end all songs, but she had

nowhere to start. She pummeled a standard opening on Moon-White, but the notes had no confidence. They wandered away from the melody. Defied the beat. Cade's mind got in the way, and her worries insisted on coming along for the ride.

What if she brought everyone together only to watch them all go spacesick, while Lee and Ayumi glared *I-told-you-so*'s? What if she let Lee and Ayumi run this mission only to lose them *and* whatever hope they had of finding a planet in one sour move? What if cutting off Xan like she had in the club made it so that Cade detached from his particles, from the good parts of entanglement, and she could go spacesick, too?

Cade vamped again. She'd started the song so many times that it was long enough to end, but she had come too far to turn back.

The crowd gave her no help. Cade had gotten used to an eager, too-willing audience, but the survivors were tired, confused, curled inside of hard shells. Cade tried to find a crew member, one point of concentration. Her mother, Lee, Ayumi, and Rennik were all half-gone. But Mira—Mira watched Cade from a cross-legged seat at the front, working so hard to listen that it looked like she might burst. Cade tried to play just for Mira. When she played for everyone she cared about, when she played to save the world, it felt like spreading her arms to hold the wind.

The song picked a direction and stuck with it, the same winding of notes she kept coming back to, unraveling inside of her. Cade wondered, for the first time, if this was *her* song. She felt it more than heard it. It had a growing and easy shape inside her, the blurry lines and gentle colors of a landscape.

It felt new and old at the same time. Known and strange.

Mira gasped, and Cade wondered if she could feel it. But when Cade checked the little girl's green eyes, they were turned to the back of the room.

There was a shuffle, and now everyone turned, pinned to a single woman who had broken the song to stand and walk toward Cade. Even the survivors who didn't know that the woman was Cade's gone-mother held themselves careful and quiet.

One step, then another. The struggling steps of a deep sandstorm, or thick water, or a night the moon left untouched.

Cade's mother stopped at the edge of the crowd, shivering with effort.

An old wish came back to Cade with a new, painfully raw edge. She needed to know her mother's name.

"Hello," Cade said.

Her mother stared out of wavering, dim eyes.

Cade had the strongest urge to reach past the wrinkles and the glass and pull her mother out. But Moon-White hung from her hand, and she couldn't pick up the song where she'd left it. What other weapons did she have?

Words. Cade had never been able to make them work like notes, arrange them in the right order and make people move to their meaning. But they were all she had now. Questions. She had so many questions. Would her mother be able to dream herself into a future where her daughter had grown up? Had her memories of Cade survived seventeen years in the dark valley of space? Did she even remember she had a daughter?

So many questions, but Cade picked the most important one.

"Can you hear me?"

Cade thought she saw a flicker move across her mother's face — recognition, or pain. Then it was gone, and Cade's mother went with it.

She collapsed, delicate as ash.

Cade ran to her side, flashing a hand to her pulse points, inspecting to be sure she hadn't hurt herself too much when she fell. People felt the shift that meant the show was over. There was no clapping, but Cade's heart made up for the noise. She knew people were talking to her, but the blood in her ears walled her off.

Cade had room for one pounding truth:

Her mother had fought — was still fighting.


Cade sent her mother to bed with Lee and Ayumi, to keep herself from prodding for hours and getting frustrated when the spacesick wouldn't budge.

As the audience drained, Cade sat down and did a thorough job of tuning Moon-White. She went through all the steps of the precise fiddle-dance that made the low E gutter, the high E shimmer, and everything in between ring just right. Cade felt balance restored.

She finally turned to go, and found Rennik standing in the door to his room. There was none of the usual paper-shuffling. He stared right at her, and didn't bother to make himself look busy.

"What do you want?" Cade slung Moon-White across her chest, like armor. "Ask for it, or go."

Rennik stood tall against the perfect curve of the doorway. He brushed a glance down at his hands, then forced himself to look up. "Do you want to dance?"

"Do I want to *what*?"

"You asked me once, and I told you that it wasn't the best time."

"And this is?" Cade got the feeling they didn't have any *best times* left.

"I was under the impression that it was selfish to think of what I wanted," Rennik said. "The promises I made, to help the human race, I couldn't put aside for something that only mattered to me. But as soon as you were gone, that night . . ." Cade wished he wouldn't bring *that night* into whatever they were talking about. She wanted *that night* to curl up and die.

But Rennik distracted her. To be specific, his hand distracted her, finding her wrist. "It didn't matter only to me, did it?"

"You get all knotted up in your honor," Cade said. The guitar hung loose between them. Cade hadn't noticed they were both stepping toward each other until there was almost no space left.

Rennik asked again. "Is that a yes or a no?"

This time, Cade didn't have a bottle of ancient green alcohol to make her brave and ridiculous. She didn't have near-death to sharpen what she wanted. She still wanted those things, and now she knew exactly how ripped open she would be when she didn't get them.

"We don't have any music." It was a thin excuse, but true — Cade couldn't play Moon-White and dance at the same time. They'd worn down the batteries on Ayumi's music-filled artifact.

"Don't worry." Rennik touched a fingertip to his temple. "I have it here."

"Are you telling me you can hear thought-songs?" Cade asked. "Because that would have been helpful, you know, this entire time."

"No." Rennik struggled a breath in, but it didn't seem like he was at war with Cade, or even himself. He was looking for the right words, fighting down the wrong ones. "I'm telling you that I have a very good recall for every song you've ever played."

So he *had* been listening.

Rennik waited, his blankness written over with a blunt fear. "Is the lack of answer all I need to know?"

Cade had been brave for him, which always looked like reckless and foolish and broken when she failed. Rennik was being brave now. It called something good up from the place where Cade had tried to bury it.

"Ask again," she said.

Rennik swallowed hard, and Cade could feel it in her own throat. "Do you want to dance?"

She looked around the main cabin. "Not here."

Rennik nodded and led her to his room without another word. Cade shut the door behind them.

When she turned, Rennik was standing in front of her. His eyes were soft, the double pupils catching light. Cade stepped closer, and Moon-White banged between them. He lifted the guitar with gentle hands, found a safe place for it, out of the way. He moved toward Cade, and they worked to fit each other's angles, but it didn't matter how they arranged themselves.

This was going to be odd.

The first steps were like walking — a soft, nowhere shuffle. Then Rennik's hands tugged in a way that drew out certain beats, and cut other ones gasping short. Cade lost herself in the good of the moments when they moved together.

And then she made the fantastic mistake of looking up. She faced the brown in Rennik's eyes, balanced with the gray. His lips so close she felt the tug of his breath. Kissing has its own laws, its own gravity.

"I can't be this close and not kiss you," Cade said.

So she did.

All of their other kisses had been cut off, but this one gained speed, until each press of his lips was a shock that spread, delivering heat to unexpected places.

"Oh," Cade said. "That's new."

Rennik's chest moved up and down with a silent laugh, so she kissed that, too—the spot where she felt air rise between them. Rennik's hand caught the back of Cade's neck. He brought her to his mouth, and kissed her until the air rubbed thin.

"Wait," Rennik said, pulling away. "I want to talk to you."

"Right now?" Cade asked, straining forward.

"Always," Rennik said, with a gentle laugh. "I like your company."

She sat back and studied him with a half scowl, but it only made him laugh harder. And then she was smiling. She couldn't keep her hands away from Rennik as they talked—about the fleet, and what came next. What it would mean if they were together. She loved that word, *together.* It meant she could keep touching him like this. Her fingers ran the length of his arms. They brushed beneath his shirt at the waist, toying with the notion of more.

Rennik pulled her back into his space, suddenly done with talking. Now Cade was glad for the conversation, because it deepened the kissing, and chased off the last of her fears.

Cade tugged at the hem of her shirt.

"Please," Rennik said. "Let me."

Cade felt the worn cloth where it danced on her collarbone before lifting off. Air slid down her skin, and Rennik's fingers followed. Cade got hasty about removing things—she was greedy for each new meeting of skin.

And then Rennik had almost nothing on, and she had nothing. Naked. In his room. Again.

Cade's boldness drained.

A slow blush uncurled from the roots of her chest. Rennik's lips chased the heat around the bend of her neck. He pulled her waist, guided her onto the bed, and settled her on top of him. Once she was up there, she had no idea what to do. But there was something delicious in figuring it out, one deliberately planted kiss at a time.

And then the kisses ran together. Their bodies started taking over. Cade's hips surprised her, like they had when she was dancing. They made demands. They wanted him closer.

She reached down, to take care of the last piece of clothing that stood between them.

Rennik stopped her hand.

Trapped it, really, his fingers underlined by hers. He brought them to his mouth and kissed the tip of each.

"There's no hurry," he said.

Time stopped inside of Cade. But it didn't stop anywhere else.

"I don't know," Cade said. "The universe tells me otherwise."

"You sound like Gori."

Cade laughed, and the happiness of that sound pushed her to kiss new places. His smile-corner. The bridge of his nose.


Cade crashed back to her bedroom in the morning, no more than a messy pulse. She had lost sleep for the first good reason in months.

# CHAPTER 16

Cade woke up to a shining new fleet.

Before she even got out of bed, she reached and felt the songs — clear and catching-bright as water beads.

She tossed off the sheets, shook Lee and Ayumi awake, and took the chute at a wild pace.

The control room bottled a new shine. Lights shone in front of the stars, near and touchable-bright. The yellow pierce of nav lights and the soft blue glow of other control rooms. The curved glint of light on the surfaces of ships.

Hundreds of ships, mostly small — shuttles, cargo craft. And at the center of it, *Everlast* swam like some great, ancient creature, little ships clustered around. This was the fleet. The real, honest-to-universe, unscattered last hope of the human race.

Renna sailed in and put them in the thick of it.

"Would you look at that?" Lee asked. The points of ship-light doubled her freckles. "I mean . . ."

Ayumi stepped up behind her, fitted her arms around Lee's middle, and finished the sentence for her. "Snug."

"Really," Lee said with a tear-choked laugh.

"Holy snugging universe," Ayumi said.

Cade spun in the starglass. It felt like standing at the bottom of a canyon, staring up at the sharp rise of wonders all around. A group of survivors joined, looking shy about it but needing to see the fleet for themselves.

Mira stood to the side, frowning. Alone.

Cade ran over to her. "It's right here," she said, waving an arm at the ships. She wanted Mira to understand. To feel it. Cade was connected to those ships and the people in them, even though she'd never seen them before, just felt them in her head. Mira was connected to them too. "These are your people," Cade said.

Mira ran a thumb over the spot on her cheek that she was always nervously tapping.

"I guess."

Cade knew that Mira's confusion would clear. The murkiness of her mood couldn't stand against all of this light.

Cade ran out of the control room to find Rennik, streaming her fingers along the wall as she went. "You did it. You're the best ship in all the systems." Renna burbled. "No modesty," Cade said. "Cabbage for you tonight."

She was so busy telling Renna how perfect she was that Cade didn't see Rennik at the bottom of the chute. She almost crashed into him, nose to chest. She threw her neck back at the last second.

"Did you see it?" Cade asked.

Rennik slid his hand to the small of her back. Right there in the main cabin. "I did." Cade pushed to her toes and kissed him.

"Do you really think this is the time?" he asked, rendering the question cute with a nervous smile.

The lights around them dimmed.

"See?" Cade pulled him to an out-of-the way spot behind the turn of the chute. "Renna agrees with me."

"We're due to meet *Everlast* in twenty minutes," Rennik said. "If we're needed—"

"Someone will make a big arm-waving commotion and find us."

Rennik kissed her again and Cade sank deeper, until she knew that it would never be over until someone stopped them. Renna tried once, with a shivery burst of indignation. Cade figured it was the ship equivalent of *Get a room.*

Cade peeled back, in the grip of a new fear. "Does Renna get jealous?"

"She's going to love this," Rennik said. "It will give her a whole new set of reasons to sulk and disagree with me."

Cade laughed. She felt a double pull—toward the new fleet, toward Rennik—but for the first time in months, it wasn't too much. Cade let herself feel the future directions and the present. Every warm and skin-sweet thing about the present.

"Really," Rennik said, not breaking his hold on her. "I should set the course to meet *Everlast.*"

"Good," Cade said, fake-inspecting him. "I wouldn't want you to stop being Rennik just because we're—"

"What?" Rennik asked, in a tone that bordered on flirty. Universe help them, Rennik was being *flirty*.

"Because we're together," Cade said.

She broke from the circle of his arms and walked off to an inner beat. A new confidence lived in her hips, pulsed in her fingers. It felt as good as any kiss, to know that she could walk away from him and he would be there when she got back.

Survivors filled the control room, taking spins in the starglass to see all the ships. They filled the mess with excited new talk. What jobs they might hold on *Everlast*. The people they hoped to reunite with.

Ayumi stood at the center of a group of survivors, talking louder and brighter than anyone else. As soon as she noticed Cade, she burst out of formation and ran, sweeping up both of Cade's hands.

"I need to take the shuttle out."

Dark spots floated through Cade's brain. "I thought you didn't need to run that mission anymore." The song had worked—the show had decided it. There was still hope to cure spacesick here, with the fleet.

Ayumi dragged out her words. "I'm not sure about that." She abruptly switched tracks, filling with the quick swell of happiness that comes before tears. "Right now I need to meet the survivors from Rembra."

Cade felt stupid and selfish and fumbled out a quick, "How many?"

Ayumi wore her tears like a badge of pride. "Every damn one." Her inner note-taker kicked in and she added, "Four hundred and ninety-six."

It was the first good number Cade had heard in a long time. "Of course you can go."

Ayumi didn't drop her claim on one of Cade's hands. She ran, almost skipping, for the dock. "You need to meet them, too! That's a big percentage of your fleet!" Cade let herself be dragged through the hold, into the flight cabin. She let Ayumi's happiness flood through her battered gates.

Cade sat in the nav chair of the shuttle, Ayumi's paintings of space all around. Earth stretched along the wall over her shoulder, blue and green and calm. Ayumi warmed the shuttle into flight mode and slid it away from Renna. They were half-detached from the ship when her eyes thickened and her body cut out. She had gone full spacesick.

Cade snatched the controls. Rage almost crashed her system —not because Ayumi had put Cade's life at risk again, but because there were so many people who didn't know what they were signing on for when Ayumi took the pilot's chair.

Cade got Rennik on the com and had him lead her into the dock, one metal-crunch at a time. When Ayumi came back, gasping, Cade was ready to fling the whole sour truth in her face. But Ayumi was already mid-babble. "I have to go. I have to go. I have to—"

"We'll meet the Rembrans later." Ayumi's explosion of

nerves forced Cade to be the calm one, which made her even angrier. "We'll get to them after we rendezvous with *Everlast*. Your people aren't going anywhere."

"No," Ayumi said. "But I am." She stood up, stacking and restacking notebooks with frantic energy, not even looking as she smashed the covers, shedding loose paper. "I have to run the planet-finding mission *now*."

"You can't," Cade said, pulling Ayumi out of the pilot's chair, ordering her hands to be gentle. "Not if you're glassing out like this."

Ayumi slammed a stack of notebooks down in front of Cade. "That's *why* I have to run it. Does that not make sense to you?"

Cade pushed Ayumi away, double-handed. "Setting you loose to die? No, it doesn't really make sense." But Cade's anger was like fire in a vacuum — a twisting burst, then gone. "Please."

Ayumi breathed for what might have been the first time since the glass broke. She gathered herself into the strong, shoulders-back posture that she saved for special occasions, when she knew she was going to get what she wanted. "This shuttle belongs to the Earth-Keeper of Rembra, and I'm the last one there is. If I can help us to a new . . ."

Cade flashed her eyes wide, daring Ayumi to use the word *home*.

". . . place to live, I have to do it."

Ayumi's confidence held, but Cade wasn't done. She knew something that could stop the mission, and keep her friends safe, while she worked on a cure. She wouldn't sacrifice them to a random glass-out or an unworthy planet. Not to anything. Cade marched straight across the dock and bellowed into the guts of the ship: "Lee!"

The sound didn't stop the celebrations in the main cabin, but Lee poked her head around the corner of the mess. It looked like she had been turning old boxes into confetti. Specks of it littered her hair.

"What?" A whoop came from behind her, and she turned like it was a hand pulling her back to the party.

Cade's voice was stronger. "There's something you need to know."

Ayumi caught up. Cade had promised not to tell her secret to anyone, including Lee, *especially* Lee. But what if Ayumi was one good fit away from glassing out forever? What if she planted Lee face-first into an asteroid when she did? Lee was the sort of person who liked to know the risks. As soon as she did, she'd recalculate and make the right decision.

"What is this little sour-fest about?" Lee asked.

"I'm sorry," Cade whispered to Ayumi. She never should have promised to keep this secret. It had gotten too big, and she couldn't hold it anymore.

Ayumi shook her head once and ran, leaving Lee and Cade alone. Cheers from the party rose around them like flames.

"Ayumi. She's . . ." Lee tracked Cade with hard eyes. She was taking the whole thing seriously now. "Ayumi's spacesick."

Lee didn't say anything for a full minute, and Cade wondered if Lee didn't believe her. What if she chose denial, or a lie from Ayumi?

But it was worse than that. Lee pressed her lips to a numb white, and when she finally spoke, the words were double-coated in disappointment and scorn. "You think I don't know that the girl I'm in love with is spacesick?"

"You . . . what?"

"I pay attention, Cade." This was what freefall must feel like. Heart-loose, nerve-spreading. "*Of course* I know she's spacesick," Lee muttered as she headed toward the line of the dock. And then she turned back.

"Here's the best part. So am I."

# CHAPTER 17

Cade kept falling.

She stumbled through celebrations, looking for a quiet place to sit, far from the dock where Lee and Ayumi sped through the last of their preparations to leave. They were back to smiling at each other in less than a minute.

Mira flitted in and out of Cade's radius, but Cade brushed her off. When she passed Rennik in the crowd, his happiness looked out of place, like a word in the wrong language. Cade skimmed over his eyes and kept moving. The common room was almost empty, except for Cade's mother, resting on pillows.

Cade shoved a stack of cushions aside and fit herself in a wall panel, where it was quiet and close and she could work out a way to get Lee and Ayumi to stay. And maybe not hate her, as a bonus. But keeping them safe came first.

The sludge of half-formed ideas was so deep that it took Cade a full minute to figure out Renna was shaking. The vibrations knocked Cade to the side, forcing her teeth into a violent chatter.

"What is it?" Cade asked, fitting an absent-minded hand to the wall. It bunched under her fingers.

"Renna?"

And just like that, the ship stopped talking to her.

Cade shifted the panel and crossed the common room to the main cabin. In the space of a few minutes, the room had emptied. Torn bits of off-white confetti littered the floor like chips of bone. The lights flickered, then returned to their normal brightness. Cade called up to the control room.

"Everything all right up there?"

Silence filtered down. Perfect silence-particles.

Cade didn't move as fast as she should have, but the silence worked like amber; it slowed and trapped her. When she hit the control room, it all rushed her at once.

Cade saw the ships.

The starglass exploded with them. The gentle, trailing movement of the fleet had scattered into bright shards. In the kaleidoscope crash of light and dark, Cade saw the repeated shape of a palm.

An attack.

But that was impossible.

There couldn't be an attack. Before, the Unmakers had known where to find the human race. There had been charts and maps, cities and towns that everyone knew about. Obvious places to hit. This time, Cade had been careful to gather her fleet in a vast nowhere, a nameless tract of space.

This wasn't right.

Cade should have defaulted to the fear of losing her friends, or braced for the sudden end of her own life, but she was distracted by something incredible happening.

The fleet was fighting back.

*Everlast* had chipped the rust off their ship-to-ship cannons and was making the most of the missile power. And the newer, smaller ships weren't cowering behind it. They had been rigged to fire from their blast-wipers.

Cade shook her head, like there was something half-buried in her brain. She'd heard these plans before. Her focus settled on Lee, at the control panels, working the com as hard and fast as she could.

"This was you," Cade said. "You armed the fleet."

"With help from *Everlast*," Lee said without looking back at Cade.

The enemy ships flew fast, hissing projectiles, yet whenever the fleet scored a direct hit, they broke apart like toys. The Unmaker defenses were particle-thin. Taking out most of the humans had been as easy as dropping a load of bombs, and now the human fleet had one thing on its side: they were underestimated.

Lee stood at the control panels, the plan to leave on Ayumi's shuttle dropped and forgotten. She rattled directions, and cargo ships and shuttles slid in and out of formations. Ship after Unmaker ship came undone.

Cade should have listened to Lee, should have heeded the words she didn't want crammed in her brain—this will come down to a fight.

"What can I do?" Cade asked.

"Get in the starglass," Lee said. "Call out the positions of Unmaker ships."

Cade rushed into the light-streaked blackness and spun, but she couldn't focus with so much exploding around her. Ships crossed Renna's path from all directions. The dramatic spark-and-shadow of the lighting made it even harder to tell what was going on.

"One at thirty-five degrees," Cade said.

Renna spun, not toward the ship but away, pulling it behind her. The pickup in speed jolted the control room. Renna aimed down a clear path and slammed toward the nearest bit of space-rock, looping a series of complicated ducks and turns. When the Unmaker ship tried to follow, it clipped the side of the rock. Crashed and spun out.

"All right!" Lee cried. "We've got some brass in us yet!" An echo of cheers and shouts rose from the crew.

But Renna, for all of her defenses, didn't have a single weapon to tilt at the Unmakers. "We have to get her out of here," Rennik said.

Renna roared her disagreement.

"She wants to help," Lee said.

Mira, who had tucked herself unnoticed into a corner, threw up all over the floor. Renna tried to comfort her, but she couldn't siphon too much energy from the battle. Mira was left to run away from the mess she'd made.

Cade wanted to tell the girl everything would be fine, but that could very well be a lie, so she didn't know if she'd be able to say it and sound any degree of convincing. Then the view in the starglass changed, and grabbed her attention by the throat.

"There's a ship," she said. It shot around them too fast for her to give a solid location. "It's closing in."

Lee jumped into the starglass with Cade.

"There," Cade said.

Lee ran a hand through her wild hair. "I see it," she said. "What in the name of every hell *is* that?"

It was different from the others — not a palm, but a raised triangle, like a dark arrow. Fear pulsed out of Cade and Lee, slid their heartbeats into the same tight rhythm.

"It's on us," Cade said.

A waterline of panic rose in Lee's dark eyes. "Go," she whispered to Renna. "Get clear of this, and don't listen to anyone who tells you different. Including me."

Cade and Lee shouted out the ship's position, eye-measuring distances. The dark arrow moved in a slick-fast, erratic flight pattern, almost impossible to track. Its black metal rendered it near invisible, and Cade lost it from moment to moment. She had to wait for the rare times when it stole light from a nearby ship or a far-off star.

Renna flew faster than fast, but she had gotten herself tangled in the thick of the fight, and getting out would mean serious flying. She wove an impressive pattern between the human ships, aiming to quit the field and shake the dark arrow at the same time.

Rennik talked to her, low, fast, and constant. He urged her on and tried to keep her anxieties in check. More than Renna, he was the one Cade worried about. He was the one whose calm focused into a hard point.

"There's something about that ship," Lee said. "I don't see what's coming out of it. No projectiles."

"So it hasn't fired yet," Cade said.

"But it took down three other ships that got in its way."

Cade shifted her focus. It did look like the dark arrow had hit targets before it moved on. Now it skimmed the top of another cargo ship. Just skimmed it. That was enough to send the cargo ship into a loose death-spin.

"Must be some kind of surface weapon," Cade said, but it came out sounding like the guess that it was.

"No." Lee crouched to look from a different angle. "It's getting close, not making contact."

Cade heard Rennik's breath before his voice, understood the fear before she made sense of the words.

"It's electricity."

"A pulse cannon?" Lee asked.

Rennik paced from the starglass to the control panels to the com, then started the rounds again.

"It has to be," he said. The first deep cracks in Rennik's

calm spread across his face. Cade couldn't shake the feeling that someone had designed a death specifically for them. She pictured Unmother sitting at the cold heart of one of those ships. She must have known that Renna couldn't stand the touch of electricity.

Rennik threw directions at the crew, hot and everywhere, like sparks. "Keep your eyes on the ship," he told Lee. "Use the com for all it's worth, and get us backup if you can," he said to Ayumi. Then he turned to Cade. "I need you to get to the engine room and keep Renna breathing."

Cade wanted to do the same thing for Rennik—rest a hand on his chest, make sure he was still in there.

Halfway down the chute, small steps called out behind Cade, two shoved in the space of one of her strides.

"What's happening to those ships?" Mira asked.

Cade spoke without turning, without stopping. "Electricity can travel through space, but not far. That ship gets close, and the other one draws the pulse. Like when the ground pulls lightning."

Mira caught up as Cade reached the panel, her brown hair swinging when she stopped short. Cade fumbled with the sliding panel, even though she'd done it a thousand times. "What happens to the people inside those ships?" Mira asked.

"The best they can do is keep off anything that conducts," Cade said, knowing how impossible that would be for people trapped inside of metal cans. The panel crashed aside, and Cade plunged into the deepest parts of the ship.

Mira spread to her full arm-span, hands running along both sides of the tunnel. "What will happen to Renna? If she gets hit?"

Cade turned and turned again, only half-sure of the path that led to the engine room. She knew Renna better than she thought. She followed a soft curve, and an open door showed her the engine-heart.

It burdened the air with an unsteady beat. The surface was hot, almost too hot to touch. An old trick from Cade's desert days came to her. She thought cool into her fingertips. Fresh-cut ice, hard rain, a sweating glass.

Mira dropped to her knees.

"I don't want Renna to get hurt. I don't want that."

"None of us do," Cade mumbled, the words automatic. Her heartbeat lived in her fingertips.

"But it's my fault," Mira said, her voice all tremble, and no solid ground. "I had to. She told me I had to —"

That word again.

*She.*

It was all Cade needed. She saw a woman, unrobed, her hair the red of an open cut. She saw Mira at the woman's feet.

"You're an Unmaker," Cade said. The words came out hollow. She wondered how she'd never guessed it before. The girl changed in front of Cade's eyes — her sweetness shed like a wrong-fitting skin. Or maybe she didn't change. Maybe Cade had layered good traits on Mira, and now they were sliding off.

"We don't have names." That tone. Harsh and honest. Cade

should have known. "Like Mira, that's not mine. I hated the sound of it, but she gave it to me. For the mission."

The girl's face made no sense, and her words made too much of it. Cade shook, and Renna's heart seized under her hands. Rennik should have sent someone else to keep the ship calm.

"I was here to learn things," Mira said. "To collect information. Not to hurt anyone. She told me to watch you, and then she got really interested when I said you were bringing the rest of the humans together."

That was why there had been no Unmaker ships since Res Minor, no attempts on Cade's life. Mira's orders had been to watch her, not put a knife to her throat. Now that Cade had a clear picture of the girl she'd taken onboard, instead of a watery-pale reflection of herself, Cade was sure Mira would have been able to kill her if it had come down to that. Dark night, cold blood, no guilt to wipe up when she was done.

But Cade had been too valuable to her enemies; she had done the hard work for them. The entangled girl who'd given up on her other half wanted to be a savior so much that she had gathered the rest of the human race into a nice, kill-able herd.

Cade got to her knees, propped Mira up, and slapped her hard.

"You did this," Cade said, "and now everyone I care about is going to die."

Cade fought against the reality that Mira wasn't the only one to blame. Gathering the fleet was her choice. Not figuring out Unmother's plan was her fault. Not seeing the spy planted in front of her might be the worst of all.

This was on Cade, and her one wish in that moment was that the guilt would crush her to death before anyone else had a chance to go first.

"I didn't come to hurt you," Mira said. Her voice broke and changed, as if she was a different person stuffed in the same small body. "Not that it should matter. Not to me. I don't care if you die. *I don't care.*"

Mira put her face down, and her hands came up coated in wet shine. "What's happening to me?" She stared down at herself in terror, like she was bleeding out. But she was crying — probably for the first time.

Cade remembered Mira's song, that stubborn curl of music growing out of her strange, rough silence.

If she told the others that Mira was an Unmaker and had led the rest of them here, to the fleet, they would find some way to get rid of her. With no safe planet to dump her on, that meant death. A quick and painless one — Cade's friends weren't monsters. But someone who drew a straight line to their downfall had to be dealt with.

"You know I should kill you."

"Yes," Mira said. She closed her eyes, like a frightened animal, her lids huddled and her body drawn small.

When Cade blinked, Mira's song was weak, and shivering, but it was still there.

She hauled the girl to her feet. "You're one of us now. You tell me what I need to know, when I need to know it. Then you tell Unmother what I want her to hear." She pushed Mira, a little too roughly. "If I think for half a breath that you're still on their side, I'll feed you to the stars myself."

Mira nodded. Cade wanted to slap her again. She wanted to do worse things, and she had to drag Mira out of that room to keep herself from doing them.

Cade brought Mira to a stop outside the control room. "Until we're out of this, I don't want to see your face," she said.

It was a reminder of Cade's own falling-down. Her mission had been to keep everyone she loved safe, and she had failed, because Unmother sent her a little girl with green eyes, a little girl who had no one.

In the control room, Lee ran to the com and hit the panels, battering them with her forearms. "Dregs, dregs, dregs." She added a desperate circle-pat when she remembered she was hurting the ship. "Sorry, Renna."

Renna wasn't listening; she was flying for her life. They had shot clear of the battle. The dark arrow was etching a close pattern around them. Lee noticed Cade in the doorway. "It's on us."

Cade walked hard for the starglass and found the sleek-dark ship. "At least we know where it is."

As if on cue, the ship became part of the darkness. Cade and Lee spun, frantic.

"Twenty-five degrees," Cade said. "I think."

"No . . ." Lee said. "I saw it at two-sixty."

"Are you sure?"

Cade looked at Rennik. He'd stopped pacing. All of his

fury had moved to his hands, desperate on the controls. Cade wanted orders from him, questions, anything to prove he was in there, that he wouldn't leave no matter how sour this turned. But he had gone dangerously silent.

"Dregs," Lee said. "I lost it."

Cade had another way to look for the ship, but it wouldn't be easy in this madness. She forced her eyes closed and wrenched herself open.

Cade struggled past the fear-spiked songs of the crew. The space around them was just that. Space. Empty, bare of thought-songs. But when Cade ran over it again, she felt rough spots, like dark circles cut out of dark cloth.

Like Mira. Pre-song Mira.

The absence of Unmakers from the human frequency had always felt wrong, and the secret was stupid-simple. Cade couldn't find the Unmakers' songs because they had none. A thought-song comes from a person's nature, and the Unmakers had tried to force-wipe theirs, start over as something other than human.

They had silenced themselves.

Cade checked again, to make sure that the darkness she felt was different from the darkness all around it.

"Two twenty-five," she said.

Renna swung hard. Cade opened her eyes and dropped to one knee. Her hand met the shaking floor. "Play it hard and fast, okay?"

Renna made a wild dash, spending all of her speed at once. She sliced in so many directions that no ship should have been able to follow the steps of her reckless dance. But the dark arrow knew its business. It hit a wide road of light. The crowd in the control room had no choice but to watch it advance with the grace of a well-made machine.

Cade's hand went wet and cold and reached for Rennik's, but he was strangling the controls.

A spreading float came for Cade's entire body. At first she thought it was fear. But the sensation hooked in and actually moved her, loosening her bone-to-bone connections, then detaching her feet from the floor.

Renna had turned off the gravity.

Rennik held the panels so tight that he didn't rise with everyone else. Cade grabbed his hand, but he was anchored fast.

"Rennik," she said.

He wouldn't let go of the panels. He held on, his hands bloodless, his face raked with a terrible calm.

"Rennik, please."

He stared up at Cade's rising body. His gray-brown eyes were the same color as Renna.

The dark arrow rushed fast, passing so close that it claimed the entire view in the starglass.

Lee screamed:

*"No one touch anything!"*

Rennik fought the rising tide of no-grav. He dug in and breathed hard, until the rasp was the only sound in the control room. Cade's hand slipped out of his. She thought that was it. She had lost him, and she would lose everything.

But Rennik closed his eyes and let go.

A pulse rocked the ship. Screamed, fast and blue-veined, through the walls, leaving a fried smell. Cade floated in the thin, charged air.

Renna was dead.

# PART TWO

# CHAPTER 18

Cade's hands were ruined.

She had played them to tatters, called blisters to the surface, cut raw lines into her fingertips, healed them, and then cut them deeper. Nothing was bringing Moon-White back from the dead.

She still started the day with a warm-up, pushing sound out of the guitar, notes that cracked grim, like bones. She gripped Moon-White's dull body, the shine faded. Cade had taken the guitar during the escape, thinking it was the one thing that would keep her connected to her old life, plugged into memories of Renna. But it painted that time in long-ago colors, the days when she had music and friends, when a fight wasn't pressing down on every minute.

The thought of all the Unmakers she had to kill today got between Cade's brain and her fingers. She could feel the sour notes coming, so she set the guitar down, jumped off the top bunk, and grabbed her boots.

Mira was waiting on the bottom bunk, framed in the endless metal of *Everlast*. She sat up like it had just occurred to her, not like she'd timed it perfectly to match Cade. Her hair was an explosion of static.

"It sounds a little better today."

Mira was a first-class liar, but she was also the only person Cade had to talk to on a steady basis.

"So what's the plan?" Mira asked.

Cade hated the innocent spread of the girl's features, the freckle-spatter that reminded her of Lee, the green eyes that so obviously mirrored her own. Even the name, Mira, had probably been assigned to make Lee and Rennik think of Moira, killed all those years ago. Everything about Mira had been chosen with care, and a mind to the mission. Cade would have been happy to let her loose in the fleet and never see her again.

But Mira was a spy. If Cade wanted to keep her alive, she had to hold the responsibility in a tight fist.

"The plan for today is to not die," Cade said, chucking Mira's shoes on her bunk. "Let's move."

Even the simple act of Mira tugging the laces, fingers weaving fast, got at Cade's nerves. It would have been easier to deal with the girl if Lee or Rennik or Ayumi were there to balance out her company, but the rest of Renna's crew was gone, scattered throughout the fleet. She felt the loss of them like fire in her chest, so Cade stopped her breath. Cut off the oxygen. Killed the burn.

"Anything new today?" she asked as they hit the hall. *Everlast* was alive at all hours of fake-morning and made-up night, bursting with fleet members on their way to the mess or their posts, detailing the latest battle.

Mira ran ahead, tossing *Good morning*s as she went. She turned back to Cade, mid-stride, and shrugged.

"Nothing."

Since her breakdown in Renna's engine room, Mira had fed Cade lots of information—the location of an attacking ship, a strategy for the day's defense. Cade used her new ability to feel out Unmakers' non-songs, predict flight patterns, learn about ship anatomy, and take them down.

The best-known killer in the fleet was a title Cade had earned fast, and Mira was her good luck charm. Fleet members shook their hands wherever they went. Matteo, June, Zuzu, and Green were already planning the entries for the history books. Mira took it in with a startled smile, but Cade felt no pride in the work. The way she saw it, she and Mira were both to blame for the constant chipping-away of what was left of the human race.

As they walked, Cade caught the twitch of Mira's fingers at her side. "What was that?"

Mira bundled her fingertips in the other hand. Too many beats passed before she said, "Nothing. Nerves. Or . . . I think I'm hungry. Do we have more of that garlicky stew thing? June said there might be leftovers."

For the most part, when Mira had inside info, she brought it to Cade, eager and fumbling, desperate to make up for leading

the Unmakers to Renna and the fleet. But now she was changing the subject.

Whatever she knew, it had to be big.

"Are you worried they'll come after you?" Cade asked.

"No," Mira said, threading her skinny arms over her chest.
A few fleet members nodded and cheered as they passed.
Cade dropped a hand on Mira's shoulder. They smiled and
put on their best double act.

Cade leaned down. "You're afraid the Unmakers will trace
the leak back to you?"

Mira squirmed ahead of her. "No."

"So the chip *did* tell you something."

That biochip was the source of Mira's info. It caused all of
the cheek-tapping and finger-twitching that Cade had thought
were nervous tics, little personal details that had made her
feel like she knew Mira better. The truth was that she'd been
wired, the whole time, with tech much more advanced than
any tracker. Cade had never seen its equal in her black market
days. When Mira wanted to transmit information, she tapped
a nerve cluster in her cheek, and the taps amounted to a code.
A chip sunk into the back of her neck acted as a controller for
one wedged deep in her brain. When the Unmakers sent back
information, it announced itself in Mira's fingertips.

Every time they flicked, it stabbed a reminder into Cade's
stomach.

"If you don't tell me, more people will die," Cade said.
"Some of them will be people you know."

Mira turned into a pebble — mouth, shoulders, everything bunched and hard.

"We'd all be in danger," Cade said. "Matteo. Zuzu." She picked the people Mira liked best, skirting the names of her own friends. Her old, non-communicating friends. But they could die just as easily.

Mira stubbed her feet as she walked, giving a thoughtful tug on the end of a braid June had wound into her thick pale hair.

"They're tough," she said. "They won't get hurt."

"Renna was tough," Cade reminded her.

A swallow stuck in Mira's throat, and she had to redampen it. It was hard work for the girl to hide her new feelings. From what Cade had gathered during the long hours in their cabin, the central point of the Unmaker plan was the stripping of human emotion. Reactions were altered, and whoever couldn't keep up with the neural reeducation was punished. Spacesicks and failures were tossed to keep them from contaminating the new line.

"Renna was nice to me," Mira said, as if that little truth held miracle status in her brain.

Cade thought of the turned-off gravity, the doors that had crashed wide so no one would be trapped when the electricity slid, unbound, through the walls. "She took care of us, down to the end."

Mira cut across the docks and took the stairwell in uneven leaps. "Well, with me, she made a mistake."

Mira had never lied to Cade about being an orphan, not knowing her people or where she was from. The Unmakers were bred in labs to cut down on the chances of attachment, but to increase their ranks over the last twenty years, a number of infants had been bought out of their cribs. Mira had been raised Unmaker, and given a mission.

She was *all* mission—or she had been until she made friends with Renna, and got close to Cade, and grew a song.

It filled Cade's mind now, while she closed her eyes to make a quick decision. Cade cut back from the control room, trailing Mira past the medical sector, all the way to a row of glass sub-rooms. Each one had its own control panel that could only be accessed with top-level code. Cade fired a string of digits into a number pad and entered airlock 7, leaving Mira on the outside.

"What are we doing?" Mira asked through the glass. She was a creature of routines, plans, schedules, and executions. Anything that disrupted them blew at her like a hard gale.

"I need to know," Cade said. She couldn't launch herself into another day of targeting Unmakers, one ship at a time, if some new and terrible thing was about to burst wide.

With Mira, the torture that would have been used on another spy was out of the question. Cade was sure that Unmother had figured that into her calculations. There were times when all of the manipulation behind Mira's presence boiled so hot under Cade's skin that she almost tortured the girl to spite the Unmakers, to surprise them, to break the patterns they were so sure they knew.

But this was a little girl, and no matter how much Cade hated her, she couldn't hurt her, because then she would have to hate herself too.

She had enough of that toxin in her system.

"The information that comes to us through that biochip is keeping us alive," Cade said. "It's our food. It's our air."

There were moments now when Mira didn't try to paste over her lack of feeling with a simulation. It was a form of honesty, but it made Cade's mouth leach dry and bad-tasting, every time.

"I'm no good to the fleet without that information," Cade went on. She locked her knees and readied herself. There was no way of knowing how this plan would play out. "You can tell me what came through the biochip, or you can toss me off *Everlast*. Your choice."

Mira looked at the controls sitting in front of her, simple and patient, the green button lording it over the smaller black ones. Anyone could figure out how to work it. You didn't want to leave room for error when it came to airlocks.

Mira rested her hands at the edges of the control panel. "What if I don't want to do either of those things?"

Cade dumped herself on the glass floor. "We'll wait."

Mira's breath leaped shallow. "I'm sorry," she said. "I'm sorry."

Mira's finger made contact with the green button, and the airlock hissed like a hurt animal as it struggled to separate its locked metal teeth. Cade ran for the door, punching the emergency override into another number pad. She latched on to the door, all of her weight on the frame, as the vacuum snatched her legs, trying to steal them out from their rightful place under Cade as she ran the snug away.

Cade hit the button that closed the door. The glass became the only thing keeping her separate from the salted black.

Mira threw herself at Cade, arms shrink-wrapping to fit her neck. "You're still alive!" Air-gulps shook the girl, top to bottom. This wasn't the sort of behavior Cade expected from someone who'd tried to kill her.

Airlock 7 had been broken for a week, and the engineers were too busy repairing busted engines and downed electrical systems to get to it. Still, one of them could have put it on the repair list without Cade noticing. She hadn't really expected to test the theory with her life.

"Remind me to keep you away from buttons," Cade said.

She breathed back to calm as Mira spilled words. "I didn't know which one was worse. If I didn't tell you, you died! If I did tell you, you would launch an attack, and a lot of other people would die. Matteo, Zuzu, other people. You said so yourself! What did you want me to do?"

Cade sighed. She was so tired that she couldn't tell exhaustion apart from pain. "Tell me," she said. "That's all I want."

"There's going to be a meeting," Mira said. "Of the highest-ranking officers."

She named the ship, the coordinates, the time. Cade's heart started up a strict, urgent ticking. Less than five hours. There was only one question important enough that she could spare the time to ask it. "Will *she* be there?"

Mira nodded.

Cade's feet pounded glass.

*Everlast* rocked as Cade ran flat out for the control room, and at first she thought they had been attacked. But this was gentle, a cradle-rock.

A ship docking.

Maybe supplies, maybe fleet members from another ship. Cade didn't have time to stop and learn the details. She had to drill this information through the right thick skulls, so they could act on it.

Four steps from the control room, a hand caught on Cade's back. She spun, sure that it was Mira catching up, but she found herself inches from honey-summer skin and searching brown eyes.

Cade hadn't seen Ayumi since the night after Renna died, when she had dropped the survivors on *Everlast*, stayed the night, and dissolved in the hectic course of the next morning. Her shuttle was gone, and for days Cade had no idea if she was running the planet-finding mission or hiding somewhere else in the fleet. Or dead — that was always a possibility. Then Ayumi had radioed once, a brief and staticky message, fake-bright with news, to let Cade know that she was joining the Rembran ships in the fleet. She was safe, and they would see each other in some vague but wonderful future.

Lee had gone with her. No goodbye.

"Hi," Ayumi said with a little wave.

Cade let the truth slip. "It's good to see you."

Ayumi clutched at Cade's arm, a big reach, like she was drowning in water that Cade couldn't see.

"I need your help."

The control room tugged at Cade. Mira's intel was going stale. "It'll have to be someone else."

"No," Ayumi said. "It has to be you, and if you can't see why, you've gone tone-deaf on top of everything else."

*Tone-deaf?* Ayumi must have been glassing out and she'd come to Cade for a quick hit of sound to keep the spacesick at arm's length.

After Cade joined the fleet, she'd spent a full night wondering if she should tell people about her music, and what it might be able to do for the spacesicks. But it hadn't brought her mother back, not all the way. It hadn't been enough to keep Lee and Ayumi close. With the Unmakers on top of the fleet, taking down ships did more good for the human race than plucking songs and playing nurse to the spacesick.

Besides. Ayumi looked fine. Slightly dimmed, nervous-fingered, but fine.

"Look," Cade said. "I don't have a guitar. We scoured the fleet and didn't find one." She dropped her voice. "So if you need help with certain symptoms—"

"It's not for me," Ayumi said.

Lee stared out of Ayumi's nav chair at the shifting metal of the fleet, but there was no way she could see it through those blank, glassy eyes.

"She flew for such a long time on the Express," Ayumi said,

perched on the arm of Lee's chair. "I thought it couldn't touch her, that she was invincible. Like you."

Cade swallowed a laugh. It sat, radiating bitterness in her stomach.

Not getting spacesick just meant that Cade had to watch everyone else do it. And she couldn't even shut off how much she cared, because that was what kept her human. Cade had to give herself to the pain, and then pinch it down to a point. Solid. Bright. Always-there.

"I'm not invincible."

"As it turns out, neither is Lee," Ayumi said.

Cade couldn't look out the window, because it reminded her of the pressing attack plans she was supposed to be making. Instead she focused on the walls, covered in Ayumi's sprawl-and-splatter interpretations of the universe. Earth glared down at Cade, the paint dried-out and shiny, heading toward cracked.

"How long has she been like this?" Cade asked.

She didn't want to look at Lee, either, and see her fallen so far from her spitting, swearing, wild grace. Cade had learned to deal with glass from her mother, and she expected it from Ayumi. But Lee was Cade's definition of human. Watching her hollow out meant too much.

"We cover for each other, so we can keep working for the fleet." Ayumi ducked her head, cheeks sparking pink. "She covers for me, mostly. It's a good system, and it keeps us out of the spacesick bay. But she's been out for half a day now. I can't keep this quiet much longer."

"Why did you wait?" Cade asked. She could have dealt with a spacesick Lee earlier this morning. Yesterday, maybe.

"If she knew I brought her here, in this state . . ."

Cade knew that she was light-years out of Lee's favor. She had told Ayumi's secret, ignored Lee's condition. Lee had every right to blame Cade for not arming the fleet, and she could even stretch that into blame for Renna's death. But Cade still felt like she was missing something.

"Like I said." Cade spread her hands. "No guitar."

For one weighted moment, Cade let herself remember the good of a working instrument in her hands; the perfect feel and the beautiful blare of sound.

"I can't help her without Moon-White."

Maybe it was better this way. Lee would be safe in the spacesick bay, as safe as she could be. Cade knew, because she had deposited her mother there before the first week was out. There was no way to keep an eye on her with the fleet swirling, Unmakers closing in. Gori was just as unreachable: Two days in he'd chosen to go into a serious rapture, expanding to the size of an entire cabin on *Everlast*. The stunt had attracted crowds at first, children who came to poke at the real-life Darkrider. Cade had thought she'd be able to wake him at some point, but so far, he was as wakeable as a stone.

And then there was Rennik.

Cade thought of him on that first night — or the last, depending on which end you looked from. He had let himself be herded into the shuttle, led to a room on *Everlast*, and assigned a new bed.

Cade didn't know what losing Renna would do to him. No one did.

When she had gone to see him in the morning, he looked wrong. Smaller, even though he didn't slouch. Off balance, even though he sat up straight and perfect, the sheet slung tight over his lap. He had stared at Cade with burned-out eyes.

"Please," Ayumi said, pulling Cade out of her old pain. "Don't deprive Lee of the thing she loves best."

"You?"

Ayumi cast her eyes to the floor. "Oh. I was going to say hunting Unmakers."

If the fight was all Lee had to come back for, Cade might have left her in her disconnected state. But Lee had Ayumi, who had slogged through a dangerous patch of space on the off chance that something could be done. Ayumi had risked Lee's wrath, and Cade knew that with Lee, a step like that was a true measure of love.

"All right," Cade said.

Maybe a fraction of the decision was selfish, too, hoping that her friend would come back to her.

"You'll do it?" Ayumi asked, her brightness back to full blast. Saying yes to her felt better than planet-bound sunshine, better than spring.

But Cade ran into problems right away. She'd promised music and had no way to make it. Lee wasn't going to be dragged from a nasty fit of spacesick with palm-on-nearest-surface percussion. It sounded nice, but it told no story. It had no heart.

"Maybe I can put a call out to the fleet and find something," Cade said. "I pick up instruments fast. But—"

Time. Ticking.

Ayumi ducked her head as if she was hiding from how stupid or obvious her idea was. "You *are* human," she said. "You come with an instrument built in."

Under any other conditions Cade wouldn't sing. She *didn't* sing. But whatever rules she had laid out for herself years ago had already been cracked or discarded, and there was no point in treating the last one standing as sacred.

She dusted off her vocal chords with a cough, and let out a weak-warbled hum. There was nothing pretty about her rough, rusty alto. Cade tried to scrounge the words to a few Earth-songs, but she came up empty-headed.

Cade was one good breath away from telling Ayumi that it wouldn't work.

But something rose to prove her wrong. It swelled when she looked at Ayumi, when she let herself look at Lee.

All she had to do was close her eyes and—

—it was like reaching out a hand, but the hand was music, and what Cade found at the end of her fingertips wasn't Lee. Cade reached past her, into a loose nowhere-place. Cast her wanting into that void. Wished new life into her friend, sewing the connection between mind and self, dragging Lee in from the wild black fields of disconnect.

Calling her home.

From that nowhere-place, something answered the call of her wanting. It matched the intensity, the need of her voice.

She pushed and it pushed back, but there was no fear of falling. This was balance. A force working with her, sometimes the same, sometimes in tension, but always with her.

Always.

*third in line and waiting*
*for the long slide into dark*
*ride the curve to day*
*again, following the*
*arc*

Cade's breath wore out.

She didn't know where she'd been. Away. But now she came back to the little ship, unsure, and Lee came with her.

Ayumi plastered the side of Lee's face with kisses. "What . . . what are these for?" Lee asked.

While she was busy blinking her dark-moon eyes and figuring out where the snug she was, Ayumi grabbed one of Cade's hands, turning it over and over like a charm. "What *was* that? It felt different."

Cade knew the song. It was the one she'd been building, a phrase at a time, before the Unmakers attacked the fleet. But there *had* been something new about it this time. Ayumi had found the right word.

*Different.*

"What's Cade doing here?" Lee asked. Her face tightened. Cade got ready for it to flick to full-on disapproval mode, but it was like something jammed. "What was that singing about?"

"Singing?"

Cade sounded even more confused than Lee. She couldn't remember choosing words, or putting them in order, but she ran back over her memories and there they were.

Lyrics.

Ayumi let Cade's hand drop and looked into her eyes. "Cadence, there was something about that song . . ."

Cade had felt it too. None of her club creations could rival it. None of her harsh alone-songs came anywhere near its beauty. The lyrics tagged it in Cade's mind as important, but the way she had felt while it poured out of her proved the matter.

Cade's throat begged her to get back to it.

Ayumi shuffled to get out of Cade's way. "We took up plenty of your time. You can get back to—"

"What's happening?" Lee asked, sensing the switch to urgency and hopping down from the nav chair.

"The Unmakers," Cade said. "We have new intel. It's our first real chance to take them down."

Lee turned one full, bewildered circle. "Then why are we sitting around here having a sing-along?"

# CHAPTER 19

Cade sat at the command table on *Everlast,* Matteo on one side, Mira on the other. She'd worried that she would have to fight to get Mira a seat in the control room, but all she had to do was keep showing up with the girl in her wake.

The crew loved having Mira around. Zuzu snuck her crinkle-wrapped sweets, and June braided her hair into long parallel lines that snapped and swung. Once, Matteo had lifted Mira onto his shoulders and given her a full tour of the ship. Mira seemed to like them too, but Cade had no idea how much of that was real and how much she'd painted on to keep Cade from throwing her out the nearest airlock.

"This new information," Matteo said, fitting the pad of a thumb to his cheek stubble. "Where did you come by it?"

Between getting swept aside by Ayumi and breaking into song, Cade hadn't had time to think of a lie. She couldn't pretend she'd heard it from another spy in the fleet. When Cade had first arrived, she'd used her knowledge of the Unmakers and their non-songs to feel out traitors. There had been eight. *Eight* Unmaker spies embedded in the fleet. At first, it had made Cade feel like the Unmaker attack was inevitable, that it would have happened Mira or no Mira. But no one else had been that close to critical information. So the spies went into the hard black of space, and none of Cade's guilt went with them.

"Cade intercepted something on the com," Mira said. Cade's brain stuttered at the ease of Mira's lies. "She didn't mention it sooner because it was double-encrypted. She spent all night cracking it."

Cade writhed under the pressure of looking like a sudden code genius, but Mira's smile seemed to make up for it.

Even Lee looked impressed.

Convincing the *Everlast* crew to act on good information was the easy part. Now came the rest.

"We have to call a quorum," June said with a quick shuffle of papers. It would be the first time *Everlast* had called a quorum since the fleet came together.

Lee and Ayumi were invited to stay. Others arrived, one docking at a time—the captains of a dozen ships, and fleet members who had made names for themselves. The doctors who dealt with the sick and wounded. The tech genius from Rembra who had stopped the Unmakers from patching into the coms. Half an hour of precious pre-attack time was spent pulling everyone together, and there was still one open seat at the command table.

Cade couldn't wait on the latecomer.

"I have a two-part plan," she said. "The first part involves almost all of the small craft in the fleet. If we send one of the warships anywhere near this meeting, the Unmakers will call it off before it even starts. But if we build a swarm of the smallest ships in the right sector—"

"And attack them how?" Zuzu asked. "We ran out of ammo for blast-wiper cannons three weeks ago."

"Which is part of the plan," Cade said. "They'll think it's recon, so they won't feel threatened."

Cade and Mira swapped a look. Mira had fed the Unmakers the info about the drained ammo, at Cade's request. It sounded like good intel, which helped her maintain a cover. It also helped set up a moment like this one.

"We go after the ship with the blast-wipers," Cade said. Zuzu started another round of objections, but Cade was ready. "*Not* the cannons. Pressurized air. We have to get close for it to work, but the Unmakers won't expect it, and all we have to do is blow through the hull once—as long as we hit the right room. Hard to hold a meeting when all of the attendees have been sucked out into space."

"Explosive decompression?" Zuzu asked, flicking at her earlobe. "Crude. But hell, I like crude!"

"Ditto," Lee said.

Ayumi drummed her fingers on the table.

"The other little ships scatter, draw the fire," Cade said, getting into a rhythm now. She stood up and paced, made a performance of it. The more confident she sounded, the more the crew would believe in the plan. The more *she* would believe in it. "Three of our shuttles are left to dock and send boarding parties. Once the rest of the Unmaker ship locks down, we have to deal with the leftovers. Make a clean sweep."

Cade knew how close this plan sounded to the Unmakers' original one. Take out the masses, round up the rest, hunt them down. A twinge lodged and spread through her in a sickening way. But Lee stared at Cade like she had never heard anything so brilliant or brass.

"Where'd you come up with that?" she asked.

Cade shrugged.

It was all she thought about. Day. Night. When she wasn't skimming information from Mira, she was planning elaborate deaths. She doubted this was what the scientists had in mind when they entangled her.

"I don't know," Matteo said. "Without *Everlast* to protect the smaller craft, it seems like a great deal of risk to our pilots."

They fought it out. Lee took Cade's side, which came as a surprise, and Ayumi watched them both with a worry-coated look. Cade wrapped herself so tight in the arguments that she didn't notice the last member of the meeting arrive. He lingered in the doorway. Too tall. Thinner, now, curves cut so deep they looked harsh.

The last time Cade had seen Rennik, in that faceless room on *Everlast,* his clothes still smelling of crisped meat, he had looked emptied out, done. But then his eyes had lit with a fever-burn.

"You can rest," Cade had told him. "As long as you need before you feel . . ." She couldn't say *better*. Renna had died and that word had gone with her. "Rest," Cade repeated, her hands clumsy and useless against the itch of his new blanket.

Rennik forced himself to his feet, clenched against an oncoming lurch. He fought it, like swallowing back vomit. "I won't need rest," he said. "It would deprive me of the pleasure of killing the Unmakers, one by one."

He stared at Cade now, and the fever was stronger than on that first night, fed by all of his success.

If Lee and Ayumi were a well-known team of pilots, and Cade and Mira had made a name for themselves taking down Unmaker ships, Rennik had made one by storming the ships and killing, down to the last.

"Cade?" Matteo asked.

She didn't know how much of the conversation she'd missed, but when she looked up, the air was thick with raised hands.

"Cade," Lee stage-whispered across the table. "You might want to actually, you know, vote for your own plan?"

"Right." Her hand shot up.

"Rennik," Green said in a dicey manner that made it clear he was wary, if not outright afraid, of the Hatchum. "Good of you to join us. We'll catch you up on the plan and then you can vote—"

"It doesn't matter," Rennik said. His tone had been stripped of calm. It was more a pulse than a voice.

*It doesn't matter.*

Cade wanted that to mean what it used to: that Rennik was on her side, and would back her. But the words had a newer, sharper edge. *It didn't matter* as long as he had plenty of metal-breathers to kill.

"Right, then," Matteo said. "It's decided."

Cade forced herself to wait until Rennik drained out before she stood.

Ayumi bolted around the table. She had been a special sort of awkward all through the meeting. "Look," she said. "About that song." Cade rushed out of the control room, but Ayumi kept talking.

The trajectory for the dock was set, and nothing Ayumi said could pause it, but a figure waddling down the hall did the job for her. He was short, robed, blinking faster than Cade's counting-down heartbeat.

"Oh, good!" Ayumi said, misinterpreting Cade's stalled feet. "So the next time you sing—"

Gori landed in the middle of the conversation.

"Sing?" Gori asked. Then he muttered to himself, "Yes, of course. A song would explain it."

"You're awake!" Ayumi said. Her arms flung high and threatened to clasp around his neck, but even with two months' worth of sleep crust in his eyes, Gori managed to warn her back with a glare.

"I had no intention of leaving rapture for several more years, but I was interrupted." Gori focused on Cade. "This song—"

Cade wanted to get her voice around it again. But she had

less than a minute to board, and less than ten before she'd be in the thick of a battle, where she would need all of her nerve endings alive to the danger.

"Look," she said. "I'm done taking requests."

"What I have to say is not shaped like a request," Gori said. "It is a gift of knowledge, a message from the universe:

"You must stop this song."

Cade tried to be patient as Gori adjusted to the hold of Ayumi's shuttle. Mira flitted in a cautious circle around the Darkrider as he stumbled. She looked double-pleased: first, that Gori was there to stare at, and second, that another fleet member was sucking Cade's attention away from her, and she'd been able to dart into the mission without a fight.

"I can't believe you brought him," Lee said from the nav chair as she strapped in next to Ayumi.

"He's one of us," Ayumi said. "Really, if I'm being fair, he's been one of us for longer than I have."

But Gori had never been an active member of the universe, let alone a useful addition to the crew. He sat and rested his head on the pucker of robe that covered his knees, and Cade wondered if Gori, with all of his dark energy chasing, could suffer from motion sickness. "I do not understand why we had to leave the great hulking metal-bellied one."

"*Everlast?*" Cade asked.

The names of ships didn't stick to Gori's brain. Too small and fleeting, on the cosmic scale.

"The metal belly isn't part of the plan," Cade said.

She had insisted that it stay in motion, which meant that if Gori wanted to talk to her, he had to tag along as they crossed the dark trench of space that divided the human fleet from the Unmakers.

"Don't waste time explaining it to him," Lee called back. "He doesn't care if we live or die."

"All things die," Gori said.

"Ugh. Proof. Thanks."

But Gori wasn't done talking or stumbling. He wove a path through the hold, putting his most philosophical hand gestures to use. "I care about matters at the scale of a single life. I also care about them at the scale of the cell, the star. This is not a lack of caring. It is a great burden of caring."

"Hey," Lee said, twisting against her straps. "You can help us with the battle!"

"Help?" Gori asked.

"You know," she said. "Nudge space around so the Unmakers get confused."

Gori blinked. "No."

Ayumi tugged Lee's strap to keep her pointed forward. "Can you sort of curl dark energy into fists and crush their ships?" Lee asked.

Gori blinked again, hard, like it might rearrange Lee's matter into something nicer. "No."

Lee flicked a switch with extra force. "What good are you, then?"

Ayumi turned to Lee without interrupting the smooth flow

of her hands on the controls. "You know, there are useful skills that have nothing to do with killing Unmakers."

"Yeah?" Lee asked, all flirt-and-challenge. "Name one."

Ayumi leaned across the space between the chairs and tugged Lee's strap again, this time pulling her in. "One," she said, and kissed her. "Two." Lee dove in hard. "Three." Ayumi brushed a line of wayward hair away from the side of Lee's face, and kissed her again.

"That's the same as one," Lee said.

"No," Ayumi said. "There's a bit of a difference." She went over the already covered territory, and Cade pretended to be caught up in the schematics of the ship they were going to board. She didn't need Lee or Ayumi to notice her bitter-tight face.

Lee surfaced from the kissing with puffed lips and a much more pleasant tone, calling back to Gori, "I still think you should go all Darkrider on them."

"I did not come out of rapture to disturb the universe for you." Gori seemed to have an endless supply of harsh stares. When he was finished with Lee, he found one for Cade. "I came to inform you that you must not do it again."

"Again?" she asked. "How did I manage the first time?"

"I felt it as a series of vibrations," Gori said, shaking his hands in a sort of crude demonstration. "But when I heard the girl Ayumi describe it as a song, I understood it was the same. A series of vibrations, shaped by a human voice."

The ship crossed the invisible line between fleet space and

enemy blackness. Cade had flown enough to know it, with the same inner ping that used to tell her when she was nearing her bunker in the desert. They were close now, and Cade needed to tack her mind to the intricacies of the mission. But she couldn't let go of Gori's words. "It upset the balance of the universe? My singing was that bad?"

Ayumi looked back from the controls, curls flying. "I knew that song was special!"

"Not special," Gori said. "Dangerous. I have never felt anything like it. Not since that day."

Cade didn't need him to specify. If this was serious enough to remind Gori of his gone-planet, it was serious enough for Cade. The last thing she needed was another atrocity on her hands.

"Fine," she said. "No song."

It was easier to say that than to mean it. Cade hadn't really known how much she cared about the song until she wrote it off with a few words and a quick wave of the hand.

"Look," Cade said to Gori, "you don't have to nudge anything. But as long as you're here, you do have to help." He started to breathe deep, but Cade cut him off. "Rapturing is not an option."

It wasn't a nice move on her part, and Cade knew it. She hoped Gori wouldn't ask why, because the reasons worked down to selfish roots. Cade wished she could have spent the last two months listening to sphere music, tuned out, but she had to stay awake to every awful thing that might happen.

If Gori wanted his opinions to count, he would have to stay awake, too.

"You can help Ayumi up front, or you can —"

"If I must make myself useful," Gori said in a dusty tone, "I will fight."

"You?" Lee asked. "I seem to remember that during training you were about as vicious as a prune."

"The danger is great now," Gori said. "I had no use for training."

Lee scoffed at the idea that he was a seasoned fighter, but there had been a time when she and Ayumi had to sit on Gori to keep him from attacking Cade, and another when Gori introduced Cade's own knife to the base of her throat. It was comfortable to think of the Darkrider as a peaceful creature, but Cade had a small scar and an old fear that proved otherwise.

"Here," she said, pulling one of her own knives. "You can borrow this."

"What sort of combat are you trained in?" Lee asked. "Inhaling your enemies? Robe-strangling?"

"Only the most desperate." Gori ran the knife-edge through a fold of robe, polishing until it glowed star-white. "I know what it is to be the last of one's kind."

# CHAPTER 20

Ayumi flew loose, non-threatening patterns for ten minutes before she started to advance on the line of Unmaker ships, drawing the rest of the attack force behind her like a swirl of comet dust.

Cade had gotten used to fighting the Unmakers, but she hadn't been this close to killing so many of them, ever. It should have electrified her, but instead it hammer-thudded through her system.

"In formation," Lee said.

"You can't be in the boarding party *and* be my navigator," Ayumi said.

"I can't?" Lee asked with a mischief-tugged smile. "I thought you said I was everything to you."

Ayumi couldn't disguise the sudden choppiness of her breath. "That's not relevant. To this particular. Time and place."

Cade watched from the hold. She'd hoped that bringing Lee out of her spacesick fit would change their loose and spreading constellation, realign them, but nothing seemed to have changed. Lee hadn't stopped Cade from joining the boarding party, but that wasn't exactly an invitation to pick up their friendship where it had left off.

"All right," Ayumi said. "Identify the ship—"

"—and we'll ask them to dance," Lee finished.

Mira surveyed the ships, most of which looked identical. She picked a slightly larger one, the palm broader across.

"There," she said.

"And the target?" Ayumi asked.

Cade closed her eyes. This was where the thought-songs came in—or the Unmakers' lack of them.

She tossed her mind, net-like, and caught the little scratched-out circles of silence. She found a concentration, a clump, with other silent circles moving all around.

"The low center of the ship," Cade said. "There's a gathering. A big one." She ran her mind over the silences to get an estimated count.

"Hundreds."

The fleet had been chipping away at the Unmaker force—two, five, ten at a time. Now they could take out hundreds with one well-placed puncture. But it was more than that. Cade had a chance to kill the woman who had ordered the attack on Renna and stolen the rest of her friends from her before they even had the chance to die. It was a real, almost-touchable hope, and it should have swelled through Cade like music. Instead, it sat like old grain-mash in her stomach.

Cade watched Mira, wondering if she was afraid for the people who had raised her or if she actually wanted to help the human fleet. She hit just the right tone with her eagerness most of the time. Her song inched louder and prickled with new growth every day.

But right now her pinched face gave Cade nothing to go on. "We have to move before they notice."

The little ship rushed forward and down to make a pass beneath the Unmakers. Metal sped at them so fast that it looked certain the shuttle would smash against it. Instinctively, Ayumi leaned in to a last-second curve. Air burst from the blast-wipers, hit the metal, dented the hull. But it didn't punch through.

"The air might not be strong enough," Ayumi said as they emerged on the other side of the ship and circled around.

"It has to," Cade said.

Lee worked the com. Reports came through — other ships were pummeling the target, but the hull stayed intact.

The little ships swarmed back to the human side of the invisible line. "All we did was step on their toes," Lee said.

"Tell them to re-form for another pass," Cade said. "We need to hit those spots again. The dents."

By this time everyone around them had woken up to their plan, and now the Unmakers spat defenses. The black around the shuttle thickened with other ships and the slick float of missiles.

"You can do this," Lee said, her hands resting lightly on Ayumi's shoulders. "You are doing it."

"Take them down," Mira said, like she meant it. Cade had to remind herself that Mira was an Unmaker, and they had always been good at putting on a show. It might be the one thing they had in common with Cade.

She marched fast to the pilot's chair. "When you get there, pull around fast. Lead our ships in, but let the rest go for the target. The Unmakers will fly hard after the ship that scores the hit, and we need to board."

"No one will board if we don't disrupt this little meeting first," Lee said, and she got so mad that she made the mistake of looking at Cade like they were friends in the thick of another argument. She tore the glance back.

The com burst on.

"*Noble* is down," Zuzu's voice told them. "I repeat, *Noble* is down."

Wreckage ran in thick streams alongside the window. Cade went electric, in all the wrong ways.

"That was one of the boarding ships," Ayumi whispered.

Which one? Cade thumbed through the last few hours, universe-bent on finding a single piece of information. Was Rennik on that ship? He'd refused to come on the shuttle even though Ayumi was one of the best pilots in the fleet. Cade couldn't help but believe that it was to get clear of her. And now *Noble* was down. That made it a one-in-two chance that Rennik was dead, and Cade didn't have time to hide how much she cared — how much care was clawing its way from her stomach, hot up her throat, scrambling to get out.

She had to land the other boarding party on that ship.

The palm came up again, so close that Cade lost its shape. Its dull metal became everything.

"I trust you," Mira said, slipping her small hand into Cade's. She had to act like that trust was real. Like it counted.

"I'm with you," Ayumi said as she slammed the controls. "Absolutely."

"What the hell," Lee said — which wasn't quite the same.

Ayumi made the pass again. Metal screamed fast at their faces, then the shuttle swerved. The other ships stayed the course, dimpling the Unmaker hull with bursts of air.

Ayumi's ship rattled, and everyone who wasn't strapped down in a seat buckled at the knee. At first Cade thought they had taken a hit, but she wasn't thrown to the ground. She wobbled to standing, and it happened again, and again, until Cade got used to the soft, gentle batter.

Bodies were raining through space.

Their fingers spread like weak imitations of starlight. Their faces, slack. Muscles so far gone after ten space-bound seconds that Cade couldn't imagine life back into them. They looked like last-stage spacesicks, like Cade's mother. Except in the eyes. There was no glass there. Nothing that held the light.

Bodies.

Hundreds of them.

"Universe keep them," Ayumi whispered.

They were Unmakers, enemies, but no one told Ayumi to take it back.

The shuttle pulled up on the far side of the Unmaker ship, and nestled against it. Lee and Gori went to work with bars, forcing the dock open. "You can't stay here," Cade said to Ayumi and Mira. The girl rolled her eyes, but there was no way she was getting on that ship. Her cover and her life would have been at equal risk, and Cade didn't want either one wasted.

"We'll clear the rest of the rooms and signal you to come back and pick us up," Cade said.

Ayumi's eyes slid to Lee. "I'd rather—"

"This isn't a time for what you'd rather," Cade said. "It's a time for you not getting killed."

"Thanks," Lee whispered to Cade. "She acts twice as stubborn when I'm the one in her way."

Ayumi twisted in her seat, calling to Lee. "You don't get to leave without kissing me."

Lee ran and leaned over the arm of the pilot's chair. The kiss was muddied with fear and ache, and Cade, for all of her jealousy, didn't want that. Having someone to love in the middle of this meant hundreds of goodbyes, hundreds of deaths. It didn't matter if all but one turned out to be fake. The dreamed-up ones hurt just as much.

Lee headed through the dock without looking back. Gori followed, knife palmed and ready. Cade walked out last.

Mira called after her. "Come home safe."

Cade forgot, for the space of a step, that Mira wasn't her friend and *Everlast* wasn't her home.

The boarding party was greeted by Unmakers, two rows deep —robed, armed, unsmiling.

"Well, dregs," Lee said, and pulled her knife.

Cade didn't want to get trapped in the dock, so she pushed forward, picking a fight with the nearest Unmaker. There were too many to face without some kind of failure, but that didn't stop Cade's muscles from going through the motions. It felt better to slash and hack, half-blind, than to give in.

Gori rushed the entire first row and took them on, three at a time. The knife Cade had given him flashed in clean, spare lines. The body that spent so much time in stillness moved with desperate speed.

Lee stopped in the middle of a knife-clash. "Holy snugging universe." Even the Unmaker she pushed off couldn't conceal that he was watching Gori take down the rest of his team. Unmakers fell in rings around him.

Gori pocketed the knife, flexed his wrinkled fingers. "I have not practiced in six hundred years."

Lee stared at him, stunned, as Cade did a quick non-song check.

"Most of the troops are headed that way." She pointed to the left. There was another presence on her radar. One silence, winding its way deep into the ventricles of the ship. One Unmaker headed for the heart of it alone had to be confused, scared, or important. Since their kind didn't believe in confusion or fear, that pretty much decided it.

"Meet back here," Cade said. "Ten."

Lee was already running. She tossed a quick "Kill some metal-breathers" over her shoulder.

Gori might have been brass in battle, but he was no match for Lee's pace. Her long legs made fast work of the hall, and he had to bunch his robes above his ankles and trot to keep up. Cade set off in the opposite direction.

It wasn't long before her sureness and sense of direction crumbled. She hadn't been on an Unmaker ship since Hades, and this one had the same white doors, the same curved design.

It brought her back to Xan, and the promises of meeting him. Those promises hadn't gotten crushed when he died, yet when she reached for them now, they fell through her mind like dust.

Cade kept running.

She heard footsteps ahead, but not the tight pounding of a guard. Erratic. Unsure. Someone unpredictable, or wounded.

Cade stopped and scouted before she rushed ahead. She found Rennik, moving down the hall.

Cade had to stop and breathe. She hadn't been able to keep the fear of his death from rising, and now relief tumbled through her like fresh water, washing her worry-poisoned insides clean.

"Where's the rest of your boarding party?" Cade asked.

"I heard someone making a distinct noise over here," Rennik said, running to check the rest of the rooms. Cade claimed the other side of the hall and started to help. "The rest of the boarding party thinks I'm insane."

A crust of meanness covered Cade's voice. "Does that happen to you a lot?"

She should have felt happy that Rennik was alive, and stayed happy. But the good feelings drained fast, and others volunteered to fill the space. It had been two months without a word from Rennik. He'd left *Everlast* on the heels of Ayumi and Lee, and Cade had tried to reach him at first. Visits to the ship where he was staying, letters hand-delivered to the rooms where he slept. She was met with empty beds and tossed-off sheets.

Cade closed her eyes.

She needed to track the non-song. Rennik was standing too close. When he got in the way, Cade felt stupid for not expecting it; not being ready, in any way, to deal with him. The comfort of Rennik's old music was gone, dissolved into a tangle of notes. With Renna missing, what had been an intricate loveliness spun into chaos.

Cade couldn't ignore him, and she couldn't blast through, so she opened her eyes and shoved past him.

The rooms were mostly sleeping cabins. One Unmaker to a cabin, everything neat, sterile, in order, with pieces of spare costumes laid out in lines. Cade prodded her neck farther and farther into each room.

"What are you finding of such deep interest?" Rennik asked from a doorway five rooms ahead.

"I need to learn more about the people who are trying to kill us."

"It's not enough that they want you dead?"

Cade didn't rise to Rennik's bait. She knew how people started fights. It was a minor art form, and she had lots of practice.

"Our forces are matched," Cade said. "We've been proving it, over and over, for months. The only way we're going to beat them is to understand them. Be smarter." She remembered Rennik's books, his carefully worded sentences. "You used to care about that sort of thing."

He turned on a heel.

Rennik's calm had peeled off, and it showed no signs of reforming. Cade remembered a time when all she wanted was to get a rise out of him, force his emotions to bubble over the edges of the politeness. Now a rise was easy to get, and she wanted the old Rennik back.

Cade had gotten so twisted up in seeing him, in seeing him *like this,* that she had stopped checking the song-map in her head. A stray five-man guard rounded a corner and almost walked into Rennik's back.

"Rennik!" she cried. "Behind!"

He planted a foot to turn, and by the time he shifted his weight, he was deep in the swing of his double blades. Cade had firsthand experience of his fight training, but when he added hate to that training, it came out as a breathless hack of blades. Rennik was unforgiving, intense, his muscles set on a fine edge and his mind over it.

Cade claimed the shelter of the nearest door and used it as a cover to lure Unmakers one at a time. By the time she'd taken on two from her protected position, Rennik had the rest on the floor, writhing or dead.

"Nice work," she said, scraping close to sarcasm.

Rennik grabbed her arm. It left her no choice but to feel him, and when she did that, she remembered.

Everything.

Cade endured the gritty feeling of not-blinking as Rennik bent over her. "This is all your doing," he said.

So he did blame Cade, or hate her, or both. Now she knew, so there was nothing left to say. Cade waited for Rennik to let her go. She told herself that she would start to forget him as soon as he let go.

His hand stayed printed on her arm.

A neat, faint scratch sounded at the far end of the hall. Cade and Rennik both ran, but she was faster. She kicked into a closed room and found a grate that had been tossed to the floor. Whoever had come out hadn't had time to replace it. Cade threw her shoulders forward, pushing into the vents without thinking.

"Where are you going?" Rennik asked.

He wouldn't even begin to fit in the choked space.

"Wait here," she called back.

Cade snaked through the vents, fighting the dimness as

much as she fought to keep moving. She closed her eyes and followed the non-song forward, forward, to the right. It was lodged. Here.

Cade opened her eyes and found a woman, her long red hair snarled with white, working to open another grate.

This was the woman who had ordered the attacks on all of those people. She had killed Renna and unbalanced Rennik. Against her will, Cade thought of Mira, and the brutal mind-shaping that had been done since the day she was bought.

When Cade's hand touched skin, she thought it would burn. But it was just an ankle, attached to a woman as small as Cade. One she could drag out of the vent and back into the room. One she could smash to the floor. Hold rough at the neck.

Kill, if she wanted to.

By the time Cade worked Unmother through the opening where the grate used to be, one of Rennik's blades was out and raised. Cade had to put her hand in the air and hope he wouldn't bring it down on her.

Confusion, disappointment, and anger showed in Rennik, as obvious as colors, blending to a form a dark shade.

He stopped the blade.

"She runs this," Cade said, holding her voice balanced and calm. "All of it." Unmother had the information they needed to end the fight. Keeping her alive was a risk, but so was walking, so was breathing. If they killed her, someone else would take her place. But if Cade pried enough intel out of this woman's twisted neurons, she might be able to end the war.

"We need her," Cade said. "For now."

Still, standing between Rennik and the woman who had killed Renna felt too much like taking her side.

"There is something you can do."

She pulled Unmother's hair back and exposed the pale-rooted curve at the base of her neck. Cade grabbed Rennik's hand and guided his fingers, running them over the strict lines under the skin.

"Biochip," she said. "Out." Cade waited for Unmother to scream as the knife worked her skin. Rennik wasn't gentle.

Unmother smiled as if she was looking at a pleasant day, or a pair of children.

# CHAPTER 21

Unmother made herself at home.

Cade had her placed in a cabin on *Everlast,* a bedroom a lot like the one she shared with Mira. The only difference was that she had Green rig a camera and feed it to a monitor that she set up in a little stub of an unmarked closet.

Rennik offered to stand guard in front of Unmother's room. At first, he offered to do more.

"You need information, and someone to extract it," he said. "Are you waiting for a better proposition?"

He had followed Cade back to *Everlast,* probably in the hope that she would go soft and let him murder someone. She wasn't going to let Rennik interrogate Unmother, not with those unsettled seas for eyes.

"Stay here," Cade said.

"So you can go find her more pillows?" Rennik asked.

Cade marched off and left him to stand there. She wondered if she would have to scrounge up a guard for her guard.

When Cade slipped into the closet, Mira was already stationed, knees folded to her chest, watching Unmother on the monitor and chewing the side of her thumb. She looked up at Cade. "Are you okay?" It was never just a question with Mira. It was part of her ongoing study: How to Be Human.

"I'm fine," Cade said.

If Mira could trick a fleet of humans into thinking she belonged, the least Cade could do was learn to tell a simple lie.

They settled in to watch Unmother. She moved in slow, deliberate lines around the room, and Mira tensed with each right angle. Unmother didn't do anything sudden or violent. She made no attempts to escape. After less than an hour, she stretched out, her hands slightly curled, and took a nap.

That was the first time Cade really wanted to kill her.

How could she sleep with that loose-breathing ease? Cade's nights seethed with dreams and startle-awake panics. Did it really not matter to Unmother that so many people were dying around her? *Because* of her? Didn't she have anyone that she needed to get back to, enough to keep her from getting comfortable?

Cade had a thousand questions, but she pinned each one in place. Her time to talk to Unmother would come. First, she had to send in the spy.

Cade touched Mira's shoulder, and she jolted. "Can you talk to her?"

Mira hoisted herself from the chair and neatened her clothes, one square inch at a time. She started up what Cade thought of as her Mission Breathing—short, focused bursts. Mira looked much too grateful for the chance to prove herself.

"I can do this."

Cade had a plan formulated, and if it went right, Mira might actually be the savior the fleet needed. Not that it would make up for Renna's death, or the blown-apart state of Cade's friendships.

"Act like you snuck away," Cade said. "Act like you're still on her side."

Mira took in the words with long, thirsty nods.

"So, full Unmaker?" she asked.

"I want you to live, breathe, and eat metal."

Mira forced the change as she walked out of the control room, shaking off emotion like mud.

Cade tacked herself to the monitor and waited for Mira to show. It was time to find the truth, hidden under the sand-shifting layers of Mira's alliances. This woman stretched out on the bed was her leader. The one who told her what to do, who to be and who not to be. The closest thing she would ever have to a mother. If there was anything left between them, one fleck of loyalty or love, it would show up now.

Mira came onto the monitor, and flashed Cade a big-eyed *here-we-go.*

She tapped Unmother's shoulder, and stepped back as the woman lilted out of sleep and sat up with a patient smile. Like she was the one who had been waiting for Mira and not the other way around.

Cade listened to Mira's song, sure that it would leap as soon as Unmother looked at her. It gathered and lifted, then settled.

Mira stood over Unmother as she worked a thumb into the crook of her shoulder, slid firm hands down her calves, pointed her toes. Mira let impatience twitch into her little flat-bridged nose, and Cade yelled at the screen.

"Keep it together!" Any leakage of emotion would be noticed by Unmother, and used against the girl.

Mira's face tilted downward, a slight scowl that meant she was holding back. Cade was surprised that she knew so many of Mira's tells.

"I came," Mira said, so flat that Cade actually cheered. "What now?"

"Don't you think it's time for us to leave," Unmother said, neat and tidy and not at all a question.

Mira flicked a glance toward the hall. "There's a guard."

"There's always a guard," Unmother said. "And there's always a way around him."

Cade tensed, ready to run and back up Rennik.

"Are you sure you want to delete my cover so soon?" Mira asked. "The captain of the ship loves me. The crew thinks I love them. The girl in charge sleeps in the bunk above mine and tells me more than she should."

Unmother laughed — a sweet laugh, rich with patience — and spelled things out for Mira like she was four years old.

"Your cover isn't necessary to the mission, and the mission is the only thing that matters." She laid a hand over Mira's. In the closet, Cade leaned toward the monitor, hand on her knife. "You did a fine job when you led us to the gathering. If you come back with me, what these people think of you won't matter. Neither will how much you've been compromised."

There was no mistaking the outline of Mira's body as it tightened.

"You won't feed me to the black?" she asked.

Unmother made space for Mira on the bed, and she sat down beside the woman, as automatic as Cade's hands sliding into place down the neck of a guitar. It didn't matter how long she went without doing that—it would always come back. "You're not that naïve," Unmother said. "And I wouldn't lie to you. Have I ever done that?"

Mira shook her head. Cade checked the song again.

No change.

"You won't live much longer," Unmother said, patting Mira's knee. "But this will be a good death."

Cade's disgust with the Unmakers was complete. It was one thing to find Xan's weaknesses, like bruises, and press on them until he gave. He'd been hurt by the universe, but he'd still had a choice.

This girl had been raised to be disposable.

Cade hit the hard bottom of the kinship she'd always felt with Mira. Beneath the green eyes and the loneliness, they were the same—brought up to be put to a purpose and then tossed aside. No matter what Mira had done in the name of the Unmakers, she could choose to undo it now. Cade would see that she lived to get the chance.

Unmother was already looking at her like a piece of rotted fruit, like a cling of trash around her ankles.

Rennik would run in at the first sign of trouble, but Unmother moved quietly, with a slithering grace. She could wrap a hand over Mira's mouth and the girl would be dead before Rennik heard one wrong breath.

"I don't know if I can get us off *Everlast*," Mira said.

Unmother wove her fingers through Mira's hair, forcing the girl's head to rest on her shoulder. "There must be some way."

"If that was true, wouldn't I have gotten back to you by now?"

Unmother's smile was short, like the clipping of a string, and it showed approval. Mira had given the right answer.

"If we can't return, there will be interrogations. I've seen several people outside who'd like a chance at my throat," said Unmother, stretching back onto the bed. "I'd prefer you kill me," she said. When Mira didn't move, Unmother strained her neck up without moving the rest of her body. "I assume you have some sort of knife."

A rough surge of emotion gripped Mira's small body. When Cade blinked, she heard Mira-song, but soured. It filled the room like twisting fingers, like fast-growing weeds.

"Aren't you going to do it?" Unmother asked, sweetly, baring her throat.

Cade shifted in the arms of her seat. Mira knew that Cade wanted Unmother in that bedroom, alive. But to prove that she was still an Unmaker, Mira either had to let her escape or kill her.

The girl fished up her knife, hands working in a broad range, from fumbling to sure. Mira ran the tip down Unmother's throat and stopped at the white pool, shaded where her neck dipped down to her chest.

She walked away.

A soft chuckle rose from Unmother's resting place. She had given Mira a test of her own, and the girl hadn't passed.

As soon as she cleared the room, Rennik checked in on Unmother. She smiled, and Cade noticed that she was as beautiful as the first time they had met. That was the second time Cade wanted her dead. Not just with the switched-on part of her brain that was supposed to want it. With her tensed muscles, with her tired heart. With every ruined part of her.

Mira banged into the closet, letting in too much light from the hall. They were alone, in a little square that had been meant to hold maintenance tools, and not two sweating, exhausted nervebags.

Mira knew Cade had been watching. There was no use in breaking down the scene with Unmother, unless she wanted to point out how wrong it had gone.

"Remember, I left her there like you wanted," Mira said. "That should count for something, right? So maybe when you do it, you can do it fast."

She scrunched her face, uncurled her palms. At first Cade had no idea what was happening. It snuck into her like a creeping-cold night. Mira was waiting to be killed. There was no putting a broken cover back together, and that meant no more intel for the fleet. Mira had outlived her usefulness as a spy.

Which meant she could just be Mira.

Cade rushed at her. "What's this?" Mira asked from the muffled center of a hug.

"Happy," Cade winched Mira tighter, smoothing her hair with one hand. "Just happy."

Mira disentangled herself and looked Cade over from head to toe. "You don't do happy like other people."

Cade dropped roughly into her seat with a laugh. "Neither do you."

Mira nodded at the monitor. "Aren't you going to go in?" Unmother was remaking the bed to suit her taste.

"I want to keep her waiting." Cade turned down the volume so she didn't have to listen to Unmother's crisp sheets. "If we march in and out of there in a line and demand to hear the full contents of her head, she'll think she's too important. She'll think she's all we have."

Mira twisted her fingers into a sickly knot. "She already knows that."

"Well, then, she needs to un-learn it."


Cade ordered Mira to get some rest, and flew across a small pond of space to spend some time with the least important member of the fleet.

Her mother.

A crude rectangle drawn on the floor in light blue chalk marked the spot where she had lived for months. Beds littered the spacesick bay, but they were reserved for the patients who could appreciate them.

As soon as the fleet-appointed spacesick nurses saw who Cade was, they tried to relocate her mother to a nicer part of the bay, with thin strips of window and clean sheets. Cade waved them away.

Ayumi sat across from Cade with the still river of her mother's body between them.

"She looks . . ."

Cade wanted to steal some of the hope from Ayumi's eyes, but there wasn't enough to go around.

"The same," Cade said. "She looks the same."

*The same* was more than she could say for the rest of Renna's crew, so maybe it could have been worse. The spacesick bay definitely looked worse than the last time Cade had seen it. Fuller, at least.

"How many in here?" Cade asked a passing nurse. It was a question Cade had dodged ever since she dropped off her mother. On that day, twenty or thirty spacesicks had milled, and four or five clear-eyed fleet members had mumbled about what to do with them. Now the bay sagged with the weight of hundreds.

"Two hundred and ninety-four," the nurse said in a crisp voice, tucked like sheets over whatever she actually felt. Ayumi cast her eyes down, like being spacesick was a form of guilt.

"I'm sorry," Cade said, seeing all at once what a sour move it was to bring her.

Cade had never gotten cleared to fly by herself. She could

have asked any of the pilots on *Everlast* to take her to the bay, but she'd wanted Ayumi, because of all the people Cade knew, Ayumi was the most like her old self. Looking at her felt like holding on to the last string of an unraveling cord.

Ayumi nodded at the nurses. "Should we ask if there's any improvement?"

"I think we'd be able to see it," Cade said.

She looked down at her mother, needing to compare every real thing about this woman's ugliness to Unmother's rigid beauty. And to see the glass — how different it was from the dull eyes of the dead.

Cade had never thought of glass as a good thing before. She'd taken it as a sign that the spacesicks were walled off from life, and for a long time, Cade's thinking on the subject had stopped there.

Now she had a different idea.

"You told me something about spacesicks once," Cade said, eager-thumbing through memories.

Ayumi sat up and pushed to the edge of her chair.

"You told me they're fighting off the disconnect," Cade said.

"It's a grab for life. Getting back to the feeling of the sun, or to the smell of things. Whatever we care about most." Ayumi's eyes drifted to the thin windows of the bay. "Or who."

That was why Ayumi's need to find a planet had gone into overdrive. Cade had thought it was all about the fleet, finding a home, holding back the darkness with land and water and sky. But it was more than that.

Ayumi had fallen in love.

Cade studied the lines around her mother's mouth and eyes, faint but sticking. She looked so much older than she should. A side effect of the fight. Cade had been fighting for months, and she could feel the drag of it on her bones, worse than gravity.

Cade's mother had been fighting for seventeen years.

She was there, under all that skin and glass. What she needed was a love big enough to pull her back to her rightful place.

Even as Cade told herself there was nothing she could do, a feeling climbed, until it reached her throat and had to be let out.

*third in line and waiting*
*for the long slide into dark*
*ride the curve to day*
*again, following the*
*arc*

*grave fingers, pulling*
*bring all things down*
*to a blue-green point of stillness*
*and still the whole is turning*
*round*

Cade could feel it this time, the singing. But she didn't feel it like words. She felt it like streams and forest and sky.

Like the song was a place, and each verse turned her around

again, so she could see more of it as she sang. As soon as she held the whole thing in her mind she would be able to stay there. Live there.

Inside of that song.

It called her mother back from the dark where she had been for so many years, and Cade saw her rise out of it, swimming to the surface. Her face blurred with effort. Her lungs held, held, then bursting.

Her eyes wavering — then clear.

Cade knew they were brown, but the color had been trapped under glass for so long that she had no idea *how* brown. They were wet dirt and bark, the sort of brown that promises green. They clutched all the light in the room.

Cade's mother looked up, her face thickened with confusion. She opened her mouth in a few weak trials.

Around them, other spacesicks broke their own glass, gasping. Ayumi watched Cade with desperate eyes. But Cade could only see her mother. She could only hold her hand, and feel the painful stirring of long-silent fingers.

She could only hear the word that her mother found in some old corner, and carried out of her inner dark.

"Cadence?"

# CHAPTER 22

Gori's room on *Everlast* smelled like rapture.

When he went into that state and stayed there, it created an odor of rock-piles and stale robes. Ayumi must have noticed it, because her breath ran shallow. But Gori wasn't rapturing now. He waited, dark eyes on the door.

"Cadence."

"Look, I came to—"

"Speak with me about this song," Gori said. "Which I have felt, *again,* even though we reached an agreement."

Her mother's glass had cleared. Only for a minute—a single word and she sank back into her previous state, with no guarantee that she would make a return visit. But if there was even the slightest hope, Cade couldn't honor her pact with Gori.

"This song works against spacesick like nothing else," Ayumi said. "Maybe it can—"

Cade held up a hand.

It was no good explaining things that way. Gori didn't care about the spacesicks, including her mother. When Cade let herself look at the whole rounded truth, she worried that Lee was right and he didn't care about humans at all.

"From what I remember," she said, working a new angle, "*you* agreed not to rapture."

"For a particular moment," Gori said. "I would not be a Darkrider if I chose not to rapture."

"And Cade wouldn't be Cade if she never made music," Ayumi said.

The truth of that vibrated deep. Music had always been part of Cade. Her first love, the one she ran back to when she needed to close the circuit and reconnect to herself. It was the only thing her mother had left her, besides her name. Cade had been away from it too long.

"So you both broke the pact," Ayumi said. "But it was a ridiculous pact to start out with, which is sort of like a stalemate."

Gori kept lancing Cade with a dark stare, like she was the one in the wrong.

"I'll write the universe a formal letter of apology later," Cade said. "I need your help now." She took Gori's lack of response and ran with it. "There's something about this song. It's powerful."

Using that word about her own singing made Cade uncomfortable. She felt it every time a note slid flat or pinched sharp or trembled because her breath ran out. But this wasn't about the perfection of the notes. It was about the strength of the meaning.

"You know I'm right," Cade said. "It was enough to shake you out of a serious cosmic nap."

Gori's stance softened. "The song is rooted in something I have felt before," he said. "Your connection to the particles that once formed that boy."

"That boy," Cade said. "You mean Xan."

She thought she had cut that connection when it got to be too much. Filled the holes he left inside of her — even if it was only with new holes. But maybe that wasn't how it worked when someone died. Maybe he was with her.

Always.

Still, the flashes from his time-loop didn't flood her days and overwhelm her nights anymore. What if Cade hadn't turned the connection off permanently — what if she could plug into it at will?

What if *she* was in control of it now?

Cade fumbled with the implications, while Ayumi raced ahead.

"Do you think entanglement could double the strength of the song?" she asked. "That's what it did with muscle power when Xan was alive. Maybe it's the same music Cade has always been playing, but connecting it to Xan somehow makes it *more*."

That could be right. It sounded reasonable. But there was one problem. This song *wasn't* the same.

It had words. It had a shape. It had weight and color and —

—life.

Gori sat on his bunk, crumpled into a tired shape. Cade had never seen him look exhausted, even though his skin was a collection of sags.

Ayumi tried again. "Do you think—"

"You *know* what I think." Gori's voice cracked. "This song is a threat to the universe, and we will say no more about it."

Cade got the feeling that this all came back to Gori's past and the long shadow of his lost home.

The story of what had happened always lingered behind him, and Cade felt like she was casting unwanted light. Maybe demanding honesty was a form of torture, but what Cade wanted was to soothe Gori. It was the strangest feeling, like wanting to hug a sharp rock. "Tell me what happened," she said. "Tell it like a story. One that happened to the universe, not to you."

His voice cracked again. "And we will say no more about it?"

Cade kneeled at the edge of the bed.

"Not a word."

Gori closed his eyes, but he didn't deep-breathe into the universe. He kept to the boundaries of his own head this time.

"The first Darkriders believed they were meant to master dark energy, use it to shape and grow and change the universe. A small group of those who had the ability did not listen to the voices of others and pushed on, even when warned to stop. They hoarded dark energy, when it is an untamable substance. What they did not understand is that gravity feeds on it, and will find it. The great store at the heart of my planet called out to gravity, and it came, crushing everything in its path. My planet. Coranna." Cade heard the music in that name, the sad swell of it. "Everyone I loved died on that day."

Ayumi knelt down with Cade and laid a hand over one of Gori's.

He pulled it back. Cade expected him to say that the universe didn't allow Ayumi to touch him. That she couldn't comfort a Darkrider, on pain of death.

He said, "You would not touch me if you knew."

Ayumi gathered up his fingers and held them tight.

"I was one of the first Darkriders. A guard, watching over the hoard. It was a lowly job. I was there on the day . . . I felt the disturbance, and understood before others did. I escaped, though I should not have."

A new understanding of Gori skimmed at Cade, like a bullet-glance. His two-month rapture after Renna's death made perfect sense. The real surprise was that he hadn't gone into one the minute after his planet blinked out, and stayed there. But he kept living, kept putting on robes every day, kept caring—in his limited, Gori-like way.

Cade kept her promise. She stood, dusted her knees, and said no more about Gori's home. But she couldn't give up on the song.

"My connection with Xan is particle-based," she said. "Entanglement has nothing to do with dark energy."

"Yes," Gori said, nudging more wrinkles into his forehead. "It is different. But it reminds me of that day."

Cade shifted her weight, but she couldn't get comfortable. Gori's words plucked all the wrong strings.

"So this isn't the universe telling me to stop," she said. "It's you."

Gori shook his head, and the look of the dangerous, self-appointed guardian of the universe dropped away. He was just another fleet member who had lost everything.

"I have wondered why I lived so long," he said. "Maybe I am the form the universe took to deliver this message. Maybe it is why I have lived all this time, walked through these many years and trials. So I might warn you."

Cade and Ayumi wound back through the halls of *Everlast* in silence.

"Maybe . . ." Ayumi said.

She flipped notebook pages.

"Maybe . . ."

Cade could tell that she still wanted to talk about the song, but Gori had deflated them. He'd done more than that — he'd taken all of the air out of the ship, or reminded Cade how thin it was in the first place.

"Maybe . . ."

The word bounced down the metal hall, stubborn and hollow.

There was nowhere left to go but the little cabin.

Cade approached Unmother's room with three knives crowding her pockets. When she got to the hall outside,

Rennik was gone, and a new fleet member stood guard. He was solid, dull-eyed, bored.

His hand sat on Cade's shoulder like a slab of wet bread. "I wouldn't go in there."

Cade brushed him off with a little more muscle than was needed. "So don't."

The guard grabbed for her waist, but Cade blocked the move, swiping his fingers in a crushing hold. She added pressure in small increments. "You know that I have clearance, right?"

The guard's smile was as hard as the stubs of his fingertips. "Just saying you might want to wait. He'll be busy for a good long while."

Cade wondered what Rennik had given the guard to keep her out of that cabin. Or maybe the man had volunteered, knowing what Rennik would do, wanting some thin form of justice for whatever had been done to him.

As Cade ran in, Rennik smashed his hand across Unmother's face, tattooing a kick to her shin. To the beat of some terrible inner drum, Rennik hurt the woman, until she flecked dark with blood.

Cade braced herself, both hands on the backs of Rennik's arms. She could hold him in place for a few seconds, but when he got loose he hit Unmother twice as hard to make up for lost time. She collapsed around her center, like a dying star.

The guard watched from the doorway as if he was being given a good show for the first time in years.

Cade launched herself at Rennik again, battering at his

back and sides with her fists. The punches glanced with the frantic rebound of hard rain. If Cade wanted to stop Rennik, she would have to hurt him.

Unmother didn't fight back, but Rennik didn't give a dreg about fighting fair. There was no standing back to wait a reasonable amount of time between strikes. Rennik didn't care about torturing Unmother for information.

This was about pain.

He bashed his fist against Unmother's perfect-molded cheekbone. The attacks built, and her screams built—edged with pain, but hollow inside, instead of filling with anger or fear. This wasn't hurting Unmother past the skin.

"Stop, stop, stop."

Cade pulled her knife and held it to Rennik's side, but he pushed himself into it, to show how little he cared. His blood spread onto her hand, warm. Memories of him, warm, moved through her. Cade tossed the blade like it stung; the guard made his first smart move and gathered it up.

Cade threw herself around Rennik's neck, lodging a choke hold against the inner wires of his throat. She held herself there even as his breathing changed. Her weight dragged him to the floor.

"What the damp hell are you doing?" cried the guard.

Cade needed to connect with the parts of Rennik that were about more than revenge. There had been so much to him before Renna died—so many complicated, beautiful, frustrating, interlocking pieces.

"I know you," Cade said. Her arms slid into an old configuration. She held him the way she had once, just once, her arms soft and strong in equal parts.

Cade couldn't let it go for long. A show of how much she cared could be used against her. And that made her hate more than the milk-faced guard and the patient, evil woman on the bed. It made her hate the whole broken universe.

"Stop what you're doing," Cade said, "or I'll have the fleet keep you out of the fighting." Rennik's face was close, and anger scratched bright red across his cheeks. Cade watched him weigh more torture now against the delights of killing Unmakers in the future.

He slackened. Cade pulled him farther across the room, but when she caught the calm, following tick of Unmother's eyes, she dragged Rennik the whole way out. Now she had to have this conversation in front of the guard, who smirked like he'd known she would give all along.

"I still haven't gotten anything out of her," Cade whispered. "That *is* what she's here for."

Rennik held an absent hand to his throat, the way he always did when he got hurt and barely noticed. "And when you do?"

"Someone can kill her." Cade looked the eager guard up and down. "I don't care who."

She turned hard and went back into the bedroom, blasting the door shut behind her. Unmother was patting the worst of the blood, soaking it with the hem of her shirt, like she'd spilled a glass of water.

She tested her muscles and sat up.

"You can leave now and save yourself the time." Unmother skimmed a glance over Cade's sweating body. "And effort."

Cade leveled a knife at Unmother. She wasn't going to use it, but it felt better to be in control of some of the danger in the room.

Unmother unpeeled her words, letting each have a moment before she moved on the next. "You came to figure out what my plan is. What I want. But I already have everything I want right here." She smiled at the beds, at the walls, at Cade.

"Really?" Cade asked, twitching the knife at the door. "You'd rather be here than with your new and improved human race?"

"We aren't better humans," Unmother said — a gentle correction, not even scolding. "We are simply *aren't* humans."

"Really?" Cade asked. "You didn't reach down deep and change your genetic code."

"Change how you act, and you change who you are," Unmother said, spreading her hands like she was the best illustration of her point. "No names. No connections. None of the things that make humans weak." She laughed at the worst of her bruises. "The limitations of flesh and blood, in most cases, can be overcome. The real problem is that humans fail to see the larger picture, over and over, because of their small concerns."

With Unmother, Cade always felt like she'd come in halfway through a lesson. She had to keep up, play along. It had always been Unmother's game. Whenever Cade forgot that, it smashed back into her, usually in the form of someone dying.

"So that's why you won't let us start over."

"Start over?" Unmother bent and tended to a cut on her ankle, licking a finger, swiping at blood. "Human history is a matter of cycles. You would make the same mistakes. You would hope and you would try and you would fail. We're saving you from that."

"You. Saving *us*."

Cade mind-gripped the irony as hard as she could. But she would never convince Unmother she was wrong—this woman had washed her own brain a long time ago. The only thing left to do, if Cade could, was to loosen Unmother's hold on the idea of the war, by reminding her that murdering everyone Cade loved didn't really matter.

Not in the *larger picture.*

"The numbers are in," Cade said. "If you were aiming for extinction, you won. There's no way the human race is coming back from this. And I don't think you want to die, no matter how much you beg for it. I think you want to go off and be the leader of this new *nonhuman* race."

Unmother looked an inch away from impressed. "You've actually learned something. How nice."

"So go," Cade said. "I'll give you a shuttle. I'll escort you, even. Make sure you get home safe."

Unmother sighed. "That's a dear little proposition. It's a shame it doesn't sit flush with the way humans work." She leaned forward. It must have hurt to push against her new bruises, but she didn't let it show. "Humans find the cracks, keep alive on gristle and hope. This will never end unless I keep a very close eye on it."

"You," Cade said. An idea prickled through her brain, the first electric strands of lightning.

Unmother laughed, the rounded laugh of someone who has never been quite so amused. "You want to believe that my people would be lost without my leadership, that if you kill me now this will be over . . ."

She trailed off, and let Cade fill in the rest. Unmother's people were designed not to care about her. They had no weakness.

"No, I'm afraid it's the other way around," Unmother said, making the struggle to get to her feet look like a promise, a guarantee that she would return some of the pain. "Your sickly little fleet wouldn't do very well without you, would they?"

Cade stepped back.

"She told me that they rely on you—"

"Mira?"

Unmother glared so hard the question fell away. She was concentrated on getting to Cade, one slow, tiny step at a time. "If I killed you right now . . ."

Unmother couldn't do it. Cade knew that. She had the knife. She had a voice to scream with, and a crew on the other side of the wall. So she should have been able to breathe, but she couldn't.

Cade backed up hard, aiming for the door, to make it look

like she had been planning to leave. Unmother had rattled her down to fear-soft bones. She should have taken the victory and let Cade go.

But the woman's voice pulled her back like fingers.

"I told the others it was time to put the endgame in motion. You must be able to guess why." Unmother dropped the lesson and it felt, for the first time, as if she was talking straight to Cade. It felt — the word slithered up from the past — *intimate*. "You're not bright, but you have a sharpened sense of self-importance. You know why this is happening."

Cade couldn't breathe, which meant she couldn't think.

"It started when I met you," Unmother said. "You and that boy."

*Xan.*

He was an echo now.

*Xan.*

Gone, but everywhere.

"Entanglement was the first sign that humans would find a way to start over," Unmother said. "We can't have that." She backed Cade into a situation that meant running away, letting Unmother reach her, or having her back hit the wall.

Cade went with the last of her sour options. A metal seam ran sharp down her back. "You don't," she said. "Xan is dead."

"The boy was kind enough to pitch himself into a black hole and save us the trouble," Unmother said. "But you." Her fingers pulsed, almost on Cade's throat. "You chose to live, which means all of these other people had to die."

• • •

Cade left the room, shaking. She didn't even know it until Rennik's hand fell on her arm and she could feel the clear, violent difference between shaking and not-shaking. She wedged herself between the wall and the floor and sank.

Rennik looked down at her. He shouldn't have been allowed to look at her like that and not touch her, but he did, staring while she shook and shook. It made her feel smaller than Unmother ever could.

She rubbed at her face with her hands until the worst of the fear came off, like she'd gone at it with fistfuls of sand.

"All right." Cade struggled to standing, keeping one shoulder propped on the wall so she wouldn't fold all over again. "You can go. I'll relieve you."

Rennik rubbed at a crosshatch of cuts along the backs of his hands. "You can't be serious."

A little bit of fight swung back into Cade. "You can't think I'm leaving you here with someone to murder."

Rennik started down the hall, then doubled back, energy spiking out in strange directions. "I went in there because—"

"You couldn't help yourself. I know."

He banged a fist on the wall, so deep that he left small crescent indents. Cade's hand ached for him, since he didn't seem able to feel it. "She was talking about you." Rennik dropped his arm, rubbing his shoulder. "Mutters, at first, but then the volume built, and the words were . . . She said foul things."

Cade trembled on the edge of believing him.

"Watch the footage," he said.

The camera wouldn't be able to lie, but it also didn't give Rennik an excuse for going against direct orders. "She was trying to bait me. Or you. It's manipulation, Rennik, you're smart enough to know that."

Rennik watched the door like he didn't trust it. "I hope you're right." Then he brushed Cade with a look so close to kindness that it almost took her apart.

"You need to sleep," she said, her hands hovering a few inches above his, without putting down.

"Find someone else to stand guard," Rennik said, "and I'll go."


Cade woke up eight times that night.

The ninth time, someone was dead.

"She killed him." A voice came into focus above her, but Cade couldn't match it to a face. "He's gone."

"Who?"

Cade's mind locked the *she* in place without effort. But which *he*?

Rennik? Matteo? Gori?

"Who's dead?"

It was Mira standing over her, dim light caught in the waves of her untied braids. She reported the news in a voice that didn't sound like hers. Grave and grown-up.

"It's Green. Someone knocked and told me . . ."

Cade shook off the waking-lag, and took the halls at a high pace with Mira close behind. They reached Unmother's cabin in less than a minute, but it didn't matter.

Green's body was pooled on the floor.

Matteo and Zuzu and everyone who should have been sleeping were there, strung in a long line. Zuzu looked like a smudged version of herself, and Cade guessed she hadn't taken a shift change in days. Matteo looked even less official in his thick cloth pajamas.

"She broke out," Matteo said.

"Of a triple-locked room?" Zuzu asked. "That tiny woman?"

"She hit him on the side of the head with something blunt," Matteo said, crouched next to Green. "Metal, by the looks of it."

There was the clang of one person running down the hall —Rennik, reporting back to Matteo. "There's a shuttle missing."

Cade ran for the docks, but it didn't matter. Her lungs screamed fire, but it didn't matter. Green was dead. The shuttle sacrificed. Unmother—gone.

# CHAPTER 23

The fleet held its breath.

And the fleet found its heartbeat, pounding in three thousand chests, as everyone waited to see what the Unmakers would do next.

*Everlast*'s crew stood in a line facing the control room windows. Zuzu and Matteo talked in strategic circles, working out offenses they wouldn't use and defenses they hoped they wouldn't have to. Ships had been sent to track the stolen shuttle, but so far no one had caught the first glint of it.

Now that Unmother had gotten away, Cade couldn't pick her out of the fleet. Her non-song would sound like all the others.

Mira's biochip stayed silent.

"There has to be *something* we can do," Mira whispered to Cade, at the frayed end of the crew lineup.

She stared at the far-off mass of Unmaker ships, bunched

her shoulders, and in general did *not* look like someone contemplating her old home. Even Cade glared at Andana with a little more nostalgia.

"What about the tapes?" Mira asked. "Maybe they can help us figure out what she did to escape."

Mira never called the woman Unmother, but she'd started answering to her own fake-name after a few slipped days. Cade remembered asking her if she wanted a new one, something that didn't have the dust of her mission on it, but Mira had stubbed her lips together, rubber-pink and unmoving. It looked like she'd gotten attached to the name she'd been given.

Cade had told her it was a very human thing to do.

"We'll track her!" Mira said, getting enthusiastic about it now, stabbing her finger in the air. How Unmother had escaped wasn't as important as what would come next, but Mira had one part right. Anything was better than staring at a cluster of ships.

Cade pushed through the element of exhaustion that heavied the air, ran back to Unmother's cabin, and rescued the most recent tape. She fed it to the tech-stack in her little closet, watching as Unmother showed up on the monitor, covered in bruises — so, post-Rennik. But there were hours missing from the playback. Unmother went to sleep. The tape scratched to black.

The bedroom came back, empty.

Mira tossed her hands, elbows angled sharp. "Great."

Faced with a fast-to-frustrate nature so much like her own,

Cade slowed the rhythm and tried to find some reason. "If she cared enough to do this to the tape, there must have been something important on it."

"And we'll never know what!" Mira's eyes flared like the green at the bottom of a sulfur flame. Cade almost let her feelings catch, almost burned the plan down because it didn't work in the first fourteen seconds.

Instead, she pressed her hands onto Mira's bony shoulders. "Why don't you go find Zuzu? I think she wanted your help with ammo inventory."

Mira heaved a sigh at being handed a concrete task.

Cade wasn't done with the tapes. That would be like taking her eyes off of Unmother again.

Green — the obvious person to help Cade figure out what had happened in those flicker-gone hours — was dead. Cade could have asked Matteo to dig another tech genius out of the fleet, but she told herself there wasn't enough time. There was someone who'd helped her with this sort of thing before. Cade knew where he slept, because she'd led him there. She lined it up so it all sounded right and reasonable in her head.

And knocked on Rennik's door.

"Who is it?"

Cade walked in. He would want to send her away, and she would argue, so she saved them the bother.

Rennik didn't look ready to thank her for it.

Cade set herself on the bottom bunk, boots up, arms heavy on her knees. She didn't need permission. Cade was the one who belonged on *Everlast,* and Rennik had chosen to leave. He was backstage at her show.

Cade held out the tape and it rattled, plastic innards against plastic casing. "The fleet needs to recover this. Green's dead and I thought maybe you could . . ."

Rennik let the tape hang between them, untouched.

"Plus," Cade said, "I wanted to make sure your new room is nice enough."

"It's adequate."

She inspected it from corner to corner, but it was just another cabin, like hers. Nothing about it sounded the old Rennik-tones inside of her. She felt the lack of his books, his handmade blankets. He looked wrong against the slick metal instead of Renna's curved white.

"You know I visited you on *Providence,*" Cade said. "And *Hazlitt.*" She hadn't meant to bring that up. It had brought itself up, dragged from some deep place.

Rennik grabbed the tape and busied himself. "I wasn't talking to anyone at that time."

"Just assorted battle cries?" Cade asked.

"You have a reputation that far outstrips my own," he said. He butterflied the tape's casing along a thin, crackable seam.

"A lot of that is Mira," Cade said, giving the girl the proper credit for the first time. She'd risked herself, every day, as a double agent.

Doubt tugged across Rennik's face.

"She gave me a lot of help," Cade said. It was the one corner of the truth she could unfold without putting Mira in trouble. It didn't matter that Mira's spy function had been null-and-voided by the recent attack. Rennik would hold the past against her. The past was all he seemed able to hold.

"Well, at least you're not alone," he said, voice dusted with bitterness. "What happened to Lee?"

"She left too. With Ayumi. Didn't you hear? After Renna—"

Rennik's hands died in midair, and the tape met the floor.

"Don't." Rennik raked his fingernails along his arms, scratching red furrows. "Don't talk about her."

The flimsy insides of the tape gushed and covered the floor. Cade picked them up and stuffed them back into the casing before Rennik grabbed the whole thing from her and sat against the wall. Cade formed a fresh indent on the bed.

"You're not invited to sit and watch," he said.

"It's not your ship. I don't need the invitation." If Rennik wanted her out, he would have to pick her up and move her. For the space of an eye-flash, she thought he would actually do it.

Rennik went back to tape-winding. "Why do you care so much about how Unmother escaped? She's gone. That's it."

*Because I hate her.*

"Because she's important to taking them down," Cade said. "I'm sure of it." There was a weakness to Unmother, somewhere, and Cade was going to dig it out, one fingernail at a time if she had to.

Rennik held up a section of see-through black tape. "This is sliced," he said. "The tape isn't salvageable."

"So that's it?" Cade asked.

Rennik studied the tape and found a reason not to give up, or at least something to obsess over. He laid the sliced part flat on the floor. "Are there other records?" he asked. "Other parts of the ship that Green taped?"

Cade winced, evidence that she should have thought of that herself. No one had seen Unmother's escape, but she wouldn't have been able to avoid all the security footage, or stop and slice the contents of every hidden camera, one by one. There had to be a record of her somewhere on the ship.

"Green covered the main halls, the engine rooms, and the control room."

"Bring that footage, and a monitor," Rennik said.

Cade slipped out, before he could change his mind and tell her not to come back.


Green's old room burst with tapes. Everywhere — tapes.

And a few pictures of his family. He had two daughters with winter-blue eyes. Cade avoided them and kept to the towers of black. Of course, the tapes she wanted were from the night that Green had died, and she couldn't be sure someone had added them to the piles.

She started in on the most recent batch and tried not to ruin the system, whatever the system was.

"What in the name of all things good and healthy are you doing?"

Lee stood in the open door, a bag in each hand. One was small, puffed out with clothes. She set down the heavier one, and it vomited notebooks.

"Same question," Cade said.

Lee dropped to her knees and tried to contain the notebook spill. "We're moving in." Her arms circled around a herd of cardboard covers, but all she got for her effort was a paper cut on the chin. "Ayumi and I heard this room was going to be cleared out and—"

"You thought you'd move straight into a dead man's quarters?" Cade wondered how many people had occupied her own cabin back in the nonhuman wars, and how many of those had died. She had a strong urge to reach the sort of future where girls could run around the decks on family trips, poking at dead airlock buttons.

"I didn't know this was Green's room until I got here," Lee said with such grit that Cade stuffed a week's worth of tapes between her hands and got ready to make a quick exit. "This wasn't my idea. Ayumi wanted the transfer."

"Why?" Cade asked.

Cade knew Lee well enough to know she was considering a lie. She swirled it around in her mouth, swishing her lips to both sides. In the end, she dropped it and told the distasteful truth. "To be near you."

But Cade had failed with the song. "That doesn't make sense."

"Oh, I agree in the strongest possible terms," Lee said. She kicked onto the bed, avoiding all things that had belonged to Green like they had death-germs.

Cade, on the other hand, was done with tiptoeing. "So you're still mad," she said.

Lee filled the cabin with the kind of silence that made screaming seem like a nice, civilized alternative.

"Why did you come back?" Cade asked.

"I told you, Ayumi—"

"Why did *you* come back?"

Lee stacked the notebooks into new piles without looking up. "I go where she goes."

Cade brought the tapes and food for Rennik, and set it in a pile on the floor—tapes on the bottom, bread and some greenish lamp-grown vegetables on top. He didn't look up from the splice. Cade wondered how long he could go without eating, without sleep. He wasn't human, but with the way he acted these days, emotions writhing strong, it was easy to forget.

Cade left again and made a monitor-lugging trip.

"Can I help?" Zuzu asked as Cade shifted the metal box across the control room, knee to knee, trying to hug all of its corners at once.

"I've got it," Cade said.

It wasn't harder to carry than her old speakers. Cade told herself that waving Zuzu back had nothing to do with wanting a few minutes with Rennik. She must have been getting better at the business of lying.

She almost believed herself.

Cade did a quick check of the control room windows.

"If they have Unmother back, and she knows our best ship inside and out, why don't they . . ."

*Attack now? Kill us all?*

Zuzu tapped her piercings one at a time, in a predictable order. Eyebrow, nose, septum, chin. "They want to make us wonder. Make us wait."

The Unmakers were playing on human emotion, again— on fear, and all the things Unmother said made them weak.

"It's getting stale out there," Zuzu said, shaking her blond spikes. "Stale, stale, stale. No move from their side." The fleet wouldn't make a move without Cade, but her stream of spy-extracted information had dried up, and she needed new ideas. Fast.

She reconstructed the monitor in one corner of Rennik's cabin.

They looped hours of tape from twelve different locations. Halls, engine room, control room, more halls.

No Unmother, anywhere.

Rennik's fingers parted his hair in deep-scratched rows. "She should show up on these. Some of them, at least."

Rennik nudged over and made space for Cade on the floor. She sat down, as aware of that space as if it were alive.

"We'll find her," Cade said.

She didn't add the word *together,* but it was there, obvious and sitting between them.


"Cadence."

The whisper came, and then the lifting.

Rennik was carrying her.

"I think you're the one who needs some rest," he said, settling her in.

To bed. His bed.

Her hands stayed around his neck longer than they strictly needed to. He pulled the sheets up. Cade curled against his pillow — the same flat-as-snug pillow that they had in every other cabin in the fleet, but somehow it felt rounder and cooler on her skin here. Somehow it felt better.

"Cadence."

She blinked awake. Rennik stood over her, with his all-the-emotions-at-once look.

"Did you figure something out?" Cade asked. She tried to pretend it was just sleep clinging to her voice, making it hoarse.

"Yes," Rennik said. "But it's not about the tape."

Cade opened her mouth to tell him to sit down, and then they were kissing. He was pushing her backwards across the bed in waves, like an ocean that they had to cross fast, or drown.

"I'm sorry," he said, breaking for breath. "I'm sorry."

Her fingers reached out and touched his face before she could tell them otherwise. "Not for kissing me, right?"

"No," Rennik said. "Not for that."

And he kissed her again, and pressed into her, the politeness gone. He drove his pain and sadness and it found her softest places. But Cade didn't let it go at that. She gathered her own pain and pushed back. Hips, arms, her heartbeat fighting his.

He slipped in words between kisses. "I didn't feel as much. Before I met you. And then Renna . . ."

It was the first time he'd said her name since she died. Cade followed an urge to bite his lip, to taste this moment, make it linger. She wanted Rennik to be this honest with her, even when it wasn't easy. The act of bravery cried out to be repaid. Cade opened even more to his kissing, found new places to touch. Stopped trying to hide what she wanted.

Rennik slid Cade under him. It had happened fast, but any patience Cade had was gone.

His hands rose into her hips like a question.

"Yes," she said.

Cade waited in the shifting dark, and then there was a sunburst behind her eyes and all through her body.

It was light and dark, the sound of him and the music inside of her. She let it be as beautiful as it was, and she let it hurt, too. Then she opened her eyes because she had to remind herself that this was real.

This was Rennik.

"I'm sorry," he said. Only now he had tears on his cheeks, round and stubborn, fighting not to fall.

"Why?" Cade asked. She held herself still, and waited to understand.

"This isn't how I wanted it to be."

Things came together. Rennik had been afraid that what

he couldn't stop himself from feeling would bleed into what he felt for Cade. The missing-ache and the anger, and sadness like a row of closed doors.

Cade caught Rennik's tears on her skin. They ran into her mouth, and she swallowed them like water.

She moved. He moved with her.

Cade asked Renna to forgive her. This wasn't perfect.

But it was right.

# CHAPTER 24

Cade fell quiet inside.

Not a soft, easy quiet. The waiting quiet of a long drop through the dark.

She had slept through almost to morning. Rennik was gone from her side, sitting on the floor. Cade could have reached one hand off the edge of the bed and touched him.

But he was already far off, tuned to a tape and its endless, boring-blank footage. The light from the monitor hit his face and formed craters of shadow on his cheeks, his neck. He watched with the same intensity with which he'd touched Cade. He rewound the tape and watched again.

He didn't even notice that she was awake.

Now it was Cade's turn to feel everything at once. The grate of disappointment, the rough knocking of need. And sadness. For herself. For Rennik. For everyone who was gone and everyone who was left.

Cade slid off the end of the bed and out of Rennik's cabin on muted feet. As soon as she was out the door, the night spread to its proper loudness and beauty inside of her. Cade needed to keep this one good thing.

She turned a sharp corner and cut across a stairwell that led down to other levels. Clatter and breakfast-flavored steam rose from the mess. Cade's stomach made a stab in that direction, but she kept moving. There were decisions to be made about what to do with the Unmakers, as soon as she had fresh clothes on.

At the end of Cade's hall, right in front of her door, she caught sight of Ayumi, looking excited even from a distance. Who knew how early she had dragged herself out of bed. Cade got the feeling that Lee and Ayumi found ways to cram into that small rectangle — found unlikely angles for their hips, vined their arms. She felt certain that they never slept alone. So why would Ayumi get up early, leave that tangled-up warmth, to come find Cade?

Ayumi must have seen fear edge into Cade's eyes, or noticed the pickup in her step.

"It's nothing!" she said before Cade even got close. "I mean, it's not nothing. But it's not the fleet exploding or someone exploding or even glassing out. I promise." Ayumi held up a battered black notebook.

"I have some ideas about your song."

• • •

Cade ushered Ayumi into her small cabin, and kicked Mira out.

"What's this about?" Mira asked, the backs of her hands like magnets to her light-sensitive eyes.

"It's a meeting," Cade said.

"So get a *meeting room*." Mira tried to pull the covers over her head, but Cade slung them off.

She knew that Ayumi was fourteen seconds away from telling Mira she could stay—her niceness dictated it. But this song was causing enough problems, and Cade didn't need anyone else attaching to it, especially Mira.

The girl beat a path around the room, plucking semi-clean clothes from the floor as she grumbled, "Think you can come marching in here after being out all night, no shift to speak of, and act like the empress of the cabin and hey, where *were* you all night?" Mira stopped rummaging. A sock hung on her arm like a tongue peeking from an open mouth.

Cade's body sang with the memories of where she'd been. It clung to the warmth and the salt skin-taste of who she'd been with. Mira and Ayumi both stopped, watching her.

"So?" Mira asked. "What did you do last night, Empress Cade?"

Cade used Mira's own tactic against her. Lies that weren't lies at all. "Inter-fleet relations."

"What does that m—"

"Go find Matteo." Cade thumped Mira lightly on the shoulder. "I think he has something for you to do."

Mira puckered her lips at the dubious order, but she

followed it. Ayumi took Mira's place on the lower bunk, then tucked her legs under and scribbled until the moment the door clicked shut.

Cade still had trace amounts of her night with Rennik in her bloodstream, heating her, swelling her with good feeling and shyness and a hundred other things that she wasn't used to. Ayumi cocked her head, studying Cade's oddness. She increased the rate of her scribbling.

"What are you writing?" Cade tried a snatch for the notebook, knowing she would fail. There weren't many things in the universe that Ayumi was fierce about, but her notebooks were high on the list.

"Is there anything you *don't* write down?" Cade asked.

"It's an old habit, and one I don't intend to give up," Ayumi said. "We'll be old ladies someday, and I'll keep records of every cup of tea you drink. You should be glad." She presented another page, this one with words running down it in uneven blocks along the margin.

"Your song."

Ayumi tore the page out, and Cade matched the paper-sharp sound with a gasp. She'd never seen Ayumi do that.

"Don't worry," she said. "I copied it out."

She handed the page over and Cade touched the words, ran her fingers over them. Seeing them like this — small, stark, without their music — made them look like tiny parts of Cade that had been torn out.

*third in line and waiting*

*for the long slide into dark*
*ride the curve to day*
*again, following the*
*arc*

*grave fingers, pulling*
*bring all things down*
*to a blue-green point of stillness*
*and still the whole is turning*
*round*

"The words don't mean anything," Cade said, but before the sentence had ended, she was rushing to correct it. "I don't know what they mean, but I know how to find them."

"When you're looking at spacesicks, you mean?" Ayumi asked.

"Not just any spacesicks," Cade said. "I mean, you're a spacesick but you're not—"

"Glassed out?"

"Right."

Ayumi's hands danced around her forehead. Her confusion was as enthusiastic as everything else about her. "Why do you think all of this connects you to Xan? He wasn't a spacesick. He couldn't even *get* spacesick."

"I know," Cade said. She looked at the lyrics again, and they were just a tangle of useless lines.

Ayumi fitted a hand over Cade's, and it held her in place better than any command. Better than a knife pointed at her face. "We can figure this out. Then we'll be able to prove the song isn't dangerous."

"And Gori won't be able to angry-blink at us?" Cade asked.

"Exactly." Ayumi smiled, creasing her notebook up the spine.

"'Third in line and waiting . . .'" she mumbled.

They ran over and over the lyrics. They tried looking at them backwards, cutting up the lines and stringing them together in different orders. At one point, they even scrambled the letters to see if Cade's brain had buried a secret code.

"Wait," Ayumi said.

She disappeared for a minute and came back with an armful of notebooks, and behind her — Lee, and more notebooks. Lee lumped hers onto the bed, while Ayumi spread the rest around the floor.

"I thought we could use some resources."

Cade hadn't seen the notebooks laid out like this since Ayumi had tried to find them a new planet.

Ayumi caught Lee in the door and tugged her waist. "You should stay."

"Matteo asked me to help with shuttle patterns for defense."

"Oh," Ayumi said. "In that case!" She proud-glowed so hard that Cade worried she might hurt herself. "You don't get to leave without kissing me," she added.

Lee knocked an unsure glance at Cade, but as soon as Ayumi's lips made contact, the rest of the room un-mattered. They kissed like they were the only people. Not just in the room. Ever.

Cade knew that feeling from the inside now, but a sting rose at the center. She didn't know if and when she'd get to feel it again.

Lee called to Cade on the way out. "See you in the control room."

Cade grabbed a notebook and buried her face near the spine, so close that the paper smell rose and edged out the slight, constant prickle of metal. "Is it just me or did Lee sound almost, on the verge of . . . *nice?*"

"Of course she did," Ayumi said, shuffling her notebooks. "You're friends."

"Lee hates me," Cade said.

Ayumi tilted her head and flicked her eyes up, like she'd switched to mental notebook pages. "Maybe, for about twelve seconds." She threw in a *you-know-how-Lee-is* shrug. "That's not why she wanted to leave. You're the best friend she ever had, *and* the one human in the universe who can't get spacesick. Lee's pride is the size of the tallest mountain on pre-blinked Earth. She got sick, and, well. Don't tell her I told you this, but she didn't want you to see her look weak."

Cade buried herself in the notebook. But a new spark made it impossible to focus on research.

"So you think the song is about spacesick," Cade said.

"I did. I mean, I do," Ayumi said. "But . . ."

"But there's more."

Ayumi inched closer, like she wanted to leap across the room but she was afraid to scare off Cade's words.

"I think it's about a place," Cade said.

"A place?"

Cade stumbled after an explanation. "When I sing it, I feel like I'm not here. Like the words want me to be somewhere else."

"Where?" Ayumi asked. Cade shook her head. "Do you know what it looks like? Or sounds like? Even how it smells?"

All Cade had to go on was a feeling. The wonder-cast shape of it. The rightness. "It's familiar, even though I've never been there before."

There was a moment of stillness, and then Ayumi went into the wildest flurry Cade had ever seen. Eyes and fingers and pages, moving fast. Matching things up. When Ayumi looked at her, the light behind her eyes was nothing less than pure-sun brilliance.

"Cade. I think the song is about Earth."

# CHAPTER 25

Ayumi was the Earth-Keeper.

The last of her kind. She was also the self-appointed champion of finding the fleet a new home. Cade tried to fight the words that blazed into her brain, but they were already out of her mouth.

"*Of course* you want it to be about Earth."

Ayumi wasn't deterred. "'The long slide into dark,'" she said, tapping at her page. "I thought that meant spacesick. But 'third in line'?" She hopped off the bed and hunted down a notebook that looked like the rest, pulling out a sketch of a solar system. Eight planets, with a tiny ice-orb clinging to the far edge. "'Third in line' could be the third planet from a sun," she said. "One." She pointed at a little cratered circle. "Two." A red-swirled planet. "Three." A crude, continent-cramped marble. Earth.

"'Grave fingers,'" Ayumi said, working faster now. "That

sounded really dire, not at all a good thing. But when you think about a planet, and you take the word *grave*, and you add the word *pulling* . . ."

Cade slammed into an idea. "Gravity. But even if that's true," she added, "every planet has gravity."

Ayumi raced ahead. "Blue, green—"

"Earth colors," Cade said. She knew that from the painting on the wall of Ayumi's shuttle.

And somewhere else. Cade was the one sniffing out a particular notebook now, hastily flipping pages. "I remember something . . ." A description, handed down from the last generation of humans to live on Earth.

*"They left before the asteroid hit."* Cade read slowly, letting herself feel the pain in the words as she formed them. *"They told their children how blue it was, how green."* She reached the point where she had clapped the notebook shut last time. *"Rich and dark, the blue and the green brighter than it had any business being. They never saw colors like those again, except sometimes in an eye. The blue of a sky on some planet might pull memories out of them, but it never quite matched."*

Ayumi held her breath. The whole snugging universe held its breath.

*"They didn't wait,"* Cade said, *"and once the ship sped up, they didn't look back. They wanted to be gone before the world changed."*

Cade closed the notebook, held it to her chest. "Maybe it *is* about Earth."

She didn't know what that meant—a song for the spacesicks, a song about Earth, lyrics that connected her to Xan's time-traveling particles. But for the first time, Cade let herself believe that it could mean something.

Big.

"I need to go tell Rennik." It felt right to have him as the default person in her life. The one she went to when it was coming together or falling apart.

Ayumi nodded. "I'll get Lee in a minute."

When Cade left, Ayumi was scribbling as fast as she could, so hard the letters must have left echo-marks three pages deep.

As soon as Cade opened Rennik's door, she knew there would be no kissing of the wild and celebratory sort.

He stood off center in a wobbling city of tapes. Their corners stuck out from the towers at all angles, and his eyes had the paste-glaze of someone who hasn't stopped looking at a screen for hours. He looked part distracted, part glad she'd shown up, and part soured that it had taken her so long. "I have to show you something."

Cade was the one with the news. Strange, enormous news. Holding it back felt like trying to shove the entire universe down to atom-size.

She moved in, trying to ignore the new things her body had to say about being close to Rennik. "Did you figure out what happened with Unmother?"

"Yes," he said. "No. I might have."

"I don't have time for all of those answers." Cade wanted to talk about Earth, not some woman whose one great wish was to make a grand exit from the human species, leaving a trail of dead bodies on her way out. Earth put Unmother back in perspective—turned her into the small, crazed ex-human that she was.

"Please," Rennik said. It was enough of a throwback to the polite Hatchum she'd met on Andana that it softened Cade's resistance. She took a seat on the floor. But she still couldn't let go of the third planet. The gravity. The blue-green.

"Rennik," she said. "There's this song I've been singing—"

"Singing?" The word was an empty echo, to show he was listening.

Would Rennik do the same thing if she started talking to him about what had happened last night? If Cade wasn't the subject of this moment's obsession, if she wasn't the focus of all of his feelings, she was nothing.

She turned to leave. Rennik's hand closed a circle around her wrist.

"Look," he said, nodding at the monitor. "Right there."

Cade flicked her shoulder and broke his hold. She leaned into the glow of the monitor and found herself looking at the engine room. The twin engines that kept *Everlast* aloft churned quiet, constant patterns. Rennik pointed to a spot near the bottom of the screen. A bit of white flashed, then dark.

"It's a . . . blur," Cade said.

That's what he wanted to show her, instead of listening to her universe-trembling news? A blur?

"Yes, good. Now look."

Rennik extracted the tape from the monitor and searched the nearest tower for a different one.

"Where did you get these?" Cade asked, feeling small in the middle of so much recorded past—which was strange, because she never felt that way when she sat in the middle of Ayumi's notebooks. They weren't cold and plastic and official. Cade felt like part of the great human mess of them, one page in a bigger story.

"I had some tapes delivered from Green's room," Rennik said. "And I redirected the crew to bring the new ones here."

Rennik slid a tape out of a tower with needle-sure fingers. When he popped it into the monitor, the control room came on the screen. Rennik sped the timeline and people hurried by on fast-ticking legs.

". . . there."

The same blur. White, then dark, flashing at the top of the control room wall.

Cade found the blanks and filled them in before Rennik said a thing. Unmother's white pants, her black shirt. Her little trip into the vents of the Unmaker ship. "You think that's how she left without anyone seeing," Cade said. "She was in the walls."

A fraction of the tightness in Rennik's shoulders eased. "You saw it too," he said. "So I'm not insane."

"No," Cade said. Unconvincing. Unconvinced.

"There's more," Rennik said. "I found her in one of the hallways . . ."

He picked up another tape, and Cade snatched it out of its

arc toward the monitor. It had numbers printed on it in thick, squat black, clear enough to see halfway across the room.

"Unmother is on this tape?" Cade asked.

Rennik leaned over her to look at the label, and his nearness sparked her to distraction, frustration, anger that she didn't have time to start a fight, because something much worse was happening. "This isn't footage from the night Unmother escaped," Cade said. "It's from three hours ago."

Those numbers stamped fear into Cade and drove the words out of her mouth.

"She's still on the ship."

Cade and Rennik moved so fast that it felt as if the halls did the streaming by instead of their bodies. No matter how much ground they covered, every turn felt like a string tossed in the wrong direction.

They had caught Unmother in the control room. The engine room. The most important places on *Everlast*.

"She was gathering information," Cade said. Like Cade had wanted to do when she brought Unmother onboard, only reversed. No wonder the woman had looked so delighted to be stuck on their ship.

It brought Cade back to the root of the failure when she had gathered the fleet. Unmother had used that idea against her, too. She claimed whatever Cade wanted most and made it suit her own ends.

"If she has what she needs, we should be heading for the docks," Rennik said.

Cade checked the nearest vent. The passages were thin, entrances tiny. Cade's hips might slide through—barely, and only at the right angle—but her shoulders would choke the passage. Unmother must have dislocated one of hers to fit. It would be like cracking a knuckle to anyone else. All Unmother cared about was blinking out the human race. Which meant—

"You check the docks," Cade said. "I have another idea."

Rennik and Cade split up, and his footsteps faded. She made it ten steps before she remembered she didn't have her knives. Cade didn't want to be right, but if she *was* right, she didn't want to be unarmed.

She swerved, doubled back a few doors, and knocked, a loud and driving beat, until Lee came out of her new room.

"Can I borrow your gun?"

"Snug," Lee said, smearing a hand across her face. "It's sort of late."

"It's urgent."

Lee pressed a look down the hall in both directions. "Where's Ayumi?"

Cade's stomach slithered cold. "I thought she was with you."

"She was with *you*," Lee said. "And a thousand notebooks."

The ice reached Cade's face and she took off. Lee didn't ask for an explanation. She didn't even slip on shoes. Cade heard the skin-sting of bare feet behind her, and the cold-clicked readiness of the gun.

She pushed her speed and tightened her heart, and hoped she was wrong.

The hall had a just-disturbed feeling, the last trouble of the wind from someone passing. In the moment before Cade turned into her own room, she heard a special sort of nothing.

A perfect lack of breath.

Cade ripped into the room, Lee behind her.

Ayumi must have fallen asleep in Cade's bed, hard at work on her Earth scribbles. Her notebook had fallen to the floor. The blanket that curled along her side hid her face from Cade and Lee. The scene would have looked normal, except for the blood. It had saturated the blanket and was dropping, red-black, from the hems to the floor.

Lee ran and tore the blanket off. Cade waited for the pain-stark gasp that would bring Ayumi back.

Nothing.

The quiet felt like blame. Cade was supposed to be the one red and silent and slipping away from life.

She didn't hear the thud of her own knees as they hit the floor. Lee ran to the bed, sopping sheets with blood in a race to find its source. Ayumi's face and neck were covered in cuts, crossing in two directions. Unmother had tried to X out the face of this wrong girl, this not-Cade. Some of the cuts were deep red channels dug across her face, nothing clean about the edges. *Everlast* and all of its metal had given Unmother her pick of weapons. She'd put the blunt side to use, too. Ayumi's head was cratered on one side, a shallow cupping of bone.

Cade couldn't help but wonder how much worse it would have been if Unmother had gotten her hands on the girl she wanted, instead of a stand-in.

"Ayumi," Lee said, her voice stretched thin. "Ayumi . . ."

She touched the hollow of Ayumi's neck. A hand went to her face, fingers frantic-tender, searching out breath.

"She's unconscious," Lee said.

Cade was sickeningly alive with nerves.

Ayumi had been talking twenty minutes ago, about blue and green and hope. Now every bright thing about her might be gone. Cade closed her eyes, racing her mind outward to catch the last of Ayumi's song before the silence claimed her. Lee's melody ran wild and thick with pain, and in the space past it—

—nothing.

Lee folded into Ayumi's side.

"You don't get to leave without kissing me," she said. "You don't get to leave."

Cade put her face to the floor.

The cold came first. Cade straightened up and found that the circle-touch at her temple was a gun.

Lee had it pointed at her face.

Everything but dead sureness had emptied out of Lee's voice. "That woman wanted you." Cade sank. Her legs curled under her, and she folded small. "She didn't want my girl-friend," Lee said. "She came here for you."

They were both crying, and then Cade did something worse. Air rose in a wave, pushing out of her.

Lee forced the muzzle, and Cade's nerves answered with a throb. "You're *laughing*," Lee said. "Tell me why. Fast."

Cade tried to stop, but she couldn't. Laughter rose out of her, warm and wrong, like blood. "Ayumi said that you and I were friends. I believed her."

Hurt and hesitation hit Lee in a one-two punch. But she didn't stand down.

Then — a breath, wet and terrible, rose from the bed. Cade turned, afraid to take her eyes off Lee, but she clattered the gun across the floor and forgot it in the rush to bring Ayumi back. Lee wiped blood out of Ayumi's mouth with her hands, her sleeves.

"My girl . . ."

Lee cradled Ayumi's bashed-in head. "Look," Cade said, with a hand on Lee's arm. "Get medical, bring them here." Lee nodded, no questions. All of the hurt she had pointed at Cade was gone. "Don't move her. I'll go and —"

But Cade didn't reach the end of her plan before Lee's eyes melted to glass. She slumped on the bed, into a nest of darkening stains.

There was nothing Cade could do to soothe a spacesick fit now. Music meant she had to summon focus, and every bit of hers reached out past the small cabin, wrapped around the woman who had done this.

Cade checked Ayumi's chest three times to make sure that she was breathing, and ran. The long hall gave her a present in the form of Mira, far off but skipping fast in Cade's direction.

"Can I get back in?" she asked, nodding at the room, "or are you still busy not inviting me?"

Cade grabbed both of Mira's wrists. "*Don't* go in there."

Mira took in Cade's stain-patched clothes, the cloud of nerves and fear that spread around her. "What happened? Cade?" Mira rattled her hands, and a shock traveled up Cade's arms. "Hey!"

Cade deliberated. Mira was light on her feet. She could reach any spot on the ship faster than Cade. Every second of medical attention gave Ayumi a better chance, so it came down to whether or not she trusted Mira with Ayumi's life.

"Cade?" Mira asked.

"Run to the sick bay," Cade said. "Now. Get everyone. And I don't mean whoever is on duty or agrees to go with you. Get *everyone*."

There wasn't even time for Mira to agree before she spun around, and was gone.

Cade headed for the docks. Rennik would have gotten there too early, and anyone else would get there too late. She had to do this part herself.

There were two shuttles missing, besides the ones that had been signed out by fleet members. Unmother must have set the first one loose into deep space before she disappeared back into the walls.

The second one was out there, now.

Cade made it through the hold in less than a breath and dropped into the pilot's seat. Every inch of the shuttle screamed Ayumi, pressing down on Cade's guilt and pain. But she had picked the ship for a reason. It was the only one she'd ever really flown.

She punched the controls forward, and the shuttle left the side of *Everlast* with a flash of speed so fierce that if Cade hadn't been strapped in, she would have sailed through the window. She drove the shuttle harder than she had ever driven a guitar, but her flight skills were amateur at best.

The lights of another ship blinked in front of Cade, sick-yellow, dotting a line toward Unmaker territory.

Catching up wasn't an option, so Cade tried to stop Unmother with sound, attacking her like she had with that slummer on Andana. A mess of notes spilled out from her head, reminding Cade of the Noise that used to make its home in her brain.

The shuttle in front of Cade slowed, twisting a dizzy curve. Cade had Unmother in her reach — but she couldn't keep producing sound and fly the shuttle at the same time. The controls danced in her hands, and the cabin sputtered.

She had to turn around and get back to *Everlast* before Unmother figured out she had lost control. Cade clunked the ship in a half circle and hit the com. It was easy to hail one of the fleet's ships. Unmother had no choice but to listen.

"You should know you failed," Cade said with a hard bite. "You should know that I'm alive, and so is my friend."

The com erupted with the sound of Unmother breathing. Cade wanted to get her hands around that slender throat.

She stole the woman's words and offered them back to her. "We will stay alive. On gristle. And hope."

Cade closed her eyes tight, to stop herself from shaking. But her mind was open, undefended.

A thought-song slipped in.

It stripped her down to her nerves. It was dissonance and drive, straight-ahead rhythms and ugly notes.

Unmother had a song now, woven thick and tight.

Strands of hate.

# CHAPTER 26

Set against the bed in medical, Ayumi looked small and clean and quiet. Her red-soaked clothes had been cut off and she wore a plastic sheet, with plastic tubes crossed over it. The blood in the tubes, the pumping and pulsing, made it seem like Ayumi's life had been lifted out of her body and was suspended above her.

"They think she might wake up," Lee said. She sat the closest she was allowed, a slice left clear around the bed for the shuffling of a nurse. Cade dragged a chair and sat next to Lee. "They think she might wake up, but they're not sure, and even if she does, it could be . . . well, besides the blood she lost, there was the bashed-in skull. So they don't know what it will be until she wakes up.

"Sorry. If. If."

Lee snatched Cade's hand and gripped it, bone-tight. Cade

hadn't let herself feel how much she'd missed Lee until now. She still wasn't letting herself feel how much she would miss Ayumi. *If.*

Lee fired out of the chair, all angles and energy. "I have to get back to the control room." When Cade shot her a soft question of a look, Lee added, "I got better before anybody showed up." So the spacesick fit was a secret, and Lee would stay out of the bay, for now.

"I shouldn't have left you there," Cade said. She hadn't even thought to stay and guard Lee against having her secret found out. There was a whole spectrum of ways to fail people.

"Are you kidding me?" Lee asked, leaping onto her toes like she always did when she had a heroic story to retell. "You went after Unmother on your own, full out. A girl who can't fly to save her own life, smashing through the black! I would have done the same thing. You know. If I could have."

Lee pressed a soft kiss onto the paper that covered the back of Ayumi's tube-fed hand. She touched the thick screen of cuts on Ayumi's face. No matter how much she healed, she would be different. But when Cade closed her eyes, Ayumi's song was the same, slow and deep, and fully threaded with Lee's.

"You know they'll find someone to cover if you want to stay here," Cade said.

"I have to get back," Lee said. "Keep busy. Do something."

Cade got the feeling that no matter where Lee went, her song would be here.

The nurse needed space, so Cade moved to the small pocket of a waiting room. Mira was sleeping on one of the chairs in a tight ball.

"How long has she been sitting there?" Cade asked a nurse.

The man's smile was tired, but he couldn't keep it from rising, like a heavy sun. Mira had that effect on people. "She delivered the message about your friend, and then we couldn't get her to budge."

Cade sat. As soon as Mira felt someone land in her space, she rustled herself awake, so efficient that Cade felt sure it had been part of her training.

"You saved Ayumi's life," Cade said.

Mira shifted back and forth on folded legs. "Maybe."

She was using the word as a buffer to keep herself from believing, which only showed how much she wanted her own goodness to be true.

Cade put an arm around Mira's shoulder, but she shrugged away. "I don't think I should let you do that anymore," she said.

"What?" Cade asked.

"Be nice to me."

Cade looked down at her hands. "You don't think you deserve it."

"It's more than that." Mira picked at the hard plastic coating of the chair, teasing it into new shapes. "It was part of the plan. Unmother said to let you take care of me. She said you would want to."

Cade hated that Unmother had been right about her so

many times. "What made her think it would go like that?"

The plastic coating burst under the pressure of Mira's nail. She hurried to hide the little hole under her palm.

"Nobody ever took care of you."

The docks beckoned, and so did the need to book a flight to the spacesick bay. A visit to Cade's mother would mean another round of empty hope, and well-earned disappointment. But it didn't feel right to log so much time with Ayumi and pretend her mother was out of reach.

Cade figured she would be able to catch a shuttle, spend a quarter of an hour in the bay, and make it back before her next shift in the control room. As she approached the docks, an *Everlast* guard swept across in a strict line, marking the boards that hung on the wall at the side of each dock.

"All non-essential flights are canceled," he said. "*All* non-essential flights."

Cade ran up to the man, locking her legs into the stance that told him she was someone important in the fleet.

"What's this about?" Cade asked.

But he didn't have to answer; *Everlast* told her instead. The ship wavered under Cade's feet, then knocked her off them. Groans flickered, irregular and weak, like dying lights. A woman who had landed near Cade's elbow let out a flaring scream as the ship rocked again.

The guard spoke from his place clinging to the boards.

"It's starting."

• • •

The control room heaved with the weight and activity of a doubled set of crew members. Zuzu and a few others ran around in sleep clothes and unlaced boots, shaken out of their beds by the constant knuckling of fire on the hull.

"Fill me in," Cade said, sliding in at the overcrowded control panel between Lee and June.

"Nothing to fill," Lee said, focused on the blips of yellow and red outside the window. "Just a little unfriendly fire."

"No word from the Unmakers?" Cade asked. She knew how much Unmother loved to send a message.

"Nothing," June said, but she tossed all the com switches to open positions to make sure they weren't missing it.

The panel was a muddle of hands, the floor thick with unsure feet. No matter how well they thought they planned for a crisis, disorder crept in as soon as the bombs hit. Cade ran to Matteo, who circled the room with a calm stride, handing out tasks like cards from an endless stack.

"Did they cross the line?" Cade asked.

"Only a few ships. The serious power is still on their side." He leaned over the shoulder of a fleet member who had his hands on the controls of a live cannon. "Divert more fire to U4, port side."

"Their pilots know our setup now," Lee said, dogging Cade's heels. "It's Evasion 101 out there."

"I am concerned about that," Matteo said, like it was a problem he'd been studying in a dust-laden book of maneuvers from three hundred years ago. "But I believe that if we change our patterns, we can still catch them by surprise. The real issue is what happens when it comes to a boarding."

"We used to have the upper hand," Lee said. "Until that woman slithered through the whole ship and . . ." Lee went so tense that Cade worried she would snap—the sort of break that there was no coming back from.

Zuzu cracked the tension by fluttering a stack of paper over her head. "New defensive protocols for everyone!"

Lee grabbed one and tossed herself into an open chair, pushing her worries into the buttons and dials. Cade followed her lead. She went back to work, her body on an auto-course, until Mira tapped her arm. The strange jitter of her fingertips told Cade an important truth, without Mira having to say it.

She had intel.

Cade pulled her aside. "What is it?"

Mira adjusted Cade to her level and channeled words into her ear. Fast, erratic, uninflected.

"Are you sure?" Cade asked.

Mira dropped into a flat, careful listening mode. "They're repeating it now, to make sure I got the whole thing."

Cade nudged Mira to the central point of command, and told her to repeat what she'd heard to the entire control room.

"The Unmakers are on the attack," Mira said three times, shedding a little bit of shyness with each bump in volume. "Hey!" Heads snapped, attention sharpened. "They're on the attack, but they're going to regroup soon. They'll leave a thin line of defense and collect most of the ships in one place to lure us in. They know we went for the same sort of thing last time. Now they're using it as bait. The whole thing's a trap."

Matteo paused in his rounds. He looked from Mira to Cade, then back again, stubbing his fingers through his gray-touched hair. "What's the source of this information?"

Cade hunted for a lie, but before she found a half-decent one, Mira hitched herself tall and spoke.

"I was a spy." The room went numb, the only sounds the click of controls and the patter of fire. "I worked for their side. Then I was a spy for us." Faces melted with confusion before setting in new molds — shock, disgust, disbelief, a few acute cases of pity. Cade knew that Mira would hate the pity most.

The girl was like a shuttle on her first trip. She had launched into her speech fiery and brave, and now she jerked through the rest, ready to land and be done with it. "Mira isn't my name, or it wasn't, but you can keep using it, I don't mind. I thought about getting something new. Like Emily. That's a good name, I think." She tamped her nervous energy into her hands. "But if I got rid of the old name, it would be like pretending the rest of it never happened, like trying to throw it away." Mira stared at the point where her fingertips met. The biochip twitches had faded. "I can't do that."

June approached the girl like she was a loaded gun, safety off. "You were a —"

"Spy."

Cade slung an arm around Mira. "Anyone who wants to deal with that has to deal with me."

The crew members looked at one another, trading discomfort. Lee strode up to Mira, arms tight across her chest. Mira took a breath and waited.

"You gave us intel last time, too," Lee said. "You're how we caught that woman."

Catching that woman had led to Ayumi, torn and silent. Catching that woman was the first step in Lee almost losing her — living with that possibility like needles embedded in her skin.

Cade waited for Lee to deck Mira. Her being a little girl would only protect her for so long.

Maybe it had never protected her at all.

Lee untucked a hand, and as Cade moved to snatch it out of its flight path, pin Lee to the ground, and take her out in less than three moves, it became clear that all Lee wanted to do was shake.

"That was something," Lee said. "Really something. Only the bravest go up against that woman."

Mira looked like she was about to go nova with happiness. She tossed herself at Lee's neck, braids flinging. Lee shifted to detach the girl, but Cade caught the moment when she softened a notch and returned the good press of Mira's hug.

A few people cheered, and Zuzu raised her paper-heavy fist high in the air. June snuck up and patted Mira on the shoulder. During Matteo's next round of duties, he stopped at her side. "We'll have to come up with a special commendation," he said. "For courage when no one can watch or thank you for it, and you have every reason to fear your friends will hold it against you."

Mira scrunched the rest of her face up around her nose. "Sounds like a lot to squish on a medal."

Matteo spared a laugh before he moved on, shouting instructions at four different crew members. "Peel topside, hard! Don't spare the ammunition! Give them a reason to think twice before they make another pass."

Cade thought she and Mira were out of the dark, and all they had to worry about now was death by Unmaker. But Rennik had been there the whole time, silent against the wall, clinging to his first and strongest reaction.

Mira ran from Cade's side and threw herself in with the cannon squad. She was everywhere, wanting to help. Rennik filled in the place she had left. The vibration of his sour feelings sat on Cade's skin.

"How long?" he asked.

Cade pretended that she was needed at the map table. She leaned low, hoping that it would toss Rennik off, but he wasn't going to give up, no matter how busy she made herself look.

"How long?"

She inched a tight shrug.

Rennik leaned down and braced his forearms against the map table, his nearness a new sort of torture. Cade wanted to be closer, fitted and moving against him. She wanted Rennik balanced and she wanted him back. But all of that got in the way of his battle, so it had to be kicked aside.

"*How long have you known?*"

"Since Renna. Right after. Well . . . during." Cade wasn't

going to apologize. She had saved Mira's life for more than one good reason. She wondered if that would still count for something when they all died in a few hours.

The anger in Rennik's face pooled to bitterness. He swallowed and turned hard, and Cade watched his back all the way out the door. She kept losing him, so it shouldn't have felt like a knife to the throat every snugging time.

"Oh!" Mira said, running a wild curve back to the center of the room. "There's something else you should know."

The crew listened to her now, not like a little girl, but one of their own.

"What is it?" Matteo asked.

"The Unmakers think I've been turned against them, or at least turned soft," Mira said. "Unmother must *want* me to pass along her plan."

Zuzu hopped onto the edge of the map table and sat cross-legged. "Do you think it's misinformation?"

Mira looked worry-sick. "I think they'll set it up like they said."

"Then why tell us?" Matteo asked.

Cade stepped in with the answer. "Unmother gets some nasty pleasure out of us knowing that we have no good options."

Mira pointed to the hull. "They're trying to get us soft now. This isn't the real strike. They have our specs, so when they make a full pass there will be better targeting on the missiles, and no question they'll try to board."

Matteo patted the wall, and it raised a memory of Renna.

Cade almost expected the hull to rumble back.

"Well," Matteo said. "Let's hope she's called *Everlast* for a reason."

The meeting took nine minutes.

Cade knew that the crew would vote to grab the offensive while they could, and cross the line with everything they had. There would be no polite folding of hands and waiting for death. Cade agreed that an attack was better than the alternative, but she still couldn't muster any enthusiasm for the decision.

June drew up new rotations and ordered Cade to take a nap. An hour later, she came back with unpinned braids and her sternest face to try again. Four hours deep, Cade finally quit the control room, weaving down the halls on heavy feet.

In her cabin, the bed was still rumpled. Unmade. Cade touched the bottom sheet, the only one that hadn't been stripped, and wondered which wrinkles had been formed by Ayumi's thrashing. It was such a dark wondering that she had to replace it. She settled on the memory of Ayumi in the same spot, eyes kindled, as she talked about Earth.

Cade rested her head on the floor and fell into a dark pool of sleep. She had no idea how long she'd been there when she woke up, alive with prickles and ache, and noticed the notebook under the bed.

It must have been kicked there when someone cleaned up. There was no question in Cade's flickering mess of a brain—

this was the same one Ayumi had been writing in for months, even in the pre-fleet days. Cade pulled it from its resting place and opened it with care.

What she found was like a map, delineating the twists and turns of Ayumi's heart. She had written long, winding sentences about falling in love with Lee. There were illustrations, too, pencil sketches of Lee in a take-charge stance and heavy boots, Lee napping against the low curve of a wall in Renna's common room. Lee at night, her eyes sparking and her hair out of its knots.

Ayumi had peppered the pages with Earth poems, descriptions, bits of history and made-up tales that connected to her own thoughts. And then, in the thick of Ayumi's words, Cade found her own.

She read them over, following with a finger as she went. The imprint of other lines on the back of the sheet pulled her to turn the page. Written there, in Ayumi's rushed slant, were the words:

*"Do I dare*
*Disturb the universe?*
*In a minute there is time*
*For decisions and revisions which a minute will reverse."*
—Unknown Earth poet, early 20th century

Disturb the universe. That's what Gori said Cade was doing when she sang. Ayumi must have agreed, or at least worried about it, otherwise she wouldn't have connected the song with this poem.

But Ayumi had *wanted* Cade to sing it. She'd been the song's biggest fan. Its only fan.

Cade tucked the notebook under her arm and took it with her on a long walk to medical. She sat in the ring of atmosphere around Ayumi's bed. A single light burned on Ayumi's broad cheeks, her newly washed curls. Her cuts had been sewn, and her head bandaged, but no one had fixed the real problem. Ayumi wasn't Ayumi if she couldn't turn up at the perfect moment with a moving pen and a half-formed plan.

"What do we do now?" Cade asked.

She read the poem three more times.

Maybe disturbing the universe wasn't the worst thing Cade could do. Maybe it was what she *had* to do. The more she thought about it, there was no way to live without disturbing things on some scale. Stirring up particles, connecting to people. Things changed shape wherever they touched. Melodies sprang up in the cracks.

*In a minute there is time*

Cade ran her fingers over the words, until the ink transferred, picking out the small ridges on her skin. She was disturbing the universe *right now.* But it was one thing to do it by existing, and it was another thing to dare.

Cade got the feeling that there was more to the poem. More to the song that sat waiting on the flip side of the page.

• • •

316

"We're playing this all wrong."

The crew looked up from the somber pushing of controls. Cade swept through the room like a fresh wind.

"We're doing what Unmother wants," Cade said. "Again. I did it when I took in Mira, and when I gathered the human race. We all did it when we threw ourselves into this fight. This is what *they* want. The Unmakers don't care if they die as long as we're gone at the end of it and a few of them can make it to a future that they like the looks of." Cade turned to Mira for backup. "Did I get that right?"

In a few hours, the girl had gone from the fleet mascot to the trusted and official source on all things Unmaker.

"Yeah," Mira said. "That's it all right."

"Unmother wants us to go after her, again and again," Cade said. "If we act like that's the only course, they win."

"So what do you want us to do instead?" Lee asked. The words floated in an answerless void.

"Ayumi had an idea." Cade held up the notebook like it was an artifact of a better world. "She was working on it when . . ." Cade stopped before she piled more hurt on Lee. There was still hope for Ayumi. For all of them.

"There's a song I need to play," Cade said.

She thought she was ready for the blank stares, but they hit her like a wall of feedback. *Everlast*'s crew didn't know Cade as a musician. Maybe they'd heard the fistful of rumors that she'd been famous once, for turning the volume up too high, kicking people's teeth in with sound. But that part of the long-ago.

Matteo shook his head. "A song?"

Cade produced a guitar pick from her back pocket, twirled it between her fingers, and a bit of the old brass came back.

"You're going to put on a show?" Lee asked. "Now?" Despite her forehead dent and matching frown, Cade caught excitement in the tug of her lips. Mira looked like she was two seconds away from hopping up and down.

"This is a new kind of show," Cade said. "One the universe has never seen."

She stared out at the sleek Unmaker ships, the mismatched human fleet, and the false calm between them.

Once the fleet had gathered, the next step shouldn't have been a battle with the Unmakers, winner-limp-away-broken. The fight had seemed like their only choice, but they should have thrown their resources at finding the human race a home. A real home. Planet-side and permanent.

"The stage matters," Cade said. "We have to get there as fast as we can."

"So we just turn around and leave?" June asked. "Let the Unmakers win? Abandon the fleet?"

"No," Cade said. "The fleet's welcome to join us."

"Where are we going?" Lee asked.

"Earth."

# CHAPTER 27

Matteo looked at Cade like she was twice as crazy as she felt.

"It's a dead planet," he said. "In a dead system."

But it wasn't dead, not inside of Cade. Earth had been growing, one particle at a time, gathering mass and swirling into blue-green life ever since she started reading Ayumi's notebooks. The control room of *Everlast* was crammed with people who didn't understand that.

"So to recap," Zuzu said as she fired another round at an Unmaker ship that wouldn't stop pestering them, too close to the engine room. "You want to take us to a blinked-out fairy-tale planet because a song told you to?"

Cade stared down the crew's confusion. When she looked for Rennik to stand with her, she found that he hadn't returned to the control room. One more thing to worry about, as soon as she could get away. For now, she had to stay focused on Earth. She didn't offer more explanation, or smatter the room with apologies. She stood back, crossed her arms, and said, "That's all I can tell you for now."

Matteo stepped in again. "We can't alter the plan—"

"I'm not asking you to. Everyone has to make their own choice. I can't tell you the risks are worth it."

Cade's short-lived stint as a savior ended here. She was a musician, and she had gotten away from everything that mattered. On the edge of the black hole she had promised Xan —promised *herself*—that she would do more than survive.

Cade pointed at the fleet members working the inter-ship com. "The one thing I do need is answers. Who wants to come with me, and who stays behind?"

"You're not just asking us to get to Earth," Lee said. "You're asking us to get there or die trying. Earth is twenty systems away. No one bothers to sail out in that direction anymore. It's a wasteland."

"Maybe," Cade said. "But it's ours."

The votes came in so fast they clogged the com. They had to be sorted and marked down, so naturally, June took charge.

Cade was surprised that anyone said yes.

"They like you," Mira said.

"Or maybe they're tired of fighting," June said. "And waiting to go spacesick, and then fighting some more."

"Maybe it's just the word," Zuzu said, rolling it around in her mouth like a blue-green marble. "Earth. Earth. Earth."

Cade focused on the votes, tick marks consuming the paper down to a thin margin of white. More *no* than *yes*, but Cade still had hundreds of people to bring with her. They trusted her, or they wanted something more than fleet-life. Either way, the burden of proof was on Cade. It winched her chest tight and made anything other than a shallow breath feel like a dream.

She did a quick check of both lists. Rennik's name still didn't grace either side, so Cade forged it. Maybe she couldn't bring him out of his broken state, but she was never going to leave him behind.

Cade spun a half circle and found Gori shuffling in the door. He never shuffled anywhere these days, so it had to be important.

"Are you coming with us?" Cade asked.

His weariness was in full effect. "I feel that I must."

Cade didn't love the idea of Gori standing over her, a chaperone sent by the disapproving universe, old as stardust, shaking his head at every note she sang. But she couldn't tell him to stay behind when everyone he knew was leaving.

Matteo crossed to Cade, looking even more solemn than Gori.

"You have to take *Everlast*," he said. "With those numbers, you'll need it."

"But—"

Matteo held up a *no-need-to-argue* palm. It was puffed and hatched, a reminder that Matteo had lived the longest life of anyone Cade still knew. But he wasn't old, not properly ancient, not even close.

"We're coming with you," Matteo said. "You'll need us,

too." Cade knew he was right. She also knew, from the stunted cough at the end of his sentence, that he was getting emotional.

"I'm going to stay," June said, capping her enormous decision with a tiny nod. "Someone has to watch things on this end." June knew how to work the operation like a machine —an imperfect, human-run machine, but still. She had turned from a chore enthusiast into someone who could head a fleet.

"I'll berth with the Rembran ships," she said. "They have a good handle on things. We'll set up a new command center and keep in touch, as long as we can." June drained fast, before she could change her mind.

"We have another issue," Zuzu said. "There are names missing from that tally."

Cade fast-flicked the pages. "What names?"

"Spacesicks," Zuzu said. The ones that were too far gone to make the choice.

"I can speak for my mother," Cade said. "She's coming with me." She wished that she'd been able to get to the bay, to sit with her mother one more time before this new trouble knocked the fleet down. There were other spacesicks, too many others. Cade couldn't leave them to fight their own quiet battles.

Lee waved an arm and stole all the attention in the room. It curled around her in the easy way that Cade had never mastered.

"I can speak for the rest," Lee said. When Cade's eyebrows

dug in, deep and questioning, Lee whispered, "Ayumi told me what you did for me that one time, with the singing. You didn't think I would wake up on the wrong ship and let it go without a little investigating, did you?"

Lee marched up to Matteo. "Whatever crazy thing Cade is doing woke up the worst spacesicks in the fleet. I happen to think that sounds better than sitting in the bay in a state of pre-rot."

"Vote?" Zuzu asked.

Hands scatter-shot the air. An overwhelming vote to send the worst of the spacesicks with Cade.

Things moved double time after that, driven by the need to get everyone in place before the fleet cracked in half. *Everlast* lost some crew members, and replaced them with new ones. The wide windows of the control room had the sort of view that couldn't be turned away from, so everyone was forced to watch when a blue-white ball of fire connected with a small transport ship. No one could escape the moment when it blew apart, to a fine grit of metal and glass.

Cade kept moving, kept working, pausing long enough to say, "Universe keep them."

Matteo shook his head at the glittering-dark spread of wreckage. "Universe keep *us* all."

June came back and threw herself into a round of fierce hugs before she departed for the last shuttle. After years of service on *Everlast,* she carried away what she could fit in a canvas sack.

"If this works, I'll get word back to you," Cade said.

June sprang at Cade and held her tight, Cade's face buried in braids, and then she was gone.

Lee and Mira took over June's workstation, collaborating on diagrams for defensive strategies. Lee had a lifetime of keeping ships safe from nonhumans, and Mira's working knowledge of the other side could finally be put to use. Lee set her chin to her fists and listened as Mira outlined a life of spacesicks thrown out of airlocks, feelings beaten out of children. Matteo and Zuzu took charge of making sure no one else took the kind of hit that the transport ship had. Gori tried to rapture in the corner, but every time he puffed a few inches, Cade elbowed him out of it.

Rennik was still missing.

Cade wanted him at her side—but she couldn't drop her plans and half of the remaining human race to go find him. Besides, she needed his trust, and that might take some time after their last conversation. Cade fought to stay where she was.

"All right," she said. "Let's burn black."

*Everlast* peeled away from the rest of the fleet, and a set of three Unmaker ships followed.

"Perfect," Cade said.

She checked to make sure Unmother was with them. The new song was there, even louder in contrast to the rough silence of the non-songs around it. Unmother had lost her footing. She'd walked a tight path of not-caring, but now she was driven by hate for Cade, throbbing with a single human emotion.

"We're not *inviting* them on this little expedition, are we?" Lee asked as the Unmakers scudded close.

"Hail those ships," Cade said. "Tell them we're headed for Earth."

"Why?" Zuzu asked.

The crew waited for Cade to offer a sound, strategic reason, and that's exactly what she did.

"It's going to make her furious."

# CHAPTER 28

Unmaker ships stayed tight on *Everlast,* and so did their fire.

"Keep them out of range," Cade said. When Zuzu tossed up her hands, Cade added, "As much as you can."

The map table became the new focus of the room as Cade tried to chart the best road to Earth. It wasn't one wide, straight black highway through space, but a badly drawn, complicated web.

Cade lifted a huge sheet of paper by a corner. "Someone thought this was useful?" she asked. "As a map?"

"It was made as part of a mining operation near Earth," Matteo said, "but their interests differed from ours. It was focused on confirming the locations of natural resources, and Earth had none to speak of."

"Also, this was four or five hundred years ago," Zuzu added.

"We might be able to use the information from Ayumi's notebooks to pin down the location," Lee said.

"Good idea," Cade said. "Get on it." She trusted Ayumi more than some four-hundred-year-old miner.

Zuzu hit the panels. "Our friends are on the move."

Cade checked the windows and the scans. The Unmaker ships had pulled wide and shot ahead.

"Good," Cade said. "If they're obsessed with getting there first, they're not firing at us."

Zuzu almost pulled the heavy ball in her eyebrow straight out of her face. "The Unmaker ships have dregs for defense, but they're lighter and, therefore, fast." She penciled a few calculations, but Cade knew the outcome.

"She's going to beat us to Earth."

"This isn't about who wins the race," Cade said. "It's about what happens when we get there."

Hours settled into a regular pace, instead of the expand-and-pinch that came with battle. The choreography of the control room tightened. Cade had almost convinced herself they were flying a simple run with no real danger clouding it, until Mira collapsed on the panels.

Water flew everywhere.

"She hit the emergency sprinklers," Lee said, diving across the table to cover the charts.

Lukewarm bullets hit Cade as she ran. Mira had knocked her forehead to a bright cherry, but she wasn't bleeding. Her hands looked wretched, though, knotted tight, fingers bloated and red.

"Crashing," Mira said. She held up one hand and her fingertips danced a sick, fast series of twitches.

"The biochip?" Cade's fingers went to the back of Mira's neck.

Mira leaked a whimper-scream. Her back arched without her permission, hands scrabbling at her own scalp. Every time Cade unstuck one hand, Mira's nails set a new course back to her face, until she was patched with raw skin and sticking blood. It was bad enough to watch from the outside, but Cade ached for whatever Mira was feeling. She wondered if the Unmakers could kill a person this way.

Mira rocked against Cade as she lifted the girl.

"Dry off and keep flying," Cade said.

Mira's hands shuddered against the back of her neck. Cade smoothed the girl's hair, clasped her tighter.

The walk to medical had never seemed so long before.

Cade bribed a nurse for the last painkillers in the drawer. She pulled a thin curtain and sat Mira down on a white bed with a paper rustle. Mira's whimpers had grown longer, more drawn out. Cade took out her knife and swabbed it with alcohol.

She tried to talk to Mira through it. Talk herself through it.

"This is going to hurt," Cade said, "but probably not as much as having the Unmakers dance on your nervous system all the time."

Cade dug into her. Mira kept her head still and her hands tight. She didn't complain.

"What is Unmother sending you?" Cade asked.

Mira winced up at Cade. "She really, really, really doesn't like you."

Cade drew a clean angle around one corner of the chip. "I've known that since the night Unmother came after me. She hates me so much that she put her own plan in danger. It's enough to make a girl feel special."

"We don't believe in special," Mira said, her breath coming in great, broken chunks. "I mean *they*. They don't."

Cade teased the chip out and held it up. It was dark, and set in rigid patterns.

Mira unloaded a sigh and straightened her neck. Her pinched fingers reached for the controller. Cade handed it over, glad to be rid of the thing. "I can't do much about the one in your brain, but—"

"This is enough," Mira said. "If they try to send new intel, it won't have anywhere to go." She fastened herself to Cade. "Thank you thank you thank you." Her words sank into Cade's shirt. When she looked up, her eyes were bright with warning. "I don't want you to fight Unmother. She's too dangerous."

The bed paper crinkled under Cade's legs as she sat down. "I have something to go on this time." She tried to explain it in her mind first, so she could get it across to Mira. When she had it worked out, she said, "If Unmother thinks emotion can only make a person weak, then it will always make her weak."

"You think it makes you strong?" Mira asked.

"Maybe it can be both things, the way a planet has two faces. One in shadow, one in sun."

Mira went stubborn-quiet. She pulled Cade down by the elbow and said, "I worry about love."

Cade raised her eyebrows, and went looking for something to patch up Mira's neck.

"It seems like the bad link in the whole business," Mira said, kicking her legs, restless already. "Doesn't love always go wrong?"

Cade still couldn't lie, even when it would make things easier.

"I don't know."

She let the thoughts of Rennik come—the softness of his eyes, and how they took so long to shade into a new feeling. The way his hands were always working, and his face offset the motion with calm.

Cade stuck a slab of thick white cotton against Mira's neck and held it in place with a snippet of white tape. "There'll be a scar."

Mira jumped off the bed and cracked the biochip under her heel. "Worth it."


Cade didn't have long to plan for the most important show of her life. She had most of the lyrics and an idea of the melody.

There were two more things she needed.

Cade headed back to her cabin and cut straight for the closet. There wasn't much in there: a set of clothes so worn and patched and worn again that Cade had tossed them aside, a few pouches of vanilla-flavored protein that she'd pocketed in the mess, and in the farthest corner, half-buried under an old bandage, the glow of a white guitar.

The second part involved Rennik. She checked his room, the control room, the mess. Panic trailed the thought that he might have ducked onto a shuttle before the fleet split, but when she checked the manifests, she didn't find his name. The docks stood quiet now, the shuttles either gone for good or put to bed.

Cade had an idea, and she didn't overthink it. She let her feet turn the steps and her fingers travel the buttons.

The dock to Ayumi's shuttle swirled open.

Rennik sat on the floor against the mild curve of the hold, his long fingers capping his knees. He didn't notice Cade at first, and she wondered if he was stuck in a memory. This shuttle had been locked onto Renna up until the day she died. Maybe Rennik could trick himself into thinking that the next time the door opened, she would be on the other side, gleaming and impatient.

Cade wanted to let him believe it, but she worried that the longer this went on, the more it would hurt when it ended.

She planted her knees in front of Rennik's face. "I need to tune this," she said. "I think you know how."

Rennik stared at the guitar with a variation on his all-the-emotions look. Love and pain and a scattering of nerves.

He touched the high E and grimaced as the guitar released a pitifully thin sound. He brushed the other strings with a thumb, but had to still them when he heard the notes, loose and rotten.

"It's part of her," Cade said. "And so are you. So, I thought maybe . . ."

Rennik turned his whole body to the task. Cade held the base of the guitar as he sank his attention into the tuning pegs. But Rennik melted from hard work into soft remembering, his gaze far off, and Cade thought he had stranded her alone in the present. She stood up and palm-dusted her knees.

"Give me a minute," he said, without taking his eyes off the smooth white. "It's been a long time."

"Right," Cade said. "Sorry."

Rennik put his ear to the hollow. "What do you need the guitar for?"

"Long explanation, lots of verses, complicated chorus," Cade said. "Please trust me."

Rennik's cheeks pinched. "The last time I did that . . ."

Cade's back went stiff against the wall. "Do you think you could stop bringing up the attack?"

It was the wrong thing to say, but she didn't have reserves of tact anymore. There was too much to worry about, and stepping around Rennik's feelings had lost its place in line.

He stood fast, Moon-White banging against his legs. "That would be nice, wouldn't it." His pacing filled the hold. "That would be a good way to live, never having to think about it. But Cade, all I can *do* is think about it." He sat down, funneling his energy into the guitar. "I know all of this is not your doing. I *know* that I'm wrong. And I can't stop." He gripped

Moon-White too hard. "You think I want that to be the case?"

Cade tried to fill Rennik's old role and be the reasonable one. But Cade was still Cade. She had things to say and no better time to say them. "I think you live by some code," she said. "Whoever meant the most to you and died, that's your lodestar. You did it for Moira, you're doing it for Renna." She dropped her voice to a mutter. "You'll do it for me, as soon as I'm dead."

Rennik looked up at her, his hands still working. "That's not true. I mean . . ." he said. "It doesn't have to be that way."

Cade knelt in front of him. "So prove it."

"We — already —"

Heat slid through Cade at the thought of what they had *already* done. But one night was a single star, one fleck of brightness against a blotted-out sky. "You have to *keep* proving it."

Rennik went back to fiddling with the tuning pegs. He didn't make a big production of it. A little this way, a little that. He had never looked so frustrated. Cade couldn't tell how much was the guitar and how much was her. When he raised Moon-White between them, Cade thought he was giving it back, but he swiped the strings, and surprised her with something better. G major.

A warm, perfect chord. It struck her like sunshine.

"What do you think?" Rennik asked.

He looked natural with the guitar on his lap, almost relaxed. "I think you should keep Moon-White after the show."

He shook his head. "Renna made it for you."

"But only because you asked her to." It was a truth Cade

had always guessed at but neither of them had ever spoken.

"You miss Renna," Cade said, "and you have every right to. She's gone." Cade touched the guitar, because she didn't know what would happen if she touched him. "I miss you and you're right here."

She set her hand along the line of his cheek.

Rennik put Moon-White aside.

He kissed Cade like he was learning her all over again. Like she was an instrument he'd given up a long time ago and was coming back to, with a needing-ache in his hands and the fear he'd get it wrong. But he touched her as if he had the time —the days, the years—to get it right. And that was enough to put the shine back. That was enough to pull it out of Cade, trembling at the surface of her skin.

Cade woke up in a little bunk, her hips at unlikely angles, her arms vined around Rennik's.

She nudged closer to him and fell into a soft sleep.

The days pushed on, full of charts and look-alike tracts of darkness.

Cade spent most of her time reading Ayumi's notebooks. Before, they had been searching for evidence of a new planet, one that would be everything the human race needed. They had chased the possibility, page after page. But what they'd needed was right there.

This time, Cade read for Earth.

She wanted the details, the stories, the memory-shreds.

They flooded and filled cracks inside of Cade that she hadn't known were there.

Nights she spent with Rennik, talking and making the sorts of plans that people make when they have a future. Neither of them brought up the too-possible ending, the short version where one or both of them died in a few days. But it was always there, like a note pitched too low to hear, the vibrations sneaking in.

Early mornings, Cade walked the sludge-gray halls, less than half-awake, and visited her mother in the new spacesick bay. The room had been designed for all-crew meetings and religious services, back in the days when people could find things to pray about. No one had a bed, but the spacesicks didn't seem to care.

Cade held her mother's hands.

Since the fleet had gathered, it had gotten easier to put her mother aside. But one broken-through moment had changed things. Cade would always have her mother like that now, real and striving. And she would have that word.

*Cadence.*

Her mother's voice had reinvented it.

The presence of Cade's mother and her glass had its normal effect on the song, stirring it up, but Cade didn't let it out. She kept the notes down when they wanted to rise. This wasn't the normal case of practice and warm-ups. If the song really was about Earth, Cade needed to finish it in the right place.

There were words that a person always had inside of her, and words she had to travel a long way to find.

Cade learned what she could by studying the song in her mind, turning it around, learning the melodic phrase and testing variations. She didn't even hum out loud, but she swore that spacesicks leaned in, bent around the burning of a secret sun.

Cade pulled aside a passing nurse. "Did any of the spacesicks who had the choice stay behind?"

"Not one."

The spacesicks knew the real fight. They'd known it all along.

And then the black outside the windows showed new signs.

A tiny ice-orb. Gas planets, one banded by rings. *Everlast* dodged and ducked its way across a thick asteroid belt.

Cade didn't leave the control room anymore. She leaned against the panels, eyes tacked to the space-black. When she ripped them away, she found that Rennik had claimed the chair on one side of her and Lee had claimed the other. Mira stood behind them, watching over Cade's shoulder.

Close, now.

And then there were no planets left. Cade had counted inward from the edge of the system, and the next one that rose out of the black should be—

Earth.

As white and gray as a dead skin-flake.

As gone as a spacesick's eye.

"Did we . . . make it?" Mira asked.

"Yes," Lee said. "You might want to work on sounding less anticlimactic."

Mira tried again. "We made it!"

So had the Unmakers. Any dreams that the enemy ships had fallen back or slammed into an asteroid were forgotten. The crew faced the truth — three ships hanging between *Everlast* and Earth's atmosphere.

That should have added up inside Cade and crashed her hopes. But she smiled, and the delight wasn't an act. Cade had never felt such a swelling rightness. This was the longed-for moment, the needed place.

Her fingertips itched for strings.

# CHAPTER 29

The new spacesick bay made a fine stage.

High windows curved at both ends, like cupped palms that rose, touching fingertips at the highest point. The window across from Cade showed where they'd been — the stretches of black, dotted with planets, iced with pale moons. The window behind Cade showed Earth. Not the Earth of Cade's song, or the Earth of Ayumi's notebooks.

But still.

"It's perfect," Cade said as she slung Moon-White across her chest.

"Are we looking at the same planet?" Lee asked.

She and Rennik shifted microphones into place, stacking the equipment that would broadcast Cade's music through the ship. Cade had tried to explain to Zuzu that she wouldn't strictly need the help, that when she played the song it would go straight into the head of any human onboard. But Zuzu insisted.

To be fair, Cade didn't fight her too hard. It would be brass to batter *Everlast* with all of that sound.

The bay reflooded with people as Cade tuned up. Whatever Rennik had done to Moon-White had worked, and the sound rushed out pure and clean. Cade remembered all of the time Rennik had spent with Renna. The careful calibrations. How much he adored her, talked to her.

Cade hung her head low over the guitar's neck and whispered, "You can do this."

Zuzu flicked a panel of switches from the side of the stage. "What do you think?"

The only option for stage light was the buzzing white overheads, but Cade couldn't have everything. This was a war-battered spaceship, not a club, and she had the one thing that mattered most: a first-class crowd.

Rennik stood in the front row, with Lee beside him. Against all odds, Gori snuck in and stationed himself against the back wall. Cade's mother was seated at the center of the room with the rest of the spacesicks.

Mira hung at the edge of the stage until Zuzu waved her over and showed her how to push at the balance and fade controls on the sound board. She nudged them with excited fingers. Cade made a silent promise to scour the girl's eardrums, call an awkward shuffle out of her feet, and make her fall in love. Not with a person, but with a song. Cade knew from experience — it was a good place to start.

The crowd did its sigh-and-settle.

Cade thought about tacking on some words in front of

her playing, some kind of fumble-sore message of hope. But for the first time in too long, she could let the music be her voice.

She hit the strings, and they spoke.

In stutters first, in long-winded sentences that started with fine intentions and faded to garble. Cade begged the guitar with her strumming, told it tenderly with each kiss of her fingers on the strings.

*You can do this.*

Cade pinched harmonics, letting the overtones find one another and huddle close. She pulled out every trick she knew, but the listeners furrowed their brows and didn't follow. Cade was trying too hard to win them. This wasn't about winning. It was about going somewhere, and taking all of these people with her.

She was knocked from the path by a disturbance near the back of the room. The crowd spread like it was taking a breath. Heads shuffled and reordered themselves, until the cause of the commotion broke through the front row.

Ayumi's face was a thicket of half-healed cuts. She looked unsure about each step, as if she were walking through deep woods. She followed the music out of the crowd, into the open space that no one ever breached during a show. Cade switched to simple chord progressions, because her brain couldn't handle anything else. Ayumi stopped right in front of Cade, her face vague, and then she smiled.

"It's funny," she said. "I was trying to sleep, and then I

heard something, sort of like the rattle of a bug in my ear."

"I'm just getting warmed up," Cade said.

Lee elbowed her way out of the crowd, but it wasn't until her arms went around Ayumi's waist and her feet left the ground that they both started laughing and crying at the same time.

"So what do you think?" Lee asked as she finally set Ayumi down.

"About what?" Ayumi asked.

Lee spread her arms to take in the room, the crowd, the planet like a white ball that could fit in her palm.

Ayumi squinted, then squinted harder until it looked like it hurt. She lowered her voice so that only Lee and Cade could hear. "I followed the sound to get here."

That quickly, the set of Ayumi's face made sense. Her eyes had lost their focus. *Head trauma,* Cade remembered from her time in medical. It could cause all kinds of damage, including blindness. Cade was worried she might have to break the news to Lee, but then she remembered how well Lee and Ayumi understood each other.

Lee was nodding, and crying, and staring at Ayumi like she couldn't be more perfect. "Earth," Lee said, gathering Ayumi's face in her hands. "We made it to Earth."

The static of doubt filled Ayumi's expression. "This is the absolute wrong time to play a trick on me."

"It's not exactly a *welcoming* planet," Lee said. "But it's one hundred percent real and very much—"

Ayumi cut her off by laughing. She leaned in and pressed a hand over Lee's heart, eclipsing every hard truth with a kiss. Lee didn't look eager to stop kissing, ever, but eventually she put an arm around Ayumi's back and led her off the stage so Cade could get on with the show.

Her head was filled with Ayumi's and Lee's tight-woven songs, so loud that she didn't even have to close her eyes to hear them. It should have thrown Cade off, but instead she decided to use it. She borrowed notes from Lee and Ayumi, then from Rennik, Mira, Cade's mother, and the remembered bits of Renna. The music of the fleet members in the crowd washed over Cade, so she used that, too, twisting it into a melody of her own design. Something simple. This was no time for showoff moves. Her song had to be carved from pure, clean heart.

Cade knew that it was working when people's hands flew to their temples. Fleet members turned to whoever stood next to them, gaping, confused.

Cade vamped — not for time, but for the right feeling. She needed to be in the center of the flow of it. To be a question rushing toward an answer that she couldn't see. She filled every note with reaching, aching, wanting-to-arrive.

When it ran out of her fingertips like water, she started to sing.

*third in line and waiting*
*for the long slide into dark*
*ride the curve to day*

*again, following the*
*arc*

*grave fingers, pulling*
*drag all things down*
*to a blue-green point of stillness*
*and still the whole is turning*
*round*

Cade reached the place where the song had cut off before, and it felt like standing at the edge of a cliff, her toes scraping the edge. One part of her clung and wobbled back, while the other strained ahead, almost out of her skin. What she needed was laid out beyond her — simple to see, impossible to reach.

She took a deep breath and the lights blinked off.

The planet behind her bloomed in the dark, white and gray and much brighter than she would have expected.

"Now that's a good stage light," Zuzu said.

Cade didn't have time to admire it, because she was too busy keeping the song from breaking apart. The music didn't hold against the urgent question of what was going on. Lights shutting down like that could not be a good sign.

The plan was for Matteo to contact them on the intercom if anything went wrong, but there was no word from the control room, so Cade forced herself to believe that everything was fine. Just a power-flicker. The overheads would be back in a few beats.

"Everyone stay where you are," Cade said.

She closed her eyes and tried to leap in the direction of the missing words, but fear blocked her, every time.

"What's happening?" someone asked, breaking the understood rule of silence.

*Everlast* rocked, hard. Metal winced, and left its shattering sound deep in Cade's ear.

"The Unmakers must have forced a boarding," Lee said. She ran to Cade, bringing Ayumi with her. Rennik followed, double blades in motion. The stage wasn't a stage anymore. It was part of a battle that was taking shape around them.

"What's going on?" fleet members asked, voice after voice piling.

Cade had an idea. She reached for the thought-songs to make sure. There should have been human songs in a ring around the bay, and a cluster in the control room. Cade felt only a few of them, faint. The rest was silence.

"Unmakers have control of the ship," Cade said.

"But there was no attack," Lee said. "No bombs, *no ruckus.* Why did they go straight for the boarding?"

Cade pulled her knives out. "It looks like Unmother wants to do this part herself."

The doors at the back of the room flung wide, and Unmakers poured in. Mira stood in a pocket of safety behind Zuzu.

"Keep the spacesicks to the center!" Lee shouted.

Moon-White swung loose and banged at Cade like a heartbeat outside of her chest. Rennik coaxed the knives out of Cade's hands. He caught Moon-White and pressed it back at her.

"Keep playing," he said.

"I can't."

Unmaker forces were biting at the edges of the crowd, and Rennik's double blades swung restless circles. "We'll cover you, Cadence. You wanted a chance to play, and this might be the best one left."

Rennik trusted Cade to finish the song, and now she couldn't. How could it ever be enough for her to play her guitar and sing while people died? She had to fight. She had to save them all. She had to —

"Play!" Lee cried.

Ayumi held fast to Lee's side and nodded.

Cade strummed at the center of a living circle. Lee and Rennik and Zuzu made up the outer skin. Ayumi and Mira and Cade's mother were sealed in, protected. Gori fought his way toward them from the back of the crowd.

Through the first eddies of battle, Cade caught a hint of red hair.

# CHAPTER 30

She held tight to the thread of the song, but when Unmother struck down a fleet member, and then another, Cade's hands mumbled on the strings.

She broke out of the circle. Rennik's hand caught her shoulder, and Lee tried to angle in front of her and keep fighting. "I can't let anyone else get hurt for me," Cade said, pressing Moon-White into the nearest empty hands, Mira's. "She wants me."

"I thought we didn't give a snug what she wants," Lee said.

Unmother turned and ran out of the bay, and Cade followed, splitting the crowd like too-ripe fruit. She knew that she was giving Unmother what she wanted. At least this would be the last time.

"Cade!" Lee cried. "Get back here!"

But Cade was already gone, through the great doors of the bay, thudding fast down the halls. When she wasn't sure where to go, she closed her eyes for an extra-long blink, and found Unmother's song. It was the ugliest thing Cade had ever heard, and it had grown more elaborate now, barbed and catching.

This woman's music had teeth.

It also lacked a sense of direction. At first, Cade thought Unmother was headed for the control room, but then she would stop, wander in a small loop, and find her way back. By the time she righted the course, Cade had convinced herself that Unmother was wounded.

Cade almost stumbled over bodies outside the control room —the shift that had volunteered to fly *Everlast* while Cade put on the show. She closed her eyes and scanned for songs, knowing it would be faster than a pulse check.

Cade sank into the sick-certain feeling that they were all dead. When she felt a song, it hit her hard. Cade opened her eyes and found Matteo, streaked with blood that had seen its bright-red days, and deepened to brown. Each breath sounded like the ripping of a knife from muscle.

Cade crouched over Matteo. "You're okay," she said, low and rhythmic. "You're going to be okay."

Then she saw the series of stab wounds in his stomach, and stopped lying to him.

"That . . . woman . . ." Matteo tore another breath and pointed at the control room.

Even though Cade knew Matteo couldn't be saved, she didn't want to leave him. Someone should be there to bottle his last moments and preserve them in memory. But Unmother was in the control room, and she had to be stopped, so Cade ripped away, leaving a small piece of herself with Matteo.

That was how it always went. Pieces of her — everywhere.

The control room was empty except for the woman hunched over the panels. She had her head cradled in her hands, fingers bored in at the temples.

"What did you do to me?"

It took Cade a second to figure out what she meant. Unmother could hear the music in her head now, like any other human, and it was doing more harm than the blows she shook off, the cuts that she calmly ignored.

"That's what you get for hating me so much," Cade said.

"Hate is a small matter," Unmother said, gritting more than her teeth. She gritted her whole body. "It's human. Weak."

"I agree," Cade said. "And I can hear it leaking out of you."

Cade was braced for another speech about how superior the Unmakers were, but if Unmother still had plans to educate Cade, she dropped them, and launched herself across the room.

Unmother's knees and nails landed, extracting air, shredding skin. Cade pushed against her, but the woman moved so fast that it was impossible to get a good hold. She was wire and force, focus and speed.

Cade could summon hate too. She thought about Xan, and Renna. Matteo dying on the floor outside. Lee and Rennik and Ayumi, who had lost too much of themselves. Mira, who had to fight to *find* a self. The people whose names she'd never learn because the Unmakers got to them first. Hate was easy.

Cade used it against Unmother, and it was better than leverage, more intense than strength. She pushed and kicked her way up from the floor, pinning the woman under her. But when she got there, hate was knocked out of place.

Cade fought to save the people she loved.

"Is there anyone you want to say goodbye to?" she asked, working to pin Unmother's lashing arms.

"I don't care," Unmother said as she swiped at Cade's eyes.

Lee ran into the control room alone, frantic, and looked surprised to find Cade alive. Cade got an idea that she knew would make Unmother writhe. "Hey, Lee. Since she's human now, what do you think her name should be?"

"Something really terrible," Lee said. "Like Roberta."

Unmother turned on Lee with a look that could have drowned a lesser girl. Lee pulled her gun and aimed it dead on.

"I know it's unfair to bring a gun to a fistfight," Lee said. "But it was also unfair when you attacked my girlfriend in her sleep." Lee waved Unmother up from the floor and Cade cuffed Unmother's wrists with her hands.

Unmother slapped Cade with a cold look. "You're going to die."

"Someday," Lee said. "But today is about starting over. A shiny new world. No you in it."

Lee cocked the gun.

"Please. Go ahead," Unmother said with one of her most infuriating smiles.

Cade flung an arm out. "Wait."

Unmother's smile hardened in place.

Cade's hands went to work, searching. She ran her hands over Unmother's wire arms, down her strongly molded legs. She got the feeling that if Lee fired, she would be giving Unmother exactly what she wanted. Again.

Cade stopped at a slight bulge against Unmother's shirt, and when she ripped the material to the waist, she found plastic packed to Unmother's skin — a thin band of high-quality explosives.

Lee's hand nodded, tipping the gun before she shored it up. A mask of sweat clapped onto Cade's forehead.

"Are you serious?" Lee asked.

"It's connected to a heartbeat monitor," Unmother said with a slight giddiness, a new set of dimples breaking the surface of her pale face. Her happiness was the ugliest thing Cade had ever seen. "If the monitor stops, or someone tampers with it, well, you both have imaginations. You can guess what will happen."

The explosion wouldn't just take out Cade and Lee and Matteo. It would grab a section of the hull when it went, breaching the integrity of *Everlast*.

They would all go down.

Cade gave Unmother's arm a fresh twist, and pushed the small of her back to force a march. If she could get the woman to the airlocks, maybe she could flush her into space, clear her out before the explosives detonated.

Matteo's breath unraveled as Cade passed him, and it reminded Cade of the people in the bay who might be dying.

It was a good thing Unmother couldn't see her face. Lee was doing her best to look like a badass while walking backwards and keeping the gun trained. It was a long way to the airlocks.

Cade mouthed over Unmother's shoulder. *"Get her talking."*

"Uh, so, what do you think the future should look like?" Lee asked. "If you know so much about it?"

"Well, there will be none of the defect that you suffer from, the one you call *attitude*."

Lee mouthed back at Cade.

*"Can I shoot her?"*

Unmother kept on about future glories, laying out the bricks for Cade and Lee. No weakness. No sickness. No imperfections, or personalities, or any of the things that make life interesting enough to live in the first place.

Around the time that Unmother described her ideas for altering all thumbprints to look the same, and body odors to not smell so offensively *personal,* Cade steered her to the hall outside the airlocks and manuevered toward number one — because it was close to the door and she knew it was working.

Lee kept backing up, and Cade wedged Unmother so she stood in the doorway to the airlock. Cade pushed the sharp knob of Unmother's shoulder. "Go ahead."

"Or you'll do what? Shoot?" Unmother scratched her way out of Cade's grip. "You see, it was an illusion that you had any control. Best to give up on it." She touched Cade's wrist, tender now. "This can be a good death."

"I don't believe in those," Cade said.

She opened her mind, sweeping music from the corners to the center, gathering force. It barreled at Unmother.

Unmother bore down under the mental weight, tightening until Cade wouldn't have been surprised to hear teeth crack. When Cade tried to knock her backwards, Unmother's arms locked and her balance held.

"It's a nice trick," Unmother said, "but you can't expect it to work every time. People build up defenses, Cadence. At least, intelligent people do." She pushed Cade off and brushed at her clothes, as if human nature might have left a stain.

Cade sounded the bottom of her plans and came up clutching the last one, hoping it would convince Unmother to let the rest of these people survive.

As Unmother moved, Lee bobbed the gun, but her arms were slung low at the elbow, tired. Cade turned to her, and the almost-tears that snuck into her eyes were like warnings not to make this harder.

"I'm going with her," Cade said.

It was Lee's job to make life bigger and better, not easy. "No. No. No you're snugging *not*."

This wouldn't be a good death. The thought opened up like a black hole with torn edges and no bright center. But if Cade had to leave, at least she wouldn't be doing it for selfish reasons, like Xan. She had people worth living for, worth dying for.

She closed her eyes and gathered her breath. In that dark space, she heard something, so pure and strong that she couldn't ignore it. Music stitched out of old Earth-songs. The same music that Cade had followed across the universe, and it was moving in her direction.

This had to be some kind of before-death hallucination. Her mother was in the spacesick bay, glassed-and-gone.

Cade reached out and took Unmother's hand. Neither of them was stupid enough to go first. They crossed the threshold and entered the airlock together.

Lee tapped the glass with her gun to get Cade's attention. "If you think I'm going to push that button," she cried, "you're insane! Every single flavor of insane."

"Do what you have to do, Lee."

When Cade blinked, the music she'd heard before was back, louder. She opened her eyes and found her mother in the door of the hall that lined the airlocks, gripping the frame with loose-skinned hands.

Unmother took hold of that second and bashed Cade's side with all of her strength. Cade slammed onto the floor, and took in the scene from a low, strange angle.

"Cadence?"

Her mother's voice settled on the folds of the name, soft, but when she turned to Unmother, her face snarled as hard as a thorn. Cade had never seen that look anywhere, but she had felt it on her own face in the Andana days.

Cade's mother ran into the airlock and crashed into the other woman. They hurled backwards. Cade struggled to get up. On the other side of the glass, Lee looked trapped, not sure whether to intervene.

Cade's mother landed on top of the small red-haired woman,

and she used that to her advantage, pinning her. Though she was larger than Unmother, in any other moment she would have been weaker. But with Cade on the floor, hurt, she was supercharged.

And she had a weapon, a slick, short knife she must have grabbed off a dead Unmaker. Quicker than a gasp, the blade disappeared into Unmother's chest.

"And who are you supposed to be?" Unmother asked, through the rising thickness of blood.

Cade waited for her mother to answer, but instead she collapsed. Her head found the glass and the rest followed. She flickered in and out of spacesick like a radio, the signal too weak, uncatchable.

"The explosives!" Lee cried. "Move!"

Unmother's life could be measured in blood. There had to be more sliding on the glass than there was left in her small body.

Cade crawled to her mother's side, curled into an unclosed circle, sinking into softness and warmth.

Lee screamed. "I mean it, move!"

Cade wouldn't do it. She stuck fast, not caring that Lee stood over her now, pulling at her, face raw, volume rising.

Her mother stared, lips drooping because the smile couldn't hold. She turned to Lee. "Take her, please."

It was Firstbloom all over again, a variation of the first unbearable loss. Her mother would go and Cade would be left behind.

"No," Cade said. If she couldn't save her mother, she would stay here with her.

But Lee wasn't having any of that. She wrestled and kicked at Cade to wake her back to fighting. And then Cade remembered that Lee wasn't some faceless scientist. Cade's mother wasn't abandoning her.

This time Cade would have to do the leaving.

She picked herself up, dressed in Unmother's blood. There was no more time for decisions. There was no such thing as goodbye.

Cade sprinted.

She stole one more look at her mother as the room burst into a crescendo of red.

# CHAPTER 31

Cade's screams were lost in the explosion. A closed door wasn't enough to stop the force. Cade and Lee ran, and it tossed them. They picked each other up and ran again, slamming doors behind them.

Warning lights flared red. The composition of the air changed. The good, breathable stuff was slipping away.

"The hull," Cade said.

"We're double snugged," Lee said. "Back to the bay?"

"That's last-stand talk." Cade wasn't giving up after all of that, not after Xan and Renna and her mother.

Her mother.

Cade felt the loss, round and whole, for the first time in her life. It had always been there, waiting for her to feel it. But she had pushed it down, and now it would have to be put off one more time.

"Can we put the ship on an auto-course?" Cade asked. "We'll head for the surface and lock down the bay."

Lee shook her head. "I thought I told you to never—"

"—land a ship on an auto-course? Well, I would tell you never to blow a hole in the side of the ship, but that would be a waste of oxygen."

Cade and Lee raced to the control room, keeping their breath as shallow as they dared. When they hit the panels, Earth stared at them through the window, empty-white. At best, Cade and her crew were going to crash-land and live out the rest of their short lives on the unfriendly surface.

But it was no use thinking about that. Lee focused on co-ordinates, speeds, vectors. Cade stretched a finger onto the crumpled chart and picked a spot. It would have been a coast, back in the days when Earth boasted oceans. Now it would be a flat strip of land near a crater. Cade would deal with the deadness of Earth when she got there. For now, all she could do was set the course.

The longer it took, the harder it got. Breathing turned from an auto-action into a chore.

"All right." Lee slammed a final button. "Let's . . ."

"Drain," Cade said, and it took every wisp of air in her chest.

Cade and Lee staggered out of the control room, in the direction of the bay. Moving and talking got easier as they went. There was more good air out here, but it wouldn't last long. They would have to lock it in or lose it.

"Umm, design flaw," Lee said, clamping her lips. "Someone has to shut the door from the outside."

Cade's answer came out fast. Pre-thought fast. "Not you."

"Don't you snugging dare," Lee said at the same time.

There was only one other person caught on the wrong side of the lockdown. Cade closed her eyes and reached for Matteo's song. It was fading. But he didn't have to fill the universe with sound. He just had to push a button.

Cade stumbled back toward the control room.

"That's the wrong way!" Lee cried. "As in, what the hell are you doing?"

Cade didn't stop, and Lee sighed and pounded after her. Once Lee saw Matteo, hand pressed to his wounds, face in the farthest reaches of pain, she seemed to understand. Cade kneeled at Matteo's side and hauled him up.

"What's this about?" he asked, the words held together by ragged strings of breath. Cade and Lee carried him between them. They stumped, fast and awkward, toward the bay.

"One more favor," Cade said.

"Short version?" Lee asked. "We need your help."

"There's . . . something . . . wrong with *Everlast*," he said. "Isn't there."

Cade gave him a quick rundown without any gloss.

"I'm a historian," Matteo said with one last stab at a chuckle. "Remember? Going down with the ship is . . . not in the job description."

"You're a captain," Lee said as they reached the bay. "And a fine one."

Matteo looked from Cade to Lee and back again. "You girls are . . . something I've never seen."

They propped him against the wall, within reach of the control pad that would lock down the room.

Cade and Lee saluted, then ran. The bay was sweat and chaos, lit by patches of white Earth-shine.

The door sealed behind them.

"Find Ayumi," Cade said to Lee. "Make sure she's safe." For that, she got the best thank-you smile in the universe.

Cade searched for Moon-White's glow.

She had a song to finish.


Mira rushed Cade, the guitar strapped to her back.

"What are you doing?" Cade asked, horrified to see her in the thick of the fight. She tried to cover the girl, but Mira ducked under her arm. She lashed out with her short knife, practiced and smart.

"I know how to fight Unmakers," she said, looking up at Cade with her best *Are-you-stupid* eyes. "Remember? I was one of them."

Cade fought to the front of the bay, Mira behind her. As soon as Rennik caught sight of them, he carved a path with the double blades. It stunned her how well he could fight even with so much worry on his face.

"I thought you were—"

"What? Ditching my own party?" Cade asked.

An Unmaker dodged at them. Rennik clapped Cade to his side and fought one-handed. "Cadence, I thought . . ."

She let the words settle. "Yeah, well, now you know how I felt every minute of the last three months." She kicked an Unmaker away from Rennik's heels as he fought off the one in front of his face. "How many minutes *is* that?"

"Thirteen thousand or so."

Rennik swung, calm. For the first time since Renna had died, it didn't feel like he was venting an unbearable heat. An Unmaker struck, and Rennik ticked the blade to the floor with ease.

Rennik and Zuzu and Gori took down Unmakers as fast as they could, but it was easy to see the truth.

"They're winning," Zuzu cried.

"One more set," Cade said.

The guitar found its rightful place against her body. It wouldn't be easy to fight her way back into the song as the battle rang around her and the ship burned a path toward Earth.

It was her mother's death that scared Cade the most. She had started the song because of her mother, dreamed up most of it just for her. The music had always been strongest in the presence of her glass.

What if her death was the end of the song?

Cade tried to focus on her crew, her friends, but they were smothered in the thickest moments of battle.

All she could do was stare.

At Lee, forced to her knees by the battering of blows, and Ayumi behind her, a few bad strikes away from being undefended. At Mira, tossing herself into the path of Unmakers, close to fearless. At Gori, putting all of his old, violent skills to use even though the universe had told him not to. And Rennik, checking every few seconds to make sure Cade was safe, without breaking the swing of his blades.

Cade kept looking for her mother.

What she found instead were words.

*come back and know the shape*
*of things*
*come back and find*
*the face you left*
*behind*

The chorus.

Cade was almost there. To the end of the song, the surface of the planet.

Everywhere, spacesicks blinked clear. Unmakers went down, the plastic molds of their false bones cracking, their robes inking the floor. Some stopped fighting and clutched their heads. The music must have found its way in.

Gori tried to catch Cade's eyes across the room. His arms waved and his wrinkled lips stretched around words she couldn't hear. He blazed forward, looking worried and certain at once. Gori's self-imposed rules were being tossed so he could tell her something.

Cade fumbled a note, regripped the guitar. She'd come this far. It didn't matter what Gori thought the song was going to do. Cade trusted Ayumi and Moon-White. She trusted the music. She didn't know where it was coming from, but she had to keep going.

Her fingers sketched patterns. Her throat reached, raw.

*here is ground as good as skin*
*underneath the staring sky*
*a breeze for breath*
*everywhere, hands*
*eyes*

*come back and know the shape*
*of things*
*come back and find*
*the face you left*
*behind*

The last note spread into silence.

The light changed from a wash of white to a gentle blue-green. Even before Cade turned, she felt it, the way a person always does. Deep, and sure, and rooted.

An unshakable sense of home.

The planet outside the window had changed. It was the crisp blue of Ayumi's drawing, the green of Mira's eyes. White curls of cloud pricked the colors bright, making them stand out. The surface drew Cade in. This was the right Earth, the real Earth, and they were about to slam into it.

Cade jolted as *Everlast* cracked atmosphere. "Everyone hold on!" she cried.

"Hold on to what?" Mira asked.

They had picked the bay for its openness, the lack of obstruction. Cade's eyes circled the room. "Whatever you can find."

All they had was each other.

One of Rennik's arms found Cade's waist and the other hooked around Lee, who had a firm hold on Ayumi. Cade tucked Mira against her chest.

She kept her eyes open as they all fell.

# CHAPTER 32

Sand.

That was the first thing Cade felt when she staggered from the ruined shell of *Everlast*.

Sand under her feet, smoke in her face.

But the sand was fine, not sticking-gritty. And the smoke was starting to clear. And when Cade looked up from her feet — water.

This was the ocean.

Cade turned back to *Everlast* and found it framed in green. Trees rose twice as high as the wreckage, turning the air thick and perfect. Cade's lungs were in love. She wanted to run to the water, wash the crust of blood from her cuts. She wanted to walk into the forest, let the sun reach for her through the leaves. This was the place her song had promised, and Cade wanted to learn every stroke of it.

But not alone.

"Rennik! Lee!" Cade ran back toward the ship. Survivors leaked onto the beach in thin streams.

The ship was destroyed, metal bent at strange angles. Cade had walked out of a hole scraped in the hull, which tipped up, almost facing the sky. The shuttles docked on the far side had been crunched like paper by the uneven landing. There would be no return trip to June and the fleet.

But that worry disappeared, like stars drowned in daylight. Right now Cade needed to find Rennik, Lee, Ayumi, Mira. She didn't know how she'd been thrown clear of them during the landing. All she remembered was opening her eyes and wandering out of *Everlast*, onto the beach.

She climbed the face of the ship, the metal hot with held-in sun. The hole was a door that had been torn off during the crash. Cade kneeled over it and looked down at the slide of the hall toward the bay. There was Lee, one arm around Ayumi.

Struggling up. Hair knots still intact.

A smile cracked her face as soon as she caught sight of Cade. She threw a hand out and they made a chain, Cade pulling Lee, Lee pulling Ayumi. They perched on the face of the ship.

"So this is Earth," Lee said, taking it in. The blue, the green, the goodness of the sun that would paint her skin with freckles.

Ayumi tapped Lee on the shoulder. "It's real? Really?" she whispered. "What does it look like?"

Lee settled her face on Ayumi's shoulder and closed her eyes.

"Perfect."

Then Rennik emerged from the hole in the ship, and something that had been knotted in Cade let go.

He stood looking at the distant point where the water became the sky. Rennik never knew how to deal with new or strange, so Cade decided to help him. She threw herself into his space and waited for his arms to close around her.

"Hello, Cadence," he said, and he didn't sound surprised at all.

As more survivors spilled out, Cade scrambled back to the torn-off door. She caught sight of Zuzu headed for the waterline, Gori shaking sand from his robes. But there was someone Cade didn't have wind of yet.

She dropped down into the metal innards of *Everlast*.

"Cadence?" Rennik called. "That's not—" Before he could say "safe," she was halfway down the hall.

She skidded toward the bay. People were headed in the other direction, and a few asked where she could possibly be going. She crossed the bay and found it almost empty expect for a few people pressing to their feet and a thin layer of bodies on the floor. Cade found Mira on the makeshift stage. She'd taken a hard fall and twisted her arm in a bad direction. Cade lifted it with care.

Mira was folded around the guitar. In the moments before Earth, she had saved Moon-White.

"Hey!" Mira's eyes flared even greener than usual. She pointed to the guitar with her working hand.

"Good job," Cade said.

She stood the girl up and tested her arm to make sure it wasn't broken. For some reason the tears for her own mother chose this moment to fall. Taking care of Mira didn't remind Cade of an emptiness anymore. It gave her the warmth of her mother's side, the last of her faded smiles. Cade had never learned her name, and now she was gone, a final gone, one that couldn't be undone.

Mira brushed a handful of wetness from Cade's face, curious and concerned. "This isn't happy," Mira said. "I was expecting happy."

Cade angled Mira under one arm. "Don't worry. I'll get around to it."

Together they helped the last of the survivors out of the ship. There were dead on both sides, mostly Unmakers. Cade got the feeling that a few of the people who climbed out of the ship, in dark pants and white shirts, had been on the other side of the fight a few minutes ago. But if there was anything to convince them to come back and give being human a real chance, it was this place. If they wanted to put down their robes and their knives and start over, Cade wasn't going to stop them.

By the time she cleared the ship, it already looked like a part of the beach. Like the metal bones of an ancient creature that had washed ashore. With the wildness of the trees and vines and undergrowth, she figured it would be crossed and coated with dark green in a few months.

The survivors sent teams back to *Everlast* to gather food, blankets, and the last of the medical supplies. Lee and Zuzu took charge, and Ayumi and Mira sorted through what they found. Cade was given a pass. People seemed to think she'd done enough for the day. But she couldn't rest with the planet awake, alive, all around her.

Gori stood down by the water, a wrinkle-blot against the beauty of the red and peach sunset. Cade joined him as fast as her burned-out muscles would let her.

"You felt it," she said. "Didn't you? Before the rest of us."

That's why Gori had tried to call to her across the battle.

"I felt the disturbance of the song each time it was happening," Gori said. "But I did not know what it meant. The explanation became clear to me while you were busy making vibrations."

"You mean singing," Cade said.

She walked in the water up to her ankles. Closed her eyes and breathed. This wasn't the kind of thing that she could take apart, piece by piece. It was too big.

"The disturbance I felt was not a planet being destroyed, but created," Gori said. "The energies are similar."

"That's why it confused you."

"Yes."

"But if the song did this before, why was the planet white and dead when we got here?" Cade asked.

Gori let his toes linger in the wet sand long enough for the water to break. He snatched them back. "The song did not hold. It was not strong enough to call forth a true change in the universe."

That explained why the spacesicks had blinked clear when

Cade sang before, but hadn't stayed that way. Part of the song's strength came from Cade's belief in Earth. She had needed to see the planet for herself.

"So it really did change things," Cade said. "And this time the change stuck." She braced against the cold and the salt and sank into the water to her shoulders. Gori stayed at the thin line between land and ocean, watching as she pedaled her feet.

This was the part where she kept getting blocked. *"How?"*

"The boy Xan," Gori said. "When his particles returned to the beginning of time, they should have been content to move along their path, as they had before, but something disrupted them."

"I did," Cade said, before she could stop herself. "I'm still entangled."

"Yes. And so you can affect his particles. Vibration is one way to do this."

Music.

The song was a question. A need. An ache for a home that the spacesicks would die without. Home had been the deepest absence in Cade, in her spacesick mother, in all the people she wanted to save. So Xan's particles, which were meant to keep Cade's in balance, had done what they could to fill the need. They had found a way to change the universe. This— all of this—had happened because Cade had dared to hope for it.

The strangeness was almost too much. But Cade didn't want to shake it off. She wanted to hold it.

"Does that mean Xan is here? He didn't catch up to us, did he? His time-traveling particles?"

"That is not in the realm of possibility," Gori said. "His particles can't move past the point in time when he traveled through the black hole. That was the end of his circle. He also could not alter this planet at a moment when it would affect his own birth, not without dark consequences. But Earth has been dead, emptied of humans for a thousand years. Xan's particles found the right moment to tip the balance of the planet toward life again, and the change has reached us now."

Cade needed a moment to take that in. She held her breath and slipped under the skin of the water. And there, in the suspended dark, it almost made sense. Gori's explanation was something she could feel, and believe in a deep place, even if she'd never be able to repeat it word for word.

She came up, spitting salt.

It looked like Gori wasn't quite done. "And this happened," he said, "because —"

Cade finished his favorite motto for him. "All time is one time."

She pushed out of the water, shivering, and wrapped her wet arms around Gori. He didn't pull away. He kept his round, dark eyes on the far distance, and pretended to be unmoved by the whole thing.

Cade almost let him get away with it.

"You told me that you lived all those years so you could warn me," she said. "But maybe you lived them so you could be here. With us."

Gori pursed his raisin lips. "The universe is strange and stretches in many directions. I have never claimed to see them all, let alone understand."

Cade tried, and failed, to stop a laugh.

She left Gori staring at his new patch of universe, and headed down the beach. Cade was in love with every snugging thing she saw. More than love. It felt like it was a part of her, or she was part of it. The colors of the melting sun and the touch of wind on her arms. The soft curve of the beach and the people dotting it in a broken line, spreading into the evening. The water that reached for her over and over.

She didn't make it far before she ran into Lee and Ayumi, sitting in the sand. Cade had expected to find Lee halfway up a tree, or swimming toward the horizon, just to see how far she could go. But she was there with her toes in the lace-white, Ayumi's hip nestled close, a notebook open on her knees, a pencil twirling between her restless fingers.

"And there's this orange crusting over the red in the sunset—" Lee said.

"What color red? Crimson? Or brighter? Vermillion?"

Lee sighed and bunched her face. "Between the red of a bloody nose and the color of bad crabfruit."

Ayumi scribbled without pretending to look at the pages. "At least that's descriptive. What about the water? And the trees? Are there bats? I heard Earth had these animals called bats. You should check the sky and—"

"Don't worry," Lee said, her hands slipping over Ayumi's. "I'm going to tell you every inch of it."

She moved on from the sunset to the water to the shoreline, picking out details that Ayumi would love. There were too many. They would run out of daylight and there would still be so much to name.

Night slid in dark blue, and the stars added just enough silver to dream by. There was still more work before everyone could rest. Cade and Lee built a fire. Mira ran at their heels, learning how to find kindling, how to vent the flame, how to add the right pieces to feed it.

Rennik returned from *Everlast* with the final supply-rescue party. He sat down and his arms fell around Cade, as easy as the dark. "I made a decision," he said. "I'll hold on to Moon-White for the moment, but only if you promise to play."

Cade said yes. Or kissed him. It felt like the same thing.

The night was difficult on Earth, shadowed and deep. Cade's back faced the woods, and she felt the weight of unknown things behind her. She played comforting songs, ones she knew better than the back alleys of Voidvil. She played fast to keep her fingertips from getting cold. The sound drew survivors from up and down the beach, and they fed the fire and kept it going. Cade played for them. She played for the people who should have been there.

And the ones who might still come.

Cade wouldn't be able to get back to the fleet. What she had was the possibility, shimmering and faint, that she could send a message. The range of her abilities was impossible to guess, but if a song could reach through time and space to find Xan, she figured that with practice, she could get one to cross twenty systems. It might take months, or years. So every night, Cade would sit with Moon-White. Let the notes and her voice tangle with the rising sparks from the fire, and the good thick air.

She would have Rennik and Lee and Ayumi and Mira, even Gori, sit with her. Cade would be one song, shining against the dark. One song, waiting, for anyone who wanted to hear it and come home.

# ACKNOWLEDGMENTS

My editor, Kate O'Sullivan, made this story better in so many ways, and supported it from her first read-through to the final edits. Thank you for sitting in the nav chair and pointing in all the smartest directions.

My agent, Sara Crowe, found the perfect spot in the universe for Cade and her crew.

HMH Kids has given me so many reasons to be happy. Rachel Wasdyke showed me the ropes, and Scott Magoon created two shiny-amazing covers. Huge thanks to the entire team.

Vermont College of Fine Arts helped me with every aspect of this story. I may not have seen the entire planet, but I am certain VCFA is one of the best things on it.

The Austin kidlit community opened its arms to me, as always. Special thanks to Sara Kocek, Varian Johnson, Cynthia and Greg Leitich-Smith, Bethany Hegedus, and Sean Petrie, who wouldn't let me fall down. (No, seriously. I almost fell down. It's hot in Austin.)

Anna Drury was there for lots of Skyping, and one epic car ride when the entire book changed. Vanessa Lee shared her home with me at deadline time, yet again. Tirzah Price gave me constant reminders that reading and writing are my favorites. Maverick brought new levels of adorable to my life, and the best kind of breaks when I needed to look up from outer space.

Cori McCarthy did more for this novel than I could ever fit on an acknowledgments page. Notably, she helped with my poetry, got everyone on my spaceship drunk, and brought Ayumi back from the dead. Lee and I have the rest of our lives to thank her for it.

Julia Blau, with her magical notecards and boundless enthusiasm, showed me that I could, in fact, make the second half work. None of my stories would exist without her.

My sisters, Christine and Allyson, and brother-in-law, Joe, made me feel like a real author every time they asked, "How's the book going?" Love to my whole big supportive family, especially Grams.

My parents, Julie and John Capetta, taught me to love books, and told me I could write them. I do not know two better gifts.